Endurance

An Apocalyptic Thriller

M.L. Banner

Toes in the Water Publishing, LLC

ISBN: (Paperback): 978-1-947510-17-3

ISBN: (eBook): 978-0-9908741-4-0

Version 2.12

ENDURANCE: Highway Book#2 is an original work of fiction.

The characters and dialogs are the products of this author's vivid imagination.

Much of the science and the historical incidents described in this novel are based on reality, as are its warnings.

Prelude
DOE Facility Yucca Lake, Nevada

July 4th, 02:10

In moments, their nuclear bombs would lay to waste America. But first, Commander Mohammad Hamid had a job to do.

His thirty-five men were among the most crucial warriors in the Islamic Caliphate in America's plans. They would be among only two teams, leading Phase Two of the operations in four days. After months of preparations, leading up to this moment, they had only to secure the base before the bombs exploded. And that would be very soon.

He tapped his fingers impatiently on the front dash of the older Army convoy truck parked on the side of Mercury Avenue, just fifty feet from the Yucca Lake Airfield entrance. Any second now, Ahmed, from the advanced team, would signal them forward.

He felt proud to have been given so much authority by ICA's ruler, Abdul Raheem Farook, their soon-to-be Mahdi, leading them to the new Caliphate on earth.

The crack of several gunshots echoed from the distant night, and Mohammad turned to their sounds. The corner of his mouth inched upward, forming a grin.

There were several flashes in front of the dark outline of one of the buildings, on the other side of the gate. Their corresponding pops sounded a second later.

Mohammad's pulse quickened with excitement; it wouldn't be long now.

He thought about the preparation leading to this moment and what his men had already accomplished and what would follow in the next hour or two. His grin grew into a smile.

Months ago, his IT warriors deployed undetectable keystroke logging software into military base computers throughout the US, including the DOE's systems inside this facility. This not only gave them access to passwords, but more importantly, a back-door into military computers at over a hundred Air Force bases. Just one base figured this out in time. Then an hour ago, they turned off the bases' systems and locked their personnel out.

Naturally all the bases affected had already put their best technicians on the problem of regaining control of their computer systems. It would be fruitless for these infidels. One or two might succeed, the remainder would not. Then when Phase One is executed, they would not have power to control them. *Soon.*

He tilted his wrist and clicked on the green glow of his watch for the hundredth time to mentally calculate when. Its luminescence bathed the cab in a spectral aura. Each time, his driver slid away from him on his seat, as if Mohammed were some sort of Jinn. Everyone was anxious to get started.

Only one hour fifteen minutes more, he calculated.

That's when they would detonate their nukes at the various cities and three military locations. Then, moments later, their Russian partners' nuclear-tipped missiles would explode over America, plunging this corrupt country into chaos. The American power grid would go down and most everything electronic—at least utilizing solid state circuits—would be dispossessed of its working components. The machinery of America would cease to function, and with it, the food and water would stop and shortly after this, its civilian population would riot in the streets.

Because most of America's military bases were directly connected to the civilian grid, many would be crippled along with its population. Much of their hardware was protected against the EMPs, but not all. For those bases with EMP-hardened equipment and not part of the civilian grid, there was Phase Two. Starting July 8th, Mohammad's team, along with a similar one in Alabama, would deliver the final blow.

Only his team knew the location of their targeted base. Even Farook did not yet know that they were at Creech AFB, outside of Las Vegas. He said it was for their protection, in the event their cell was broken up by the American government or if there was a mole in their organization. As this cell's leader, Mohammad chose the base and what to tell Farook. Soon it would not matter. Once they took over this base and the bombs fell on America, even if the other base in Alabama didn't participate, his team would bring honor to Allah.

He could hardly wait for their time of glory to begin. He glared at the radio. In response, it crackled a hiss and then a voice speaking Arabic told him their entrance to the base was clear.

Perhaps he was a Jinn, he thought before picking up the portable off the dash.

"Thank you, Ahmad," he said; then to the driver, "Forward."

The driver huffed a sigh of relief, fired up the truck's ignition and they lurched forward. The other dozen Army trucks followed in a train of vehicles that snaked its way through the gate and onto the airfield.

Their part of this war had just begun.

Phase Two

"Islam isn't in America to be equal to any other faith but to become dominant."
- Omar Ahmad, Co-Founder CAIR (Council on American Islamic Relations)

"America must be burned! America is no good at all."
- Louis Farrakhan, Leader of the Nation of Islam

"Then wait you for the day when the sky will bring forth a visible smoke, covering the people, this will be a painful torment." - Qur'an: Verse 44, Sura 10-11

"And this profound smoke will be unleashed by our warriors, raining terror upon the Infidel's military. And the Infidel will collapse under our boots."
- Imam Ramadi, July 8th, Crystal Waters, Florida

Chapter 1

Hasta Army Base, 15 Miles from Endurance, Florida

July 9th

"Come on, you pansies. Double-time!" Drill Sergeant Reynolds yelled at Bravo Squad.

The thuds of their boot falls grew immediately louder as Bravo increased their pace, hugging the fence line. The practice field was now coming into view, and therefore the end of their run. It was then that they all knew they would make it.

"I heard we may be shipping out today," Private Davis huffed. He was always hearing things.

They rounded a corner, each darting over the many fronds cast off from the ubiquitous palmetto trees ringing the base.

"Where?" Private Simpson puffed. The smallest of the squad's three women, she was known for her toughness and economy of words. She focused on keeping her breathing rhythmic.

"What diff. As long as we get to kill jihadi scum," Davis answered.

"We'll get our revenge," PFC O'Malley said calmly behind them, seemingly not winded.

They were pulled up to their starting point, after a full ten laps around base, a total of twelve miles with full packs. Although tired, they were all feeling pretty good.

"Hooah, sir," Simpson bellowed.

Reynolds had turned ahead of them and was waiting. "All right, gentlemen and ladies." He tipped his hat to his squad. "Halt!"

They all stopped and promptly bent over, lungs heaving for air.

"Drop packs and pair up."

Having been through this exercise before, Bravo Squad complied immediately. Time for their daily hand-to-hand combat drills.

O'Malley was having trouble with a strap on his pack. So he took a knee and held back from the rest of his squad that had already trotted out to the middle of the open practice field. He knew there was another run to follow and this might be the only chance he had to adjust it.

The sound of a motor fluttered in the distant sky, coming from the north. It was faint at first, but quickly became more pronounced. It had speed and the wind behind it.

Their heads tilted upward, curious more than anything. Since the bastards nuked them, they'd had no power for five days; they'd seen only a few of their older vehicles working, and few things that functioned on electricity; certainly none of them had seen or heard anything in the air that sounded like an aircraft.

"Is it a plane, Drill Sergeant?" yelled Davis from the field.

"No doofus, it's smaller," chided Simpson. She was mostly oblivious to the small craft: instead she wanted to show off her hand-to-hand skills. Snickering, she warned her partner, "Get ready."

"It's a drone," Reynolds mumbled mostly to himself. He was surprised that a drone would be flying near them: they were over sixty miles from the nearest Air Force or Army base with a drone program.

They watched the craft, only a hundred feet in the air, pass over the admin and dormitory buildings on the other side of the practice field. Then it banked hard right and headed for the Gulf.

"What the hell was ..." Davis started to ask, before he coughed twice. "Damn, my—" His face twisted into tortured wrinkles, like he'd been just sucker-punched.

O'Malley pressed a bandanna against his mouth, immediately suspecting the drone was the cause. He glanced at his sergeant, kneeling next to him and doing the same with his shirttail.

"Sir," pleaded Simpson. She sucked in a deep breath of death and then clawed at her skin, her mouth cast open wide like she was trying to scream. Another gasp emptied the remaining good air held by her lungs.

"Gas!" Reynolds yelled through his shirt. He pondered for only a second, watching two more of Bravo fall to the ground, gripping their throats. "Run! Water!" He pulled up O'Malley, and they ran for the fence line closest to them, hoping all would follow.

A few attempted to run. But it was more of a drunken stumble. They seemed disoriented, unable to plot their direction.

The remainder fell over or were already on the ground.

Reynolds glanced back. He was shocked to see none of his squad was following them. His toughest soldier, Simpson, was on the ground, convulsing with a final spasm of pain. He knew once they started exhibiting symptoms, there was nothing he could do for them. But it still pained him to see.

Reynolds and O'Malley catapulted themselves up and over the section of fencing closest to them, ignoring the bites from its barbed-wire crown. They hopped down and slogged through the thick threshold to the ocean.

Reynolds kept moving. "In the water," he yelled, and then he flopped in and swam away from the base, not sure how far he had to go, only knowing he needed more distance.

He heard O'Malley behind him, splashing and coughing.

"Take your clothes off. They're covered in poison," Reynold coughed again, kicking vigorously while ripping at his own shirt.

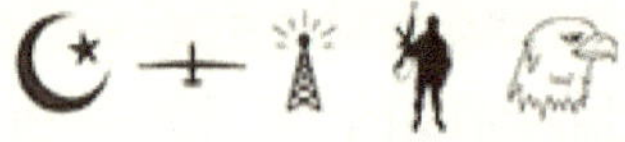

The MQ-9 Reaper drone banked again to compensate for a stiff southeasterly wind and followed its course to the next target, ninety-three kilometers further.

Its operator, Tariq Al Ufari, sat comfortably in the pilot's seat some 389 kilometers away. A counter on his giant control screen counted down the distance to his next target.

His hands were steady as he guided the drone on a straight path, the counter on his overhead display ticking down one kilometer every nine seconds. When he was within one mile, he would once again depress the button with his left hand while maintaining the yoke with his right. Then, he would release the button after only a few seconds. It would be just enough time to release a concentrated dose of sarin gas over the next base. That is all he would need to kill everyone on the base, and move on to the next one. Well, not quite everyone.

Of those on the base, 63 percent would die within minutes from inhalation or sarin saturation on just a small percentage of their epidermis. Another 20 percent would die within a day if they didn't receive an antidote that few carried.

He gleamed at his effectiveness as a soldier.

It was far better doing what he did than putting himself at risk by killing only a few infidels on the ground with a rifle. He'd prefer not being a martyr as thousands of his brethren would soon be.

And with electronics and power down at most bases, and the promise of Allah, his drone would avoid detection from radar equipment or anti-aircraft munitions. As long as the drone had enough petrol and there was no pilot error, he should be able to bring it back to base for refueling and then send it back out for several more runs before the end of the day. By his count, he would be responsible for eliminating the personnel at least thirty-five military bases.

Between this base and the other at some location unknown to him, and with the help of their Russian partners, they would have neutralized most of the US military before they knew what hit them.

Beep-beep-beep.

His proximity alert to target (PATT) went off, telling him that his drone was within three kilometers of the target. He'd already forgotten its name.

He removed his left hand from the release mechanism and tapped the control panel bringing up the details: MacDill Air Force Base.

Clicking another button on his control panel brought up the drone's underside camera feed. A window popped up with the live feed of its canisters, nested in the much larger front aerial feed, showing the upcoming base.

The counter, set to go off at five hundred meters, turned from flashing red to solid red.

Tariq punched the big red button and watched the lethal spray cascade out of both canisters. Within seconds, it would rain down on the 12,000 military and 1,300 civilian personnel below. By the time his drone maneuvered to his next target, 63 percent would be dead. That's almost 9000 lives he'd exterminate in a matter of minutes.

He grinned at the thought.

Chapter 2
Sunbay Cove, Florida

Lexi

"No!" Frank barked at Lexi. "None of that limp-wristed stuff, come at me with all you've got."

She glared at him, first taking in his leg brace; then the sling on his arm to prevent undue movement, which might tear at the healing gunshot wound in his shoulder; and finally his bruised and puffy face. He looked really old today, not much of an opponent against a lethal weapon like her Gerber survival knife.

"Don't worry; your blade won't even come close to me, no matter what you do." He motioned her forward with the fingers of his free hand.

It was just a little taunt, but she bit.

She lunged at him with her serrated blade. This time, with much more balance, her wrist stiff, the blade a natural extension to her arm, she thrust.

Twisting from his waist, he blocked with his immobilized arm and grabbed her wrist with his free hand, while spinning and pulling on her, using her forward motion against her. The old man was a blur.

Both the knife and Lexi ended up on the ground. Her head bounced hard off a patch of dandelions, startling up a bouquet of seedpods. Like the burst from a white chalk-line on a baseball diamond, the wispy pods erupted and enveloped her.

Frank stood over her, concerned by the way she'd struck her head. But when he saw her face was filled with disgust and not pain, he forced back a grin while offering a free hand.

She pushed herself up instead, forgoing his assistance.

When she stood up somewhat hunched and shrouded in dandelion seeds, but definitely unhurt, he snickered. His chest started an involuntary quiver that undulated throughout his body. His hand, still outstretched, even though she obviously didn't need it, picked up the humorous tremor.

Her scowl, framed in a crown of delicate seed-heads, was too humorous for him to hold back any longer. Her attempts to look serious probably didn't help. A belly laugh grew until he couldn't restrain it anymore.

She batted away at his still outstreached hand and attempted to shoo away the innocent flowers, as if she were trying to bat away bees attracted to her sweat. Several remained glued to her sticky brow.

It took a moment, but he finally regained his composure.

"Listen, it takes most trainees days to get the hang of this. You're actually doing quite well after only a couple of hours."

"Sorry if I don't take your words to heart. After all, you're practically disabled and a senior citizen."

It was Travis who now laughed from behind both of them, sunning himself on an Adirondack chair in the grass. It was also the first time she had heard him laugh in a while.

"You've got an evil wit about you; I'll say that. All right, we're done for today's hand-to-hand."

Lexi had never been in the Army, but suspected from movies that you never heckle a drill sergant. Still she prodded. "What, you getting tired?"

When Frank's expression changed, she knew she pushed it too far.

"We'll see who's tired. Now, you're going to run that way"—he thrust out his forefinger north, toward the front of the property—"and you're going to keep on running for one hour. I don't want you to stop even for a break. So, you'll need to pace yourself. Based on your height, weight, and physical fitness, you should have no problem making it to a sign at mile-marker 23, less than Three miles north of here. Memorize what that sign says and only *then* you can return. If you don't stop, you'll be back here in"—he checked his chronograph—"sixty minutes. Go!"

He clicked the first of the three buttons on the watch's side, starting its stopwatch second hand, and glared at her again with a look that said "What the hell are you waiting for?"

Lexi stared at him as if he had given her instructions in a foreign language. "How could you possibly know what it says on a sign three miles from here? You've never been here before either."

"We passed it last night. Being always aware of what's around you is one more thing you'll need to learn." He glanced at his watch. "You've got only fifty-nine minutes now."

"Shouldn't I take water?" She still hesitated, unsure. She swung her head in each direction, her eyes finding Travis for some encouragement.

"No! Only your gun and your knife. Do not talk to anyone on the road, just run around them."

"And what if they stop me?"

"Shoot 'em!"

"Geez, some patriot you are. It might be an old person like you needing help."

"You're wasting time. Fifty-eight minutes."

"All right, all right," she huffed, shuffling toward the side of the house.

Lexi jogged from the rear of the dwelling to the front driveway and followed the meandering private road through the thick growth that seemed even denser than it had last night when they arrived, if that was possible. She reached for and then glanced down at her holstered .357 Rossi silver revolver and tried to adjust it, fearful the gun would fall out during her jog.

Apparently her father had kept a holster for this very weapon; Frank had found it in a workshop off the garage. Moving was much easier with the gun holstered, rather than stashed in her back pocket or tucked in the waistband of her pants at the small of her back. Of course, the FBI running shorts she'd borrowed from her daddy's wardrobe didn't have pockets, and the holster was held to her waist by a man's belt, also her father's. Frank had punched extra holes in it to accommodate her much smaller waist.

She felt silly wearing the damn belt and holster, as it didn't exactly look flattering on her. Not that flattering was as important as safe. After the past crazy five days, safety was far more essential than style. And Frank insisted that she wear the thing everywhere she went, even around the house. He said she needed to become intimately familiar with the gun and its feel, and to always have it available. That way, if anything arose, she'd be able to respond. He constantly reminded her, "A loaded gun is worthless if it's not with you." It was hard to argue with that logic.

She burst out of their driveway and onto a road, which was barely wider, and then finally onto the highway north. The same highway they had come down last night.

It felt good to be running, with her thoughts her only company. In the five days since terrorists attacked her country, she had almost never been alone: always looking after her brother, or worse, in the company of the lawless or of Abdul and his band of terrorists. She shivered just a little at this. Thankfully, the sun filled her with warmth again.

The Florida humidity hung on her like her already wet over-sized clothes. Frank promised they would go into town in a day or two and trade for a few things more her size.

This struck her as funny, and then sad. She wasn't sure when or even if there would be a time when they would be able to go to stores and buy—using money, rather than bartering with other things considered valuable such as food or ammunition—frivolous items such as pretty clothes and makeup. Frank had said he thought the grid might be down for good. That even if they no longer had to worry about Islamist invaders, it would take many years to rebuild what had been damaged by the EMPs.

Their lives had changed so quickly. Only five days ago, she was worried about only herself. And she was filled with hatred for so many.

These thoughts seemed so trivial now. She just felt glad to be alive, the nightmare of her Uncle Abdul behind them, to have her brother, and to have her godfather, Frank, looking after them. She felt "blessed," as Frank would say.

Before she knew it, having gotten lost in the thoughts churning around in her head, she was standing before the sign. It was right after mile marker 23, just like Frank had said it would be. She shook her head in disbelief, amazed that he remembered this. She swore that she'd pay better attention of everything around her from now on—to be "aware of everything or person around you," as Frank told her.

The green sign said "Endurance 5", as in it was five miles to Endurance, Florida. That was all. No expected secret message or trite saying like "Buckle Up" or "Bicycle Crossing." Just "Endurance 5."

She had not realized—until now—that Endurance was the name of the town they now lived in, or rather lived closest to.

Pivoting on her heels, her mission complete and yearning to get back before her hour had expired, she jogged back the way she had come. She felt pretty good, although she also felt like... *what did Travis call it? That's right, "a big sweat-ball."*

When she found their private road again, the sign announcing Sunbay Cove, she felt like she had time to spare. So, she slowed her pace. With her gait at a trot, her holster started to move funny, and the heavy gun nested inside began rubbing her thigh raw.

While she bobbed up and down with each stride, and trying to avoid the many tree branches that threatened to tear at her skin or the potholes that worked at sucking her down to her ankles, she monkeyed with the gun and the oversized belt.

At what she remembered was the first zig in their narrow driveway, the damned revolver popped out of the holster. *Maybe if I hadn't fiddled with it so much ...*

She lunged for the airborne gun, intending to catch it midair and fearful she'd damage this gift from her dead father. As her hands grasped for it, instead she batted the gun away—the soft tissue of her already sore wrist and the back of her hand connecting hard—sending it sailing into the bushes. It spiraled away rapidly; little glints of sunlight sparkled off the chromed finish. Then it was consumed by a mass of green. A single thud told her it came to rest on the mossy floor inside the tropical barrier.

"Shit!" she grumbled, clutching her hand, now bleeding from where it had connected with the gun. It throbbed painfully.

I'm such a klutz.

Lexi ducked under a clog of branches and stepped into the thicket, hoping her weapon hadn't landed too far away. Only a couple of steps inside the thick mass of trees, bushes, and vines, it opened up some. A burst of light worked its way through the denseness. She pushed her head out through the mass, into the small clearing, and saw something odd.

She expected to see a shiny gun, but instead there were two dirty tennis shoes facing her.

She followed the shoes up. They were connected to dirty ankles, which were bound to dirty legs, which were joined to filthy shorts...

"Ya looking for dis?" said a high-pitched voice in the distinct twang of a man who lived his whole life in this backwater. She shot a hurried glance up at the young man and saw: *he* had her revolver.

It was pointed at her.

Frank

"Where the hell have you been?" demanded a joyous Grimes. His voice crackled from radio interference.

Frank's face exploded into a giant smile. "Oh man, I cannot tell you how great it is to hear your voice."

"We can talk about that later. First, are you both all right? The gas hasn't gotten to you?"

"Gas? What gas?" Frank played with the knobs of the transceiver, afraid the atmosphere would muddle Grimes's words.

"Oh shit, you may not know this. The enemy is gassing military bases with what we believe is sarin gas. It started this morning, with drones and some say jets."

"We saw a couple of planes in the sky last night ..." Frank recalled when he and Lexi were sharing beers by the dock, maybe a couple of hours after they'd arrived, and she had pointed out the two streaks in the sky from jets. But they had thought this was the sign of something good. Maybe it was just another phase of the enemy's attack.

Frank's heart skipped a beat as he considered if this was the Phase Two they worried about.

"Well then, count yourself lucky for not being by a military base." Even over a radio's static, he could hear Grimes sounded relieved. But Frank became more anxious as he chewed on this new information.

"Uncle Frank?" Travis's small voice blew in through the back door, left open but screened. He had been listening while Travis had been playing outside, so that he could hear Lexi's return from her run, which should be soon.

Frank cocked his head out, so that he could better peer through the doorway of the radio and food storage room. He peered through the living area of the house and out the screened door. Only a few feet away, Travis was hovering over something on the ground. But otherwise he seemed fine.

"Wait, what did you say?" Frank focused once more on what his friend was telling him over the radio. "Only military bases are being hit?"

"It appears so. We've had reports from ham operators and a few bases we've been able to connect with that there were multiple strikes—"

Ding!

The cheap kitchen timer's bell ratcheted up his anxiety, already heightened from what Grimes was telling him.

The timer was set to ten minutes. That way they'd spend only that long on their pre-selected frequency. He heard a similar chime on Grimes's side of their radio conversation. Without saying a word, Frank rapidly twirled the circular dial to the next frequency. "—ya got your ears on?" It was Grimes, already there—no doubt he had a newer-model digital transceiver, with programmed pre-sets.

"I'm here," Frank replied. He felt his heart racing. He wanted to get to the logical conclusion of this conversation, and yet he feared what that might mean for them, and then for the rest of his country.

There was a thump on the roof. He suspected it was a heavy cat pouncing on something; maybe it was hunting. Frank had seen a couple of feral cats already, so he dismissed the sound and turned his attention back to the radio.

"Uncle Frank?" Travis called out, a little louder than before.

Frank moved his rolling chair sideways this time, craning his neck out farther, stretching the microphone's cord. He was closer to the workshop doorway, getting an even better view. Travis was still outside, though he had moved closer. Once again, he was bent over examining something on the ground.

"I was saying," Grimes continued, "I heard from several military bases and a few ham radio operators reporting the same thing. One base reported that their people were fine one minute and then the next they were clawing at their skin, followed by convulsions, and then death. The attacks seem mostly concentrated around military bases, but some of the surrounding populations are getting hit with this too."

Two more thuds on the roof. *Three cats, all hunting at the same time?*

"It appears to be sarin gas. Anyway, I'm glad you're not next to a military base, otherwise you might have been affected."

"So this has already happened? I mean it's over?" Frank asked as he hurriedly pulled back to the desk where the radio sat and examined a topo map of the area. He had pulled it out earlier this morning from one of Stanley's many bookshelves in this radio area. His finger searched its surfaces.

"No, it's still ongoing. We just got a report from Tyndall Air Force Base in Panama City that—"

"Uncle Frank?" Travis's voice, now much louder, had taken on a tone of panic.

Frank's finger landed on a spot on the map. It was not a publicly known military base, but Frank recognized the boundary markers as Army. Hard to tell on a civilian map what it was, other than military and off-limits. More disturbing, it was only a couple of fingernails away from the house: at the most, a dozen miles.

Two more thumps: one on the roof and the other outside in the yard.

These weren't the practiced sounds of predators. These were the sounds of nonliving things dropping from great distances.

"Uncle Frank!" screeched Travis.

Frank bounded up and saw Travis backing into the house. The door was propped open, but he was still facing outside, as if he was drawn to an accident occurring right before him.

Frank dashed to the door, pulling Travis in, but from what he didn't yet know.

There were a couple of flopping dark masses on the ground, and then a splash out in the bay.

They were birds.

He watched two more tumble to the earth and crash, dead or dying.

The sarin gas!

"Travis!" Frank hollered, pulling him from the doorway, and scooting him back toward the radio room. "Get inside there and close the door. Do not come out until after I return." He demanded.

Frank grabbed two gas masks from a table in the living room and two blanket throws on the couch and bounded out the door, slamming it shut behind him.

He had to get to Lexi, before the gas got to her.

Chapter 3
Off the Coast of Florida

"Dammit, Sarge, my throat feels like the inside of a roasted pepper," PFC O'Malley huffed while treading water.

"Beats the shit out of the alternative," Sergeant Reynolds stated matter-of-factly, while scanning the skies, as if talking to himself. He wasn't worried about O'Malley; he'd survive. They both would if they could get to the antidote quick enough. He was sick about the rest of his Bravo squad, and all the men and women on their base. But as a soldier, he was most concerned about his country. This war had just been escalated, and they'd just lost another battle.

"They're all dead, aren't they?" O'Malley said, gazing at the shoreline where they had jumped into the water.

"Yeah."

"What was it?"

"Sarin."

"You mean like the sarin gas terrorists used in train stations or Bashir used on his own Syrian people?"

"The same."

They treaded water for a while, not saying anything much, both lost in their thoughts and sorrows.

O'Malley had known he'd see death, being part of this special unit. He expected to witness it firsthand. He also knew that death would have probably found some of his band of brothers and sisters, when they took up the fight against their attackers. He'd just never expected this. Everyone he had trained with was gone. And they didn't even get a chance to kill even one of their enemy. It felt like some giant weight pressing down on his chest, making it hard to breathe.

Reynolds had larger concerns. He knew he couldn't do anything more for the dead; his concern was for the living. He started to wade toward the shore.

O'Malley followed. "What now?" he asked quietly, keeping his splashing down so that he could hear.

"We need to get you an antidote, but first we need supplies."

"Wait, what antidote?" He asked this, immediately not wanting to hear the sergeant's answer. Involuntarily, he found it even harder to breathe.

"Sarin is a nerve agent. Once you come in contact with it, in a large enough dose, you have to get a counteragent in your system within twenty-four hours, or you're dead. Sooner is better. The only source I know for the antidote is on base, which won't be clear for a couple of days. So, we need hazmat suits. I can think of only one place close to here that has at least two of them. I'm hoping it hasn't been saturated in sarin too."

Reynolds pulled himself out of the water and stood up on shore, adjusting his brown-green briefs. He was thankful for being stationed at a base off the Florida Gulf, with its warm waters, rather than someplace on the freezing Atlantic.

"Do you need help, Private?" Reynolds sounded empathetic, but his hands on his hips spoke of impatience.

"Sorry, Sarge. But ... I'm naked; you told me to take my clothes off. I thought you meant everything." He said sheepishly.

"This is no time to be embarrassed about your privates, Private. Get out of the water!" Reynolds watched briefly as the embarrassed private trudged out of the water, coughing. Reynolds hadn't noticed till now, but O'Malley's face and forearms were an angry shade of red. They needed to get moving.

Reynolds turned and quickly paced along a northwesterly trail that hugged the coastline, on the other side of the base's boundary fence. He listened to confirm O'Malley was following, and he was. He could also hear the private's labored breathing.

It didn't take long for them to reach the fenced rear yard of a small cottage, the home of the base commander and his wife.

After passing through a small unlocked gate, they walked side-by-side up the stepping stones, leading toward the house's back patio, where they both stopped abruptly.

Locked in mid-step, both were dumbstruck by what they saw.

O'Malley spoke first, "Uhm. Sorry to bother you, ma'am." His palms quickly converged over his crotch. The situation painted his face an extra shade of crimson.

The bikini-clad woman pushed herself up from a lounger in the sun, and moved her sunglasses down the bridge of her nose. Her lips curled into a sly smile. "To what do I owe this pleasure, gentlemen?" Her eyes flitted from man to man.

Reynolds immediately recognized Sheila Thompson, a woman whose beauty was renowned around base. But, this was no time for pleasantries. "Sergeant Robert Reynolds, ma'am. We're sorry to bother you, but the base has just been attacked. We barely made it out alive. Our clothes were covered in sarin, so we had to remove them."

Mrs. Thompson jumped out of the lounger as if it were suddenly molten hot, throwing a towel around her shoulders. It was a quick show of a modesty that hadn't existed moments ago. The playful smile was gone. "Is my husband all right?"

"I don't know, ma'am. But we plan to check. The reason we stopped here first is that Colonel Thompson kept two hazmat suits here for both of you in case of a gas attack. The private and I need them to return to the base and see if we can find any survivors and to get the antidote. Unfortunately, if we don't take it soon, we'll both be dead."

O'Malley shot his sergeant a quick glance. His face momentarily tightened, then he returned his gaze forward, attempting to hide his concern.

Mrs. Thompson just stood, still in shock over the prospect of what she'd just heard.

"Please, we need to move now," Reynolds said, ushering her to the back door of the house.

E ven Reynolds wasn't prepared for what they witnessed next.

After gathering what they needed and calming down Mrs. Thompson, they suited up and exited the cottage's main entrance, walking quickly to the base's front gate. That's where the killing fields started.

The sliding aluminum gate, crowned with razor wire, was slightly ajar. PFC Woo lay just beyond, dead. Other dead comrades were everywhere, strewn about like in a disaster movie. Similar to Woo, most were clutching their throats, their eyes wide and terrified.

Sarin gas was the most volatile nerve agent known. It caused its toxic effects by preventing the proper operation of an enzyme that acts as the body's "off switch" for glands and muscles. Without the "off switch," the body's glands and muscles are constantly being stimulated. Most infected die within minutes, typically from asphyxiation.

"Sarge," O'Malley asked, out of breath, his voice obscured from his hazmat suit, "do you think anyone's alive?"

Reynolds slowed only slightly, craning his head to examine O'Malley's red face, now covered in a sheet of perspiration. Both men readjusted the bunch of towels and blankets each had slung around their backs, secured by a make-shift blanket satchel, all procured, from the colonel's cottage. "Yeah, I do. If anyone stayed out of direct exposure, or got out of it quickly like us, they'd make it."

"So, what, we check all the buildings?"

"First to the clinic for the atropine. Then yes, we clear each building, until we've accounted for everyone.

Luckily for them, the clinic was the second closest building within the twelve-building complex.

Before entering, they'd counted out loud fifteen dead soldiers. There were forty-eight on base. Three squads: Alpha, Bravo, and Charlie, each with their compliment of eight men and women. The remainder was support for their squads.

Reynolds knew they were the only two who made it out from Bravo. He knew Alpha and Charlie were also on the field and he hadn't seen any of them running, although he only glanced once. So, they probably didn't make it. That left only maybe four more potential survivors. He was starting to lose hope.

Inside the two room clinic, they found two survivors, although they were barely hanging on.

They were two young privates from Alpha Squad. Each rested in a heap in the corner of the reception room, their faces covered in a thick sheen of sweat and mucus. Both drew shallow breaths.

O'Malley bent over them, desperate to help his fallen comrades.

"Come on, PFC O'Malley. Let's get the atropine. Then we can administer aid," he said while pushing through the door of the clinic, hoping the doctor was here. He wasn't.

"Look there." Reynolds pointed to a locked cabinet, with glass doors. Behind it, medicines were perfectly lined up like little platoons of Army efficiency. "We're looking for either atropine or pralidoxime."

O'Malley picked up a reflex hammer resting on a table. Using the metal end, he speared the middle of the glass case, shattering it. His oversized gloved hand probed the inside, knocking down several vials. Gingerly grabbing one bottle from each column, he read aloud the drug's title.

Reynolds hurriedly rummaged through a different cabinet of drawers. His internal clock told him they were running out of time.

"Got it," yelled O'Malley.

"Grab all of it. I have the syringes," Reynolds said, scooping the couple dozen hypos from the shallow drawer. He tossed them on the same table O'Malley had swiped the reflex hammer from and pulled off his satchel of blankets, wrestling from it a beach bag Sheila had given him--she'd said they'd picked it up on a Regal European cruise during their honeymoon, before she started to leak more tears of worry.

"Toss the hypos and the atropine in there. Also grab some morphine, but hold that aside. Then, follow me."

Reynolds strode back out to the reception room. "Privates, get your asses up, on the double," he yelled at the two nearly lifeless forms on the floor. He rushed to a water cooler, grabbed the full bottle by the door and ripped off the top. Sloshing a little water on the path to the two men, where he made his quick assessment. One was struggling to raise himself, while the other barely moved, his breaths getting shallower.

Reynolds laid the bottle down and tugged at the standing private by the sleeves. His faceplate up against the struggling man, he demanded, "Son, you need to take your outer clothes off, now."

The private half nodded and started to unbuckle his pants and Reynolds ripped his shirt off. Then while the private was trying to navigate out of his trousers, he hoisted the water bottle and poured sloshes of water over his head and face.

"Scrub your hands."

O'Malley came over, breathing heavily and waited for direction from his sergeant.

"Switch out. Pour some of this onto a rag and wipe his face." He grabbed the beach bag of medicine and set up the first and then the next, and then another syringe. He counted the doses and figured they had maybe ten total. He jabbed the first needle into the private, while his face was being cleaned by O'Malley. With the second hypo, he jabbed O'Malley through his suit. The young man didn't even so much as flinch. He was tough.

"What about you?" O'Malley asked.

"I'll get mine last. I didn't inhale much." *I probably misstated their need for an antidote,* he thought. O'Malley looked like he'd probably survive without the antidote. But he was more concerned about the long-term effects to O'Malley's system, so he figured it wouldn't hurt him to receive the injection, and it might even save him. As for himself, Reynolds figured whatever was going to happen to him would happen. He was more concerned about the other survivors.

"All right, son." Reynolds laid a gloved hand on the arm of the panicked private, who was starting to come alive, going from barely breathing to almost hyperventilating. "You're going to feel your pulse race," he said, this time including O'Malley with a look. "It's okay, it's part of the drug's effect. You stay here," he said to the private, whose eyes were still wide with concern. "And don't go out for a few hours. If no one comes to get you, wrap this blanket around you and run out the gate and to the hospital in Endurance. You got it, Private?"

The young man's head nodded.

"O'Malley, let's go."

"Sir, what about the other one?" O'Malley motioned to the other private. But he knew the answer. The man—he thought his name was Fortuno—received too big of a dose and they didn't have enough of the antidote to go around.

Reynolds didn't answer. O'Malley quietly followed him out of the clinic and to the next building to find survivors.

They both hoped they'd use all of their remaining doses.

Chapter 4
Sunbay Cove, Florida

Lexi

The man was a boy really, maybe her age, though by the way he carried himself he looked even younger. He had a poor excuse of a goatee clinging to his chin, like a dirty string of saliva. Regardless, his holding her gun against her made him just as deadly as any other man.

He gave her a gross smile as he ushered her out of the thicket, back onto the driveway.

"Where you goin in such a hurry?

She didn't say anything. Frank had already taught her to pay attention to an enemy and to everything around her, but to say little to reveal her situation. Besides her footsteps and his, she heard his heavy breathing—he seemed jumpier than she was.

"Yah live here? We're spose to stay away, but Jonah got a report of a car driving in heah yesterday."

She stopped in the middle of the driveway, and readied herself for his next move.

He pressed the gun's barrel into her side, and it was like he'd hit her "on button." She reacted exactly like Frank had taught her.

"You goina talk or are ya—"

She spun around to her left, while hitting his gun hand away from her with her palm. With her right, she flicked out her knife and slashed at his forearms. Frank called the move "defanging the snake."

The man-boy was caught by complete surprise. He dropped the gun and fell on his ass, clutching his bleeding forearms.

She quickly snatched the gun from the ground and turned it on him as he scurried backward, kicking away from her like a wounded animal.

Her head was pounding so hard and she was breathing so heavily that when something exploded right in front of her, she thought for a moment that it was her head that had ruptured.

She screeched and so did the man-boy. Both backed further away from each other and the object flopping before them.

Their fear turned to shock and so for a moment, they could only gawk at the massive beast of an animal floundering in between them. It was as if some prehistoric monster had fallen from the skies.

It's just a pelican. And it's dying.

Its beak opened, extending unnaturally wide, gasping for one final breath, before letting out a raspy squawk. It shuddered once more and then stopped moving.

"What the fu—" Lexi 's head popped up, alerted by the man-boy's movement. He was already stumbling down the road, hugging his reddened arms to his chest.

Deciding the threats had passed, Lexi turned and jogged a couple of paces away from the dead bird. She'd tell Frank about both incidents.

Her head still pounded, but her senses were on high alert. So, even before she came to an abrupt halt, she reflexively leveled her pistol, pulled the hammer back, and readied herself to put a bullet into the newest threat before her.

The thicket rustled and then an elderly man released himself from the heavy growth, only ten yards in front of her. Once free, his hands shot up. In one hand, he gripped an old lever-action rifle.

"Don't shoot, please," he pleaded. "I'm Jasper, your neighbor." His dark face was covered in a thick gray beard that framed a warm smile. He seemed much older than Frank, but had the same knowing eyes.

He appeared unthreatening, but Lexi still kept her pistol carefully trained on the skinny man's chest. "What are you doing sneaking around here with a rifle, spying on us?"

"First tell me, what's your name?" The smile unflinching, but he tilted his brow, like he was chewing on a thought.

"You answer my questions, and then I'll answer yours."

"Fair enough; you're holding the gun ... I was asked by this property's owner to watch the place." Jasper noticed the change in Lexi's face immediately. "Do you know him?"

"Wait, you know my father?" she chirped.

"That'd make you Lexi Broadmoor," the man said grinning at his deduction.

She lowered her gun and returned the smile.

"L-e-x-i!" a muffled voice hollered from down the driveway, in front of the house.

Both Lexi and Jasper turned. Somebody was running toward them. He had a towel over his head and a gas mask over his face. It was Frank. "Come here!" he yelled again, his voice muffled and foreign from the mask.

Another white form fluttered from the sky, crashing near them. It flopped violently, its beak slicing at the air.

"It's gas," Frank screamed, again almost impossible to hear. "It's gas," Frank screamed again, pulling his mask up as he approached.

"What kind of gas?" asked Jasper.

Frank glared at the stranger and yanked Lexi away, toward the house.

"I'm your neighbor. Stanley asked me to watch the place. What kind of gas?"

Another bird dropped from the sky.

"Sarin!" Frank blurted, thrusting the extra gas mask at Lexi.

"My house is right here, quick. We might not make it all the way back to Stanley's place." Jasper was already through the trees, headed down a small path that led to a small house, not more than forty feet away.

"Come on," Frank insisted to Lexi, now pulling her the other way, and they followed Jasper.

Cain

"Help," the young man gasped, falling through the swinging door of Jonah's office, the front of his shirt and his two arms covered in blood. Two hurried men with military rifles followed close behind him.

Jonah leapt out of his chair. "Cain, what happened?" He reached out to him on the floor.

"Some woman slashed my arms." His voice was weak, his face pale and swimming in sweat.

"Get some bandages," Jonas growled at one of his men, who spun on his heels and ran out the door.

"Who did this?" Jonas asked as he whisked up the young man and lowered him onto his couch, grimacing at the amount of blood.

His other man had calmly grabbed a couple of towels from a closet and started to wrap them around Cain's arms.

"It's a woman at the Smith place. There's someone living there and she stabbed me. And I was doing nuttin."

Jonas carefully peeked at the wounds, before tying off each towel so that it was tight. He couldn't tell how bad the cuts were, but he felt sure Cain would live.

A man appeared in Jonah's doorway, "I can't find any of the first aid supplies. What can we do?"

"He's been cut pretty badly on his arms," Jonah said. "Help me."

"You want me to take him to the clinic?" asked another man, calm and reserved. The other men hovered, not sure what their boss would order.

"Thanks Peter, help me get him in the 'Vette. I'll take him to there. Em will fix him up."

Peter grabbed Cain's legs and Jonah held the young man's arms, and carried him out of the warehouse, toward Jonah's car.

"What would you like me to do?" Peter asked, being careful to not let go.

Jonah didn't say anything as they loaded Cain into the seat, every jostle eliciting a groan.

Jonah walked around the front of the car and opened up the driver's side door, and glanced up to Peter and his men. His face was full of violence.

"You"—he pointed to one of his me—"get into the back and keep pressure on his wounds." Then to Peter he snapped, "You take some men and go get that bitch who cut my boy."

"You want her alive, don't you?"

"Yes. If my boy somehow dies from this, I'll want to kill her myself."

Chapter 5
Sunbay Cove, Florida

Travis

Travis spun around in the chair, letting the inertia of each spin pull his head outward, like the Whirly Bird at an amusement park. Using the feet of the rolling desk chair to push off against, he spun himself around faster with every successive spin, enjoying the momentary light-headedness each time. He counted each revolution, trying to beat the last one, which was slightly further than the one previous, getting almost up to five total revolutions with the last push.

"The crowd was anxious to see if a world record, F I V E revolutions could be accomplished by the young Travis Broadmoor, the current record holder. The crowd has quieted down, holding its collective breath."

His right heel ratcheted into one roller leg, the back of his left heel hooked to a leg opposite this...

"He looks ready..."

His leg muscles tightened.

"And he's off—"

Travis pushed-pulled so hard the chair tilted backward, and for a moment, he and the chair hung suspended before he flopped hard onto the floor with a large *crash-thunk.*

Epic fail!

He chuckled out loud, once he realized he wasn't hurt too badly.

On his back, staring at the underside of the work table right where his Uncle Frank had been seated just before the birds fell out of the sky, he considered what he did wrong in his record-breaking attempt. The outline of something drew his eyes. Scrunching his brow, exaggerating a squint, he tried to make out what was mostly hidden underneath the table.

Sloughing off the overturned chair, he pressed his face up to the underside of the table and knew what it was right away.

It was a gun.

A pistol, actually, held to the base of the table by Velcro straps. He freed it and held it in his hand, his fingers naturally wrapping around the handle. It felt good.

His lips curled into a grin.

He examined the barrel of the gun, careful to not look into it directly so he didn't accidentally shoot himself. He read this before, and besides what idiot would point a gun that might be loaded at himself? Frank was going to teach him today how to shoot a .22. And this looked like a .22, based on the size of the hole coming from the barrel. He held it close to his face, scrutinizing every line of the Ruger. Then he thrust it outward, pointing it at a big can of catsup on one of the many shelves of food, maybe five feet away.

"Bang," he said pretending to fire, but not squeezing the trigger. He couldn't wait for Uncle Frank to get back.

A loud screech blared out of the desk's speakers and it startled him so badly, he almost touched the trigger. Relieved he didn't accidentally kill their supply of catsup (because he didn't want to be forced to eat mustard instead), he pointed it away and glared at the radio. Its dials had just lit up by themselves.

"I repeat. F are you there?" blared from somewhere in the room.

Travis leaned into the radio, as if he wasn't sure the sound actually came from it. He reached over with his other hand and pressed the microphone button down. "Hello?"

"Who is this?" the voice asked.

"Um, this is Travis." He pushed the chair out of his way with his foot. "Who are you?"

"You can call me G. I'll call you T, if that's all right?"

"Sure."

"Where are you and your parents, T?"

"My parents are dead and my godfather Frank is taking care of my sister Lexi and me."

"Where is F? Are you and your sister all right?"

Travis was getting the hang of this. "Sorry, but F isn't here right now. Both my sister and I are all right. Uncle Fra ... I mean F told me to wait in here. He was pretty worried about something. He ran out the door and said to not open the door for anyone else, but he hasn't come back yet. They've been gone for a while now ... Hey, how do you know my godfather? I call him Uncle Frank. Sorry."

"I'm a friend of your uncle. I was worried something had happened to him, but I'm sure he's fine."

Travis set the chair back upright and crawled into it, swinging his elbows over its back. He laid the gun down. "Are you in Florida too?"

"No, T, we're in Texas, F's home town."

"Cool, that's hundreds of miles away, actually less for the radio waves, going across the water. But it's still pretty far."

"So you're in a safe pla—"

There was a ding sound in the background and G stopped speaking.

"Ahh, T? Do you see a little sheet of paper taped to the radio, with a list of frequencies?"

"Yes."

"Good, go to the next one. Can you do that?"

"Piece of cake, G." Travis spun the dial and found the next frequency. G was already speaking.

"T, are you there?"

"I'm here, G."

Travis gave his chair a spin.

Stowell, Texas

Grimes

G rimes gave Travis some information for Frank on his return, insisting that he write it down so that he wouldn't forget. He had already quizzed Travis on his situation, happy to hear that he appeared to be in a safe enclosed space with water, food, and even a bathroom. Travis, who seemed like a bright boy for ten years old—he told G this proudly—promised to stay put for up to two days, or until someone came and got him, before going back outside.

Grimes had to be careful not to say too much, sure the enemy was probably listening. Luckily for him, Travis seemed to know this stuff intuitively, picking up their frequency process without much difficulty.

"Ding!" It was the second ten-minute rotation, and Grimes still had other work to do, even though he was reluctant to let the boy go. He heard the signal on Travis's side too.

"I've got to go now, T," Grimes looked forward, as if the boy were directly in front of him. "Can I talk to you tomorrow at the same time?"

"That would be great, G." Grimes had a mental picture of the boy smiling. He sounded like he was having fun.

"You know the frequency, right?"

"Duh, G. This is T, over and out, good buddy."

Grimes smiled now. It was the first thing he had to smile about since he heard Frank's voice hours ago.

Aimes burst into Grimes's radio room. "Anything?"

"No, but I did talk to Frank's godson in Florida."

"What happened to Frank? Is he all right?" Aimes seated himself in a side chair against the wall, and rested his rifle against the wall beside him. He unlatched his tactical vest to give his broad chest more room to expand.

"I honestly don't know. I was trying to not scare Travis—his godson—but Frank left our conversation so quickly ... and because he put Travis inside and ran outside, I don't know if they were gassed or not." Grimes pushed himself away from his desk, crowded with radios, microphones, books, and a project: a tangle of wires that were the guts of a radio. He rubbed at the fatigue in his eyes.

"But there isn't a base beside them."

"I know ..." Grimes stretched his arms upward, and then tilted his chair back.

"And no word from Porter or the others?"

"Not a damned thing." His chair *flumped* back to all fours. He stared at Aimes with worry.

"Shit, buddy, the world ended. It's not too easy to just drive back. I'm sure your son is being careful. He's a smart boy." Aimes tried to give his friend a welcoming smile of assurance. But he knew it wouldn't help.

"I know. I just wished to God I'd hear something from them, or at least one of our men on lookout."

Ten Miles Northeast of Stowell, Texas

Paul

Paul Skidmore worked the crook out of his neck from being in the same position for so long without moving. He was thirty feet up in a giant antenna tower, on a small platform—way too small for him—peering through binoculars along two stretches of highway. He was watching for bad guys.

It was literally a bird's eye view of I-10 all the way to Beaumont, and 124, the county road that mostly ran parallel to the highway.

His job was to not only look for any enemy that may come their way, but also for any bands of thieves or miscreants who might be a threat to their little town. Finally, he was watching out for Robert Grimes's son and a few soldiers who were coming to help.

The world resolved itself through a Leopold scope attached to his 30-30. Although he was quite a good shot, having bagged a whitetail every year now for twenty years, he was told not to shoot anyone. If he saw anything, he was supposed to just call it in to Grimes and let the others take care of the threat. Luckily, there had been no threats so far. The only folks he'd seen were the occasional small family or couple walking along the road, probably trying to find their way home. But that was over a day ago. Since then, nothing; longer since he'd seen a working vehicle.

So now the watch was monotonous as there was nothing to look at except three dead bodies on the road, only one of them human. Of course they didn't move, much. He pointed his Leopold at the dead woman; the scope was more powerful than the binoculars. He lined up the black cross-hairs on her handbag, just above her head, and stared at her some more.

It was not right the way she'd been left there, half-naked, her throat slit. She must have had a pretty face, although it was all swollen now. He was thankful that part of her shirt, although torn and revealing, covered her chest. The rest of her was exposed and he couldn't stand it.

A large black form landed in his field of view. It was blurry, but he knew instantly what it was.

Paul adjusted the power back slightly and then refocused; it was a damned turkey vulture, about ready to dine on the woman.

He'd already shot two of these things before they could chow down on her. He wasn't going to let this one add to the dead woman's indignity.

Breathing slowly, he cycled a round into the chamber. His finger touched the trigger, ready to apply the proper two pounds of pressure.

The carrion eater flapped away, just as he had coaxed the round out.

He missed.

"Damn!" he said to the winds.

He once again zoomed back so that he could see ten yards around the dead woman. The vulture was definitely gone.

The sound of a door closing alerted him to something beyond the body.

Paul pulled his head away from the eyepiece and was shocked to see a caravan of vehicles, with dozens of men on them. The wind was blowing from behind him, so he hadn't heard their approach.

Two men moved to the woman, their faces filled with evil smiles. He glanced back at the others, and then lifted his eyepiece back so that he could better assess who they were and radio it in to Grimes. He needed to let them know a threat was coming their way.

They looked like a group of crazed men who were taking advantage of a new world without any more laws. Certainly they weren't the terrorists he was watching for.

A flash of light blinded him for a moment. He pulled his eye away from the scope and then looked back. On the hood of one of the trucks, an older model Ford, a man was pointing a rifle in his direction.

It was pointed at him!

Paul's eyepiece shattered, the round piercing his brain. A half-second later the percussive sound reached him, unheard.

Chapter 6
Endurance, Florida

Jonah

The man's frantic voice arrived before he did.

"I need a doctor!"

He burst through the clinic's doors, clutching a boy blanched of all color. The boy's mouth was welded in a permanent cry for help; his eyes seared wide with fear, were lifeless.

"It's my son. He can't breathe," the man croaked.

No one seemed to hear him over the reception room's chaotic din.

Endurance Health Center had a staff of two doctors, three nurses, a dozen support staff and several volunteers. All were there and all were occupied, trying to save as many as they could of the town's people afflicted by a mystery illness. Even the janitor was giving CPR to an elderly man who had stumbled in and collapsed.

"I'll get the doctor," said an aged volunteer, who had come in on his day off. He rose slowly at first from his seat, softly patting the head of little girl crying over her unconscious mother next to her.

The elderly aide moved briskly for his age and disappeared around the corner. But he came to a stop almost immediately, in front of one of the two doctors.

The senior physician on staff, Dr. Emily Scott, was arguing with another man. Of course it wasn't just any man. The aide could see it was the famous, or more appropriately, infamous Jonah Price.

"I need you to get me more supplies," Dr. Scott barked at Jonah. "We're of course out of everything since the power went out five days ago, and we haven't had a delivery in a week. So, we need everything. But now we need every milliliter of atropine or pralidoxime you can get your hands on."

Jonah shrugged. "Hey, Em, do you think I'm some sort of medical supply company?" he said, almost meekly.

Her return glare gave him his answer. And she added, although it was unnecessary, "Please don't treat me like one of the bimbos who keep you company at night." She looked up at the frantic volunteer, and then back to Jonah. "Remember, I took in your son as a favor to you, over all these people who need my help more."

Jonah bored holes in his feet with his gaze, feeling the sting of her words. He glanced up past Emily to the room behind her, where his son was resting comfortably, even though his injuries were not life-threatening. He then scanned around the wide hallway, and saw for the first time the frantic pace of everyone attempting to deal with the crisis.

"I need to go, Jonah. Just do what you can, please." She said as she brushed past him.

Jonah started after her, making his way into the waiting room. "I'll do my best, Em," but she was already attending to a boy, his father clutching the child's lifeless frame. Jonah knew the man well as he had had several run-ins with him: Rory Thomas, the town's sheriff. She shook her head and the man buried his head into the boy's chest. The rest of the waiting room was packed with the sick, the dying, and the dead.

Something horrible had just happened to their town, worse than the power going out. And although Jonah believed it was every man for himself, and many more would die when they ran out of food. This was his town. It was the town he grew up in. He went to high school with Emily's eldest brother and Rory. He knew half the people in the waiting room, especially the older ones.

Jonah hovered in his place, watching and listening to Emily work. His two men, who had helped him get his boy to the clinic, waited impatiently beside him.

A strikingly beautiful woman blew into the open doorway. She scanned the room, found Dr. Scott and rushed over to her. The words fell out of her full lips, "The Army base has been gassed. My husband, the base commander, is there. I don't know, but maybe they're all dead." Her eyes welled up, ready to overflow. "Can you get someone to check on them?"

Jonah was now standing behind Emily. "How do you know they were gassed?" he asked the woman.

Dr. Scott glanced at Jonah and then the commander's wife.

"Two of his men came to my house and said it was attacked by a drone. They watched it fly over. They took our two hazmat suits and went in to save as many as they could. They were going to get some sort of antidote and bring as many survivors over here as they could." There was no holding back her tears now.

"I'll take a couple of my men and check out the base for you, ma'am," Jonah said to the woman. Then to Dr. Scott he added, "And Em, I'll get you the meds you need. One of my men will bring them over shortly."

"Thank you," the woman said, offering a weak but beautiful smile.

"Thanks, Jonah," Dr. Scott said. Her smile was warm and genuine.

"Come on." Jonah corralled his two men and they hurried out the doorway.

"Stue," Jonah said, hurrying past others standing near the clinic's entrance, "you go get two more men and get a mix of medical supplies, say about ten percent of our total, and bring them to the clinic and give them to the doc."

Stewart remained at his side, staring at his boss like he had grown horns. He knew that Jonah was sweet on the doctor, but to give away so much when their supplies were getting more valuable by the day was foolish. And it was dangerous to all of them.

"What are you waiting around for?"

Stewart, as if electrified, turned away and trotted off the other direction, to a warehouse only a few blocks away.

Jonah stopped at his '58 'Vette, motioning his man to get into the other side. Jonah got in and started it up. The 'Vette grumbled as Walters swung into the passenger seat. Jonah turned to him, making sure he was listening. "I'm going to drop you off. I want you to grab one of the trucks and load it up with hazmat suits, enough for everyone. But first call Peter. Tell him to meet us at the base ASAP."

Jonah drove out the clinic's parking lot, navigated around the stalled cars, and pulled onto the otherwise empty road.

"Aren't Peter and his men out getting the one who sliced up your son?"

"Yes, of course." He'd already forgotten about the knife-wielding woman, after realizing the danger had passed. "Have him bring her too."

"What are we all doing at the base?"

"We're going to look for survivors of course. But if they're all dead, I want to grab all their supplies, before someone else thinks to do it."

Walters nodded his head in agreement. There was a reason why Jonah ran this town.

Chapter 7
Sunbay Cove, Florida

Lexi

"I'm sorry to tell you this, but my father died five days ago." Lexi's whispered words affected her more deeply and stung harder than the real-time event had.

She fought back her tears, unwilling to surrender to them. The event hadn't changed, but she had changed since then.

The sting must have been fresh for Jasper, who only just heard this. He seemed to sink into his ancient recliner, lost in thought. His palms fell onto the chair's arms—each branded with a gray X made by two strips of duct tape, as if they were marked to remind him where to put his hands.

"Most men don't live the life they were meant to, Stanley Broadmoor appeared to be the exception," he said.

Lexi eyed him for a while, not sure what to make of his comment and waiting for something more. But the strange man must have needed to process what she'd just told him.

As the moments passed and her eyes wondered, she noticed that Jasper's house didn't have any lights or anything that indicated he had power. She had almost taken

for granted that most folks wouldn't have been as prepared as her father or godfather.

She also noticed that all the vents were sealed with
cut-out pieces of black plastic and tape, and there was no
circulating air. It was hot as the blazes inside.

All of the living room's light poured through one giant
window, framing Jasper where he sat, with a perfect view
of the inlet to the Gulf. Any other time, this would have
been a idyllic spot to read a book or just stare off contemplating life. But those days were gone.

Frank fidgeted next to Lexi in a love seat facing Jasper,
in the middle of the living room.

He scrutinized every point where the air from the outside could get in: the doorway, the large window, and
the vents. His gaze moved around the room trying to
find a breach, while a few flies nervously bounced off the
window, wanting out.

Jasper had assured him when they had first entered
that the main living areas of his home were sealed up
tight as a drum. He described his preparation for things
such as nuclear fallout and poisonous gas. Hearing how
well he had prepared, Frank was dying to compare notes
with the man when they had a free moment to do so.
Instead, he worried.

Based on this stranger's say-so, they were resting—not
that Frank could sit still—while they waited for the sarin to
dissipate. It could take hours. Maybe days. He just didn't
know, and that made him very nervous. Leaving Travis

alone amped up his nervousness even more. But what really got to Frank was depending on one more person, and a stranger to boot.

It's not like we have a choice. Make the best of it, he told himself.

Frank huffed and laid his rifle on his lap, while his left toe tapped a rhythmic beat to match his restlessness. Getting up and pacing would only make Lexi more anxious than she was. So to get his mind off of their situation, he finally took some time to regard their host.

Jasper was an odd-looking man with a full Duck Dynasty beard and a Confederate cap resting off-center on a crown of fine, curly white hair. His left eye was normal enough, but his right one was both strange and telling. Both were intense and felt genuine, but his right one drifted on its own each time the left moved, like it wasn't properly connected to the rest of his head.

If the eyes were a window to one's soul, then what did that unhinged eye say about this man? Frank's left toe tapped more rapidly.

Jasper had spoken of being in the military and definitely appeared to be able to handle himself, even with his wiry frame. And in spite of just meeting him, Frank knew it was necessary to trust this man. Again, they had no alternative. It was certain death out there.

But when he considered their situation objectively, there was a red flag he couldn't disregard: wasn't it a little too fortuitous for them that Stanley would end up with Jasper next door? A prepper and ex-military man like him, as a neighbor?

He had to push this thought away. They'd deal with that later.

His hands reflexively squeezed his rifle: a physical re-assurance to his psyche that he was ready to put it into action the moment it was needed.

No, he wouldn't relax, no matter how long they were holed up here.

Lexi's eyes were drawn to Frank's tapping. But then she noticed droplets of red, escaping a sleeve and sliding down Frank's left bicep. "Shit, your shoulder's bleeding," she blurted, her gaze riveted to Frank's left shoulder where he had taken a bullet only two days earlier. His camo-colored T-shirt was stained with wetness that she'd figured was sweat—they were all covered in sweat from the exertion and sitting in a nearly 90-degree house with no fan or fresh air circulation.

Jasper looked up at Frank and Lexi, and rubbed away the wetness from his eyes. "I think there are some fresh dressings in the cabinet behind you."

Lexi rose from the love seat, moved around to a dark wormwood chest, and searched the drawers. "Off with your shirt, major," she demanded, mimicking his own drill-sergeant tone.

"It's really nothing. Besides what do you know about field dressing wounds?"

After clanging around for a moment, Lexi stood up and stepped behind Frank. She dumped handfuls of gauze pads, medical tape, and scissors on a small table abutting the back of the love seat. "I was constantly hurting myself, and I didn't want to tell anyone, so I got quite good at patching myself up. More importantly I sped-read one of Daddy's books, First Aid for Soldiers by The Department of Army."

"You speed-read the entire First Aid for Soldiers book?" He twisted and glared back at Lexi with disbelief. "Okay, what page addresses my particular issue?"

Lexi scowled back at him. "You forgot I have a nearly photographic memory. Page 2-32, specifically section 2-16 deals with Entrance and Exit Wounds. Below that, is a detailed description of Field Dressing. *Okay*?"

Frank turned back to Jasper—he offered a shrug, followed by a shallow but genuine grin. Reluctantly, he slowly removed his shirt. Even though he tried to repress it, each movement was followed by a muffled grunt.

Jasper just watched the show. His unemotional stare turned into a smile... then morphed into something resembling disgust.

Lexi's eyes fell to Frank's back.

"Oh my God," Lexi stepped back from Frank and the couch, as if she were afraid of contracting a disease. Her palms pressed against her mouth, to hold back the contents of her stomach that threatened to come up, while her eyes nearly burst from their sockets with concern.

Frank's back looked like something out of a horror movie. He was covered in bandages, all crimson-colored. In between the multitude of reddened gauze, were butterflied bandages holding together opened gashes that oozed. The remaining portions of his unbandaged skin that hadn't been recently tortured were a weave of scar-tissue.

It was an omnibus book of real-life horror stories that screamed of pain and cruelty.

"Sorry, I should have warned you first."

Lexi instantly lost all feeling of nausea. *He's apologizing to me?*

This man, who's risked his life and body to protect her and Travis, who never complained once about his torture and about being shot.

Suck it up buttercup! her mind commanded.

"No worries. Just ... a surprise." Lexi bit her lip and ignored her own frailties. She could do this.

She reached over to the darkened bandage, covering the bullet wound in his shoulder, and peeled back the tape. The stitches were still intact, holding together the damaged tissue, only seeping a little blood now. The front entry wound was even better, as it was a lot smaller.

"It doesn't look too bad, actually. The stitches have held, and it doesn't look infected. It's just bleeding a little," she announced confidently. "I'm just going to replace the dressing around your bullet wound."

"Thanks, doc." Frank said, unable to repress a grin.

Lexi laid out strips of tape, and set up the dressing. Then blotting the sweat and blood with a clean pad, she applied the first bandage to the entry wound.

"If you don't mind me asking," Jasper said, "so what happened to your dad? I mean"—he paused and looked empathetically at the young woman—"how did he die?"

"Car crash," she rattled off, like she were repeating a recipe. "We were in the car. Best I can figure, we were headed here, driving west on I-10 when they set off the bomb in Jacksonville. Its flash must have blinded him and he ran into a street sign that ... killed him."

Jasper nodded, as if knowing her pain, but he said nothing.

She applied the bandage to Frank's back, smoothing down the folds of tape, to make sure they'd adhere.

"It's okay. We buried him by the highway," she said softly, and then addressed Frank. "You can put your shirt back on, soldier."

"Your father sounded like a man who cared about his children, setting up his home, and trying to bring all of you here where you would be safe. You were lucky to have him."

"I really didn't know my father." Lexi's voice cracked a bit, but she felt stronger talking about this. "He went away after my mother died, or rather was killed by my uncle."

"Abe killed your mother?" Frank blurted, his mouth somewhat crooked, as if he were amazed by this revelation.

"Yep, dear old Uncle Abdul, the leader of the terrorist group who murdered millions of Americans, also murdered my mother eight years ago." Lexi hadn't had time to tell Frank this, so now was as good a time as any. "My father realized that Travis and I were in danger." She stopped abruptly and then glared at Frank. "Are you sure Travis is all right?"

"Yes, of course he is. He's locked up in the radio and storage area. He's got food, water, and even a bathroom. It's sealed against gas. I noticed that when I did an inspection this morning. I told him to wait for us. He'll wait."

Frank said this with certainty. But his face seemed to say otherwise.

The two men sat silent for some time, when Frank spoke to Jasper, "So tell me, Captain—"

"—just Jasper, please Frank."

"Oh sure. So, tell me Jasper, since we're going to be here for a bit longer, what's the status of the neighboring town? How are they dealing with the lack of power and supplies?"

Lexi had put away the remaining medical supplies and sat back down next to Frank again, eagerly wanting to hear what their host had to say on this.

"Endurance? Oh, they're doing better than most, I guess. Many of the residences, like yours and this one have some sort of back-up power and have some stored up food. Everyone here is prepared for the next hurricane.

"But those who live in town, at least those who didn't plan for that rainy day, they get their food from Jonah. I imagine most of the town will at some point."

"Jonah?" asked Lexi. "You mean like from the Bible?"

Jasper was a lot more animated now. "I imagine so. Jonah Price is one part opportunist and one part thug. What he doesn't own, he takes. When the lights went out, he started trading food for labor, or other favors for his men."

Lexi's face twisted into a painful scowl, when she asked, "Other favors?"

"Let's just say, the women in town, the pretty ones especially, offered a different kind of labor than the men. Sorry, young lady." Jasper's shoulders sank and his head dropped.

It was hard to see all of the features of his face with the bright light behind him and his full beard, but Lexi suspected it was as red as his dark skin would allow.

"What kind of labor did the men provide?" asked Frank. Lexi was sure he'd changed the subject slightly for her benefit.

"I don't know, Frank. He has a lot of businesses and warehouses. I'm guessing he had them working in one of his warehouses."

"So this thug, as you called him, is forcing people to be slaves in exchange for food?" Lexi didn't hide the anger in her voice: she hated seeing people prey on others.

"Well, I guess it depends on how you look at it. Most Americans haven't prepared and only have maybe a week's worth of food or less in their cupboards. Jonah is just offering them his food, but not for free. But with Jonah, there's no limit to the price he might charge."

"I definitely need to meet this Jonah, after this threat passes."

"What?" Lexi asked. She didn't like the sound of this man at all, and although what he was doing to others in this town—now her town—made her angry, she wasn't eager for any of her family to engage him. The man sounded like a bigger version of Clyde, someone she wanted to forget about, and put behind her.

"I'm sure he'll be coming to you soon enough."

Both Frank and Lexi glared at Jasper; their faces begged the question.

"Yeah, it was Jonah's son that Lexi cut earlier."

Chapter 8
Sunbay Cove, Florida

Peter

"Check," crackled the radio. It was the last man to check in from his detail. "I still don't see any movement."

Peter and his men had the house surrounded. They had been waiting for a long time, but there didn't appear to be anyone in or around the place. All the window blinds were open in back, so they would have seen if someone was moving about. He guessed no one was home, and would have just waited, but something told him to check further.

It just didn't feel right.

There were maybe a dozen dead birds around the house and grounds. They hadn't seen any on the way into the property. Not knowing what had happened here amped his tension to a level thicker than the normal humidity.

He couldn't stand holding any longer. Waiting would be the safe option. But with Jonah breathing down his neck to get the woman who sliced up his boy, there was no time for safety. "All right, move in slowly," he whispered into his headset.

Peter and one of his men raised their SCAR 17 rifles and crept toward the door. Another man kept watch of their perimeter, in case someone came at them from their flank or rear.

Peter saw from his periphery that two other men—one on each side—approached the home as well. And he knew two more were approaching the front of the house.

He reached up with his left hand, still keeping the beefy SCAR pointed with his right, and tried the screen door knob. It twisted without resistance.

Pulling at it slowly, he winced as the screen door groaned. If someone was here, they heard that for sure.

Sliding forward while bracing the screen with his knee, he turned the solid wood door's knob and it too opened. It was unlocked.

There had to be someone inside, as he didn't think they'd leave the house unlocked. They must be close by.

He turned his head back to his man behind him and whispered, "Tell the others if their points of entry are locked to hold their positions. We're going inside."

He waited till his man radioed his order. Then he pushed the door open and stepped inside.

Lexi

Lexi really didn't know Frank too well, at least not yet. After all, it had been years since she had seen him, and that was when she had been a different, much younger person. They'd been together now barely more than a day. Yet, Lexi already knew Frank didn't show much emotion, except when he was agitated, and then it was obvious. He was agitated now. And because Frank was, so was she.

They both rose from their seats. Frank started to pace around the room, and Lexi just remained standing in her position, in front of the couch. Jasper eyed them both.

Movement outside the window caught Lexi's eye.

She saw it clearly, but it wasn't making sense to her at all, and this filled her with more angst.

Right outside of the giant picture window was an ancient-looking bird feeder, dangling off of a large elderberry in Jasper's yard. Dozens of little birds were feeding from it. It felt odd, but she didn't know why.

Then it hit.

"Frank! Look!" Her forefinger shot out like a bullet toward the window. "The birds ... they're fine."

It registered instantly for Frank too, who dashed back to the love seat and grabbed his rifle.

Jasper didn't yet understand why that excited them so. Frank brought him up to speed. "If the birds are alive and eating, that means the outside isn't contaminated, if it ever was."

"Wait," Lexi grabbed his arm, "what do you mean, 'if it ever was?' We saw all the dead birds."

He squeezed her hand, and pulled it away. "It's okay, the birds that died were probably part of a flock that got a dose of it in the air. They were probably coming from the Army base just north of us and died here. I don't think our area was hit. But we've got to move. Travis is alone and

I don't want him to be there if Jonah or his men come to the house."

Lexi didn't need any more coaxing. She unholstered her pistol and followed Frank to the door. They both looked back at Jasper to see if he was coming.

"I'm right behind you. Wanna grab a bigger gun."

Frank and Lexi bounded through the door and down the side path to their home.

Jasper

Jasper took longer than he wanted, but he really didn't think Jonah and his men would be here this soon, so he didn't rush. He changed into some camos, just in case, and grabbed his Thompson Submachine gun. He'd procured it from the previous homeowner and preferred it over his AK. He was told by Jonah to keep it hidden since it didn't possess the proper ATF stamp. It had a full fifty-round drum attached, making the gun incredibly heavy. But if the shit hit the fan—he always loved that euphemism—it was a worthy companion, regardless of the weight. This he slung around to his back.

Next, he grabbed an M1 Garand, also the previous occupant's, and slung around him an ammo belt with twenty pre-loaded stripper clips. Finally, he flung a few additional items into his camo pack, including a couple of gas masks, and tossed the pack over his shoulders. It was overkill, but he liked to be prepared.

He bounded out the door, pausing only briefly to lock it and then raced down the side path, being careful to not make too much noise.

When he arrived at the opening to the Broadmoors' property, he stopped abruptly and slunk down behind a thick bush for cover. He raised his Garand and followed his target through the gun's peep-sight. Slowly the man approached. But then there were others behind him: Frank, Lexi, and a boy. They had their hands raised and were walking in Jasper's direction.

Frank looked directly at Jasper, as if he could see him behind the cover. Frank shook his head; it was his way of telling him "Don't try it."

Jasper lowered his rifle, but moved his head closer to hear what was being said.

Frank asked, "So where are you taking us?" It was obviously for Jasper's benefit.

He recognized the man who replied. It was Peter, Jonah's right-hand man. "I'm taking you and the girl to talk to my boss. He has some questions for you about what happened to his son."

"And where is that?"

"We're going to his—"

Peter's radio crackled and he held it to his head.

"He wants us to do what?" He listened, and then nodded. "Yeah, we have the girl, her brother, and her godfather."

They passed by Jasper, following the Broadmoors' side path toward the driveway.

Jasper stuck his head out, trying to make sure he heard as much of the conversation as he could.

"He wants us to go to the front gate of the base? All right, tell Jonah we're leaving now."

Jasper waited until they were out of sight, and then he trotted back to his place. He rummaged around and found the boat keys, and then hopped into the little boat. He idled it out of the metal boathouse and into the inlet. When he was in the Gulf and sure that his engine wouldn't be heard, he throttled it forward and headed north toward the Army base.

He wanted to get there before Peter and the others did.

Chapter 9
Crystal Waters, Florida

Randall

"In Ramadan, there will be a Sound." The fiery imam raised a hand up to an ear and tilted his head toward the heavens, as if he could hear Jibrail himself speaking directly to him.

To Randall White, the man looked more like a TV preacher than an imam. But that was his style, and his style was what drew them all in, including Randall.

"They said: O Messenger of Allah, is it in its beginning, in its middle, or in its end?" Imam Ramadi continued.

"No, in the middle of Ramadan."

He paused and looked out at his followers. Most of those in the mosque stared back eagerly. Some like Randall looked back with dread, a reflection of an almost prophetic sense of what was coming next.

"This day my friends, as you all know, is the middle of Ramadan." He was setting up his followers for the rest of the prophetic message partially taken from the *hadith* about what they could expect during the end days.

He tilted his head back up to the ceiling and to the side.

"Then, there will be a sound from the sky that causes death to seventy thousand.

"They asked: 'O Messenger of Allah, who will survive from your nation?'"

The imam paused for a long moment and then peered at the men standing in his mosque and then at the women, separated by a wall so that neither group could see the other.

"It is the *true* believer who will survive, my friends. Is that you?" He pointed his crooked forefinger first at the women, and then the men, his eyes following his finger's accusatory scorn.

Randall felt sure that the imam's finger stopped, pointing directly at him. The man's severe eyes knew what Randall felt in his heart: that this imam was evil.

When the prosecutor's twisted digit and critical eyes moved past him to the next accused, Randall's mind wandered to how he got here.

After retirement from baseball as a respectable hitter with a .242 average, he felt a big spiritual hole. He was raised Southern Baptist—a family tradition that stretched several generations and included two pastors—but it all felt false to him. It was the speaking out of both sides of their mouths that got to him most: at church they'd sing glowing praises to God, and then at home, they'd spew hateful things about their fellow congregants. And yet, this very manner of conduct was despised by God, when James warned, "Do not speak evil against one another, brothers." It was the incongruent actions that rubbed away at him, causing him to first miss an occasional Sunday—always with a believable excuse—until he stopped attending altogether. After a time, he became spiritually lost.

Then a baseball friend of his talked to him about Islam. He was immediately drawn into the concept of being submissive to Allah—the Muslim name for God—as he believed obedience to the Almighty was important. But the other pillars hit him as right too, especially the daily prayer. His friend invited him to mosque and he listened, and started to read the Quran. Oh, there were passages that bothered him in their book, just as many Old Testament passages in the Bible made him uncomfortable.

One day, he found that the community, the commitment, and the prayerful supplication to Allah moved him spiritually, and this led him to become a Muslim. His wife, Leticia saw the change in him and the other men's wives worked on her, explaining her role in the family, which was similar to the one outlined by the Baptists. She slowly came around, but it was mostly because of the noticeable change she saw in him.

They were attending mosque on a regular basis, when an Imam Ramadi visited their mosque and spoke. He told them of the coming end times and of what they needed to do to prepare. This was a different version of the same speech he heard spoken from the Baptist pew before. And they, too, recognized the Second Coming of Jesus, who would appear with the Mahdi to bring changes to the whole world. The imam spoke about his mosque in Crystal Waters, a small community in northern Florida that was almost entirely Muslim; where everyone took care of each other. The charismatic imam charmed Randall and his wife instantly.

At a big dinner where both his and his wife's families attended, one of them brought up their conversion to Islam. They had all avoided this conversation for months.

But at dinner, the accumulated bile toward their faith erupted, and each family member spewed forth angry words about their actions and their newfound faith. Randall and Leticia, stomped out in tears. The next day, they put their house up for sale and moved to Crystal Waters, where they made friends and became completely immersed into the community. That had been less than a year ago.

When the power went out, Randall thought their decision to move was even better. While reports—via the imam—came in daily about violence and rioting in cities, they experienced none of that. Imam Ramadi had already warned them about the coming hard times, and that it was important to store up food and water for the coming days. Then those days arrived, and the community almost seemed excited about it, as if its members were chosen personally by Allah to survive this apocalypse. But there was so much more to this that he hadn't heard.

Then yesterday, Imam Ramadi declared in his daily message at the mosque—where they received all their information about the world outside their community—that sharia law was being instituted immediately. It was necessary, he had told them, because Allah was testing their obedience. Further, he told them, there was no more America and therefore no more American law, so they had to police themselves.

A couple of his neighbors spoke about a few public dissenters and the consequences of their dissent. But he thought it was just rumor. Then, this morning, on the way to mosque, Randall and his family were shocked to find two dead men hanging by their necks, in the middle of the town square. Each dead body bore a sign that said "Treasonous Infidel."

The message was clear. Break any of the community's laws, and your punishment would be swift and absolute.

It was like the proverbial frog, at first comfortable in the pot of warm water, totally unaware that his pot was being brought to a boil until it was too late. Only after arriving this morning, and now hearing the imam's words, did Randall come to realize that they were the frogs and the pot was this community, and it was about ready to boil over.

There were many other signs, which they willfully ignored, but they should have seen. The *Matawi* were a perfect example. These "volunteers" were chosen by the imam to help teach the community what was right and wrong under sharia. At first, they were very kind and gracious, offering instruction on how a man should treat his children, or how a woman should dress in public. But then there were changes, all noticeable if anyone wanted to recognize them.

The pot started to simmer.

One day, last week, Leticia was walking alone from the store with her head uncovered. The hijab she had chosen that day was black and wholly unpractical on a day when the sun was particularly brutal. One of the *Matawi* brought it to her attention and she said something sarcastic back to him, and the man struck her. This incensed Randall so much that he marched over to the man's house to give a physical rebuttal. But several of the *Matawi* were with him then and instead of beating this man up as Randall had intended, he left for fear of his own safety. He would take it up with the imam directly. But that never happened. And he knew now it never would.

The pot was boiling.

The imam's booming voice continued. "It has started, my friends. From the air, Allah's armies have cast down death to the infidel armies. But it will not be seventy thousand dead. It will be seven hundred times seventy thousand.

"But that is just one more step in the end-times which have begun.

"The Mahdi has already been identified. Mahdi Abdul has already begun his reign, commanding his army against a corrupt country and after this the rest of the corrupt world."

Randall backed up through the horde of men surrounding him. They ignored him, and happily took a place closer to the imam in an effort to soak up more of his poison.

"I have been in touch with the Mahdi ..."

Randall stopped in his tracks and peered up at the man who once again seemed to be looking directly at him.

"He has chosen our community as one of the places to host his army. And in a few short days, when that happens, all the men in this community will be called by Allah to take up arms against the infidels and become his warriors ..."

At that moment, the pot boiled over.

He backed away slowly at first, his heart racing to a full panic. Then, he burst from the frothing pack, leaving them snarling and lapping up the imam's words.

Happily, he had found his wife already in back, moving away from the women, her face full of fear.

They shot knowing glances at each other. Without speaking a word, they made their way out the doors. They would collect their children and head home, where they would try to leave unnoticed.

Ramadi

"**A**sasah Salam."

"Salam Asalah," Imam Ramadi said to Fidel.

"We have word from Mahdi Abdul." Without desecrating his imam's robe by touching it, Fidel ushered him toward the imam's private office, away from the crowds that wanted to thank him or simply be in his presence.

Once they were inside and the door was closed Ramadi asked, "So, what happened? Why has our Mahdi been out of touch for so long?"

Fidel held his head down. "Mahdi Abdul was injured during an attack on his base, which was lost to the infidel army. However, we are told that he will survive. Several of his men survived, and they are in hiding until the third phase begins."

Ramadi had already removed his cloak and parked himself in his desk chair, where he considered Fidel's report.

"Anything else?"

"Only that our warriors will be descending upon us in two days."

"Good. Is the sign ready?"

"Yes, it was posted just before you concluded."

"And you have the three men that will be executed tonight?"

"Yes, two Christians and a Jew."

"How did you catch them?"

"Our security cameras in each family's home first caught them praying and reading their holy books. The *Matawi* then studied their activities. They often gathered for tea and had quiet discussions. We have taped audio and video feeds of their discussions to assassinate you."

"Excellent. Then everything is as we had planned."

"Yes, it is, my imam."

Randall

"So are we doing what I think we are?"

"I'm afraid so," he said grimly. "We'll get our kids, and then grab a few things and leave."

"But where will we go? Our home, our friends are here, no matter how bad it is."

He looked at her to make sure she understood. She did, but still didn't want to accept it. He didn't either. "You know it will get much worse?"

"Yes, I do." She looked down, filled with sorrow and then back up to her husband. "But where will we go?"

"We'll stay with Emily. She's offered many times."

"But that was just for the weekend."

"She loves the kids and adores you. She'll welcome us."

"All right." Her eyes already wet with tears, beamed acceptance and strength. "I'll pack a few things for our walk to Endurance."

Chapter 10
Hasta Army Base, 15 Miles from Endurance, Florida

Reynolds

Reynolds and O'Malley fell into a plush couch in the commander's office.

Both wheezed through their full-face respirators. Each was covered by a fully encapsulated front-entry vapor-protective suit. They were Type A-level suits, impervious to sarin gas, but they were designed to be worn for twenty minutes. The men had had them on for over an hour.

Their tanks were still pumping air, but they were breathing high concentrations of CO_2 back into the suits.

Normal oxygen concentrations at sea level were just under 21 percent. The National Institute for Occupational Safety and Health defines an "oxygen-deficient atmosphere" at below 20 percent. Per NIOSH studies, at 16 percent inside a suit, users can expect some impairment in judgment and coordination. At 14 percent, fatigue and emotional distress. At 12 percent, nausea and vomiting and a significant decrease in judgment and respiration. At below 10 percent, unconsciousness. Their readings had just dropped below 10 percent.

For a while, their chests rose and fell in quick succession, adding an odd crinkly sound to their raspy but inadequate attempts to pull oxygen into their lungs.

Their faces and bodies were drenched with perspiration. The insides of their suits were a tropical forest during rainy season. They gazed out through their faceplates, but a mist hung on everything inside, not unlike the fatigue fogging their minds,

"Is that all of them?" O'Malley exhaled.

Reynolds was just then mentally going through the base map, struggling to think of any other rooms, in any of the buildings they might have missed clearing out yet. "I think so," he huffed.

"I count ... forty-one dead ... one most likely dead ... So, that's forty-two." O'Malley paused a long time, taking in a rapid series of breaths. "Only three are living; that means we're missing two."

"Correct." Reynolds tried drawing a long breath, but it was no use; there was too much CO2 inside. He jumped slightly as O'Malley surprised him by jamming a needle into his arm. "What the hell?"

"We had five doses left ... Knew you wouldn't agree, so made decision ... Need you to survive past today."

Reynolds did his best to study the private first class through his faceplate. As if inside a steam bath, he was invisible in the haze of his suit. But he didn't need to see him to know he was suffering from hypoxia. They both were.

A rivulet of perspiration ran down, momentarily revealing a small sliver of a view, before it was immediately consumed by the condensation.

He looks pale, Reynolds thought.

"You're going to make a great officer someday."

Reynolds unzipped the front of his suit and the office air, with whatever sarin it contained, rushed in.

Jonah

"Where are my hazmat suits?" Jonah blared out the window of his '58 Corvette to the truck parked in the opposite direction, alongside of him.

The anxious man in the truck's driver's seat glanced at Jonah and then at the ground just outside the window. The man hesitated, his thick neck straining, the blood vessels bulging across his head. It was obvious to Jonah that his man was using all of his limited mental powers to decide his next action, before he finally rolled down the window. "Sorry, boss. Whadya say?"

"You buffoon. We're safe here, that's why we parked a couple of blocks away from the base. You don't see any dead animals or people here, do you?" Jonah was getting impatient waiting for his trucks to arrive. "Give me your damned radio. My battery conked out."

The Dwayne Johnson look-alike again nervously glared down at the asphalt as if to tell it not to get any sarin on him, and then gingerly stepped out, tiptoeing onto the blacktop. Like a NFL center doing his ballerina act, handing off the football to his QB before being pummeled, he thrust his own handset through the Corvette's window and leaped back into his truck.

Jonah wanted to laugh at how silly his man looked, but he had more important matters to attend to. If they were going to grab what they could from the Army base, they'd needed to move quickly, before anyone else did. "Where are my damned hazmat suits?" he hollered into the radio.

The static background sounds were broken by the clear sound of an open microphone. There were two voices whispering something and gears being ground, followed by "We're pulling up right behind you boss."

Jonah's car was pointed toward the gate, so he immediately glanced at his rear view mirror and saw his truck appear from the next block.

Jonah was already out of his seat before the truck stopped, slamming shut the 'Vette's door. He momentarily paused and hovered, loving the sound it made. "Great engineering," he'd tell anyone who listened.

He marched over to the big yellow box `truck. One of the perks of owning a franchise is that he had, at any one time, practically an unlimited number of box trucks. Of course that had been before the EMPs fried most of them. He was thankful that several of his trucks had been parked inside one of his metal warehouses, getting serviced, before the EMPs hit. They survived, and were probably among the few such working vehicles in all of Florida.

The truck's two occupants scrambled out of their front seats and out the cab's doors, racing to the back, in an attempt to arrive before their boss did. One quickly released the big roll-down door to reveal several blue suits hanging on hooks from a tall suit rack inside.

"Did you bring every suit I own? There are only four of us," he bellowed.

"Sorry, boss. But you said Peter and the others were joining you. I thought it was better to bring more than we needed."

Walters was right, of course. He forgot for a moment that Peter would be arriving with his men and that woman who had sliced his boy up pretty badly. He reflexively looked at his wrist where his digital watch would have been, wondering where they were.

He gazed at the dozen or so hanging hazmat suits. He must have had fifty of these things at the warehouse. One of the businesses that rented from him was going to take advantage of the Ebola crisis that had swept the country some years back. The owner of the business had spent $50,000 on the Lakeland Interceptor Suits alone, which were considered top of the line. The next month, the owner welshed on his rent and Jonah took possession of all the tenant's assets, including the suits. At the time, Jonah laughed at his luck, since the rent was only a couple of thousand dollars. However, when he tried to sell them on eBay, he couldn't get any bids higher than $50 each, so he held on to them, figuring that one day they might come in handy.

Today was that day.

He hopped up on the truck's gate. Walters had already prepared the suit for him to hop into.

It took about ten minutes to get the three men into their suits with masks on and comfortable. With gloves and boots secure, the only thing left was to zip up the front, they were ready to go.

Jonah jumped out of the truck, but was already feeling hot in the thing and was glad the cross zipper was opened for ventilation. It only weighed nine pounds plus the oxygen tank. It took a little getting used to.

Just then, Peter pulled up in his pick-up with another box truck following. He could see the young woman, a kid, and an old man in the truck bed. Two of his own men, holding rifles, were there in the truck bed, guarding them.

Jonah trudged over to Peter's truck bed. Her punishment would be based on what she said next.

Jasper

Jasper had been in a panic.

He had found himself doubled over in the middle of the T of a residential intersection, the cross-street leading to the base's gate, when Peter's truck—with his neighbors in back—pulled onto the street. He glanced to his side, and was shocked to see a box truck parked near Jonah's 'Vette, its gate opened, pointed in his direction, with several men busy inside.

He had been trying to catch his breath after having run four blocks from where he had beached his boat. Because the trucks had been coming fast, and fearing Jonah and his men might see him, Jasper had dashed into a back yard.

He had tried to hop over a hedge, but its branches conspired against him, tripping him up and causing him to fall face-first into an overgrown lawn. Righting himself quickly, he passed through another yard before he was finally able to stop and take a breath.

His navigation was spot on, as he was only a few steps from the big box truck's opened back.

Peter's truck and another box truck pulled behind the parked one, just as a man in a giant blue chemical suit hopped out and trotted over to Peter, stopping to face him and his neighbors in the truck's bed. *Jonah's in that suit*.

Jasper lifted his Garand, wiggling his shoulder to adjust the heavy Thompson machine gun slung to his back, which had moved when he had fallen. He'd brought the Thompson, just in case things got ugly.

Through the peep sight, he focused on Jonah's head through the visor of the blue suit. He wore a gas mask underneath, but he knew Jonah's blue eyes and close-cropped hair anywhere.

Jonah was about to address Lexi.

He looked angry, like he was trying to settle down before he said something.

Jasper considered taking the shot, thinking at first that Jonah might try to harm her, but then decided to watch how this played out.

Lexi

"**S**o, you're the one who sliced up my innocent boy?" Jonah scowled at Lexi, his voice agitated but muffled and almost unintelligible through his mask and suit.

"Oh, that boy was your son?" Lexi stood up in the truck bed, forgetting that she was addressing the big, bad Jonah. Anger filled her chest, and with hands on hips, she took a step his way with elbows thrust back. "Did your *innocent* boy tell you that he was trespassing *on my property*, and that he took my gun from me when I was coming back from a run, and then threatened me with it? And it was only then that I sliced his arms in self-defense to take back my gun before he shot me. Is *that* the innocent boy you're talking about?"

Travis

Travis's mouth was at first ajar. Then, only his facial muscles—taut from his anxiety—pulled in a vain attempt to hold back a grin. He watched in awe as his sister verbally took down this man dressed like a blue alien. A part of him was glad that for once his sister's anger wasn't aimed at him.

"What do you mean, your property?" the blue alien asked. "The property you were on is owned by Stanley Smith, a friend of mine."

Lexi looked perplexed, sucker-punched.

She couldn't understand how her father could have been friends with this, as Jasper described him, "thug."

And why was he calling him Stanley Smith? Smith was her aunt and uncle's last name. Their father's last name—their last name—was Broadmoor. How many more secrets did her father carry with him to his grave?

The blue man continued his muffled interrogation. "So what's your relationship with Stanley Smith?"

"He's my father. And he's dead."

Now it was the blue man's turn to look like he had just been socked in the gut.

He turned his giant blue head to the driver of their truck, gabbling something Travis couldn't hear. The driver shrugged and said something back.

The blue man turned back to them, fumbling with something like a zipper across his chest. "All right, you may be correct." The zipper didn't seem to want to go up as he tugged on it. "But, I have more important things to do—"

"You ever wear one of those things?" Frank asked.

"You some sort of expert?" Blue Man protested, now trying to grab the zipper with both hands.

"He's an army specialist, who served many times in the Middle East. He probably knows more about your blue suit than you do," Travis blurted in confidence. He could do angry, just like his sister.

"Okay, little man, then I guess Mr. Army Specialist and your sister get to wear one of these and come with us."

Reynolds

I t wasn't a long sprint.

After all, the four hundred yards from the farthest building to the gate was usually a warmup for two men who ran at least ten miles every day. But Reynolds and O'Malley were physically exhausted: after searching every nook and cranny of the base for survivors, but finding only three; after subjecting themselves to a dose of sarin and then atropine, which had to play havoc with their bodies; and finally dealing with a bout of hypoxia, because they wore their suits too long. At this point, they could barely stand upright, much less sprint four hundred yards through a mine-field of more sarin gas particles, which had no doubt adhered themselves to everything. But they knew they had to.

They had collected two of the three survivors in the complex, moving them to the building exit closest to the gate. The third soldier, who was supposed to wait for them, was already gone. Maybe she was done and had already run.

After shedding their protective orange suits, they did what they told the others to do—wrapped blankets around their bodies, and clean shirts around their faces. They would make a dash, and once they had passed the gate and any signs of contamination—that is, dead people or animals—they'd shed their outer clothes and find a way to the clinic in Endurance.

"Are you ready?" Reynolds asked, not because he wanted to know—they were—but to warn them it was time.

All gave an accepting nod.

"Let's go." Reynolds pushed through the door, holding the arm of the private they'd first found. Reynolds guessed that he looked stronger than he felt. Maybe he should be holding the private's arm to steady himself. They broke into a running trot. O'Malley held the arm of a corporal who definitely needed the help, and followed directly behind.

Four of the five survivors of the gas attack on Fort Hasta raced over sidewalk, road, and lawn, around the bodies of their comrades and dead birds. It felt to all of them like the most surreal and macabre obstacle course they'd ever run. And even though all were ready to fall over, their lives depended on their completing it.

As they neared the gate, Reynolds almost stopped. The others had been looking at the death around them and not at the gate in front of them.

All their heads swung forward. At first they were shocked, then they felt a sense of relief. Two hooted their excitement, and he was pretty sure it was O'Malley, covered in a pink blanket, who yelled "Help us."

The world was spinning to Reynolds.

Although he muttered some words himself, he wouldn't remember them. The last thing he remembered thinking was *perhaps we will make it after all.*

Chapter 11
Stowell, Texas

Grimes

Robert Grimes sat hunched over his microphone and peered into the dial of his Kenwood, as if he could mentally push his broadcast to every corner of his crumbling country.

The microphone was clicked open, awaiting his repetitive words.

"Repeat. The enemy has begun the systematic gassing of all US military bases with sarin gas, using our own US military drones. If you live near a military base, do *not* go outside. Tape up your vents, doors, and windows and remain inside for no less than three days. We've been getting reports all over the country of mass deaths in and around various US military bases, starting early this morning.

"Sarin gas is a nasty neurological toxin that can kill you in seconds. However, sarin dissipates outside over time. Our information is that three days is an appropriate amount of time to wait for it to dissipate. But, if you see a drone, and you're near a military base, please seal yourself inside.

"To everyone with a weapon, if you see a drone, shoot it down, even if it has US markings. The enemy has captured many of our US drones and is using them against our US Military with sarin gas.

"We will bring you more information as we receive it from our sources in the field.

"You are listening to the American Freedom Network, broadcasting reports from the front lines of the war against America."

He clicked off the microphone and waited. After two minutes, he spun the dial to one of the freebands that had been frequented by the survivalist community prior to the attack. When he found 27.425 USB, he repeated the same message. He'd now broadcast something similar to this bulletin on over a dozen commercial, military, and ham frequencies. He even transmitted on the NOAA emergency weather channel of 162.4 MHz, abandoned by their local broadcast station when the war started. In each case, he waited exactly two minutes before moving onto the next channel, in the event someone responded.

After he finished the freeband broadcast, he shut his eyes and let his head fall back. His heavy frame accepted by his chair, which receptively creaked into a resting position. He couldn't help but wonder if some of that creaking wasn't from his tired body.

A staticy buzz bled through one giant speaker: a lifeless haze of empty frustration as so few people transmitted now on the freeband or anywhere for that matter. But he listened anyway, just in case someone answered. It had been more than a day since the last person had reached out on one of these channels.

He fought a mind-numbing fatigue. His consciousness was tugged at by dark worries making it hard for him to focus on any one thought. He could so easily go to sleep, which made sense since it had been over a day since he had slept more than a few consecutive minutes. But there was so much to do.

Grimes often waited longer on or around this frequency because it had the highest potential for broadcasters; the freeband was accessible by many CB radios, which didn't require a ham radio license to operate versus the nearby 10-meter band and so many others, which required licenses. Not that broadcasting without a license was anyone's concern during a time of war. It was simply a numbers game for Grimes. There were millions of CB radio users in the US before the war, but less than 700,000 ham operators. Since most radios were fried from the EMPs, this range offered the best chances of his finding the radio-operator needle in the radio frequency haystack. Besides, a lot of preppers—those most likely to have hardened their units—often frequented this band.

Yet, it had been silent for a long while.

When he was done waiting, he would return to the thirty-six frequencies he monitored. These were the only frequencies, anywhere, on which he had heard consistent broadcasts since the EMPs. Some of these frequencies were sources for his reports from those on the ground, ranging from the hotspots in the Midwest and East, to sometimes catching someone from the US military.

The military had been noticeably absent since the first attacks. That was mostly explainable because the two EMPs took out the civilian grid, which in turn brought down the power to most military bases, as they were often dependent on it. It was perhaps the US military's Achilles heel. Add to this the fact that most everything with solid-state circuitry was fried, in addition to many military vehicles, communications, high-tech weapons systems, and so many other things run by electronics. With the nuclear bomb-blasts in DC and at least three other military bases, the enemy seemed to have taken down much of the military's and therefore the US's command structure. Now the sarin attacks were further chaos at military bases.

And there didn't seem to be any help from overseas, at least based on reports Grimes received from the BBC. US forces seemed to be tied up with the Russians, Chinese, and North Koreans, and so were Allied forces. And to make matters more difficult, economies all over the globe were in a free fall. It all meant one thing.

They were completely on their own.

And somehow, Grimes and their American Freedom Network—a name coined by Aimes after yesterday's broadcasts—had assumed the mantle as the central repeater of both emergency and military information across the US. All the information he thought was safe to share, was curated into alerts which he broadcast at least once every two hours on his preselected frequencies.

It was no wonder he was so exhausted.

He tried to concentrate on the buzzing haze of his main speaker. But his mind quickly floated to worry he felt for his son, Porter. It had been more than a day since he'd heard of his and Frank's defeat at Ft. Rucker, then their triumph over Abdul and his army, and finally his plan to come home to Stowell, minus Frank, but with a new friend from Ft. Rucker, a Lieutenant Wallace. But that was a long time ago. He glanced at his wall clock, an old Mickey Mouse. But as hard as he tried, he couldn't calculate the number of hours it had been.

All he knew was that they should have been home by now.

Waiting for Frank only made it worse. He hadn't heard back from Frank since he ran off to save his goddaughter from what he thought was a sarin attack at their house in Florida. Then, it was Frank's godson, Travis. Now silence.

He couldn't stand all the waiting!

"Is there anyone there?" boomed his speaker. It was unbelievably clear, like the person broadcasting was next door.

Grime's chair sprang forward, practically catapulting him out of it. He punched his microphone. "Please state your name and the purpose of your transmission."

"Ahh, I'm Corporal Ben Sparks, sir. I was stationed at Ft. Benning Georgia, but my entire base has been wiped out. I heard your broadcast and wanted to thank you, sir, and ... I don't know, see if I could help."

"How did you survive the gas, Corporal?" Grimes wondered out loud.

"I was on patrol outside the base, when the drone flew overhead. I called in and they were all dying, sir. I heard them screaming and choking. Someone yelled that they were being gassed and to close ourselves inside where we were until we were told otherwise, or take ourselves outside the perimeter of the base. I drove as fast as I could."

"Where are you now?

"I don't know, by a pond southwest of the shooting ranges."

Grimes thought quickly of when he was on Ft. Benning, many years ago, and tried to come up with some way of testing this young man to make sure he was who he said he was. This was an open frequency that he broadcast on often. "Corporal, think of how many weeks your Basic was and go down that many kilocycles from where you are right now. Do you understand?"

"Yes, Sir."

"If I don't hear from you in one minute, I'm switching the channels again. Go there now and ask for Lieutenant G."

Aimes burst through the door of the studio, which had once been his bedroom. He was out of breath.

Grimes held up a forefinger and then twisted the dial to 27.325, ten kilocycles below the previous frequency, representing the ten weeks of Basic. Hopefully, the enemy didn't know this offhand.

"I really need to interrupt, sir," Aimes said. His body was in constant motion as he shifted from one foot to the other.

"Twenty more seconds," Grimes said watching the second hand of his Mickey clock.

"Lieutenant G? Is there a Lieutenant G there? This is Corporal Sparks, are you there?"

"Hello, Corporal. It's 15:46 your time. At 16:00 call me at 27.10 MHz. If you don't hear from me, call at 17:00. Until then, stay in your truck. You got that, Corporal?"

"Got that, sir. Out."

"Okay," Grimes said to his nervous friend. "Why in the hell are you so worked up?"

"They found Paul... or everything, but his head."

"What? Who did this?" Grimes asked, hoping he had dozed off and was having a nightmare. He was very much awake now.

"Don't know. Paul didn't call in at his appointed time, so we sent John—he has lookout on I-10 West—out to check on him. His body, was by a cell tower, he used as his lookout. It looks like he somehow fell out of the tower and then ... he was beheaded."

"What the hell did they—who ever this was—do with his head?" Grimes gawked at his friend. Aimes was usually in prime physical shape. But now, Grimes felt like he was looking at a mirror image of himself: Aimes was worn out.

"Don't know." Aimes paused his face grew grimmer. "The news is worse."

"Okay, hit me."

"Winnie is in flames."

Grimes considered this new grave piece of information. "So, you think that..."

Aimes finished his conclusion, "Whoever killed and be-headed Paul, probably destroyed Winnie, just two miles north of us. And that means—"

Grimes interrupted, "—they, whomever they are, should be arriving in Stowell any second now."

Chapter 12
Hasta Army Base, Florida

Lexi

"**O**h God. There's so many."

Lexi's gloved hand clamped down onto Frank's harder, and he squeezed back. It wasn't enough.

Her eyes burned as she struggled to see through two layers of protective plastic, already coated in a fine mist from her breathing. Not that she really want to see: everywhere she cast her gaze lay the tortured forms of formerly living, breathing soldiers in the US Army.

So much death.

In only a few short days, she'd already become way too accustomed to seeing the dead, often not even glancing at a corpse by the side of the road, any more than she used to pay attention to a discarded beer can. But it also seemed that each day her eyes were assaulted by a sight more horrific than the previous day's. This time it was a mass death on a semi-secret Army base, only a few miles from their new home.

Her eyes were drawn to their faces. Each seemed to have been grasping at their throats—some even had claw marks—with their mouths opened wide, searching for oxygen but finding only more poison. Their tortured eyes were seared in place for all eternity.

"Why didn't we end up like them?" she whimpered through her respirator.

Lexi felt like she was on the verge of another full-on panic attack, even though the suit's radio deepened her voice and made it sound less terrified than she was. Her mind kept considering that only little pieces of plastic separated Frank and her from this horrible death. She hoped Frank's words would put her at ease.

"I believe a drone sprayed sarin gas directly over this base. The spray didn't reach us, but some of the birds flying in our direction got some of the sarin on them and fell on your property, before they died."

"Glad Travis isn't here," she huffed.

"Keep the chatter down," Jonah bellowed through his comm.

Jonah's voice already sounded deep. But through the suit's radio and respirator, it was as if Darth Vader were here in the flesh. But his was all the more menacing because this voice was real, unlike the fantasy that Travis said he loved. She glanced at Jonah, and then the three other men following them; two carried rifles, and one a hand-held radio wrapped up in a giant zip-lock.

She still didn't understand what she was doing in this place, or why this man was putting her and Frank through this torment. Maybe it was his way of punishing her for slashing his boy. But she was sure it was more than this, reasoning it was Jonah's way of keeping tabs on her and Frank while they searched for what, she didn't know.

It was better than being shot.

She pushed this thought out of her head.

There was movement, in the distance, in front of them.

More than movement. It was four figures, wrapped in multicolored blankets, running their way.

It was more oddity, in an already surreal situation. They appeared as if four differently colored human-sized carnations were blowing in their direction. "Look." Lexi pointed.

Jonah's two men swung their rifles up and aimed at the four figures flying right at them.

Adding to the black comedy of the moment, each of Jonah's men struggled, unsuccessfully, to get their gloved fingers into their trigger guards. It was obvious the thought of how to shoot their guns while wearing the suits hadn't occurred to them before they put them on.

One of the figures, a man wrapped in red, yelled something in their direction. But with his mouth covered, it was impossible to hear.

Another figure pulled away the blue blanket covering his mouth and face. "Help us," he shouted.

The quartet slowed only slightly, angling to get around Jonah's group.

The lead man, wrapped in pink, who was steadying a female soldier, pulled back his blanket. "We need to get off this base and into a pool or the ocean ASAP." He said this as he and the other three fuzzy blooms raced by Lexi and the others, back down the path they had just come, toward the front gate.

"Peter," Jonah hollered through his comm to his man holding the baggied radio. "Take Lexi and follow them. Get them to the clinic and make sure they get whatever help they need." Jonah snatched the baggied radio from him.

"Come on!" Peter said to Lexi, who looked up to Frank for confirmation.

"It'll be okay," he assured her. "I'd feel better if you weren't here any longer." Frank squeezed her hand once more before letting go.

Travis

"Have you killed little boys with that gun?" Travis asked the man sitting next to him on the box truck's bench seat. The man, whose name he'd forgotten, had a rifle restively bouncing in his lap, pointed away from him. The man's foot tapped away a silent tune of impatience. "Have you killed *many* people for your boss?"

Travis was staring directly at the man, his own posture demanding a response.

"Would you kill your own son if Jonah asked you to? Would you use a knife or—"

"Shut up, kid! My God, you ask a lot of questions," the man huffed in frustration.

Travis didn't care. He was tired of waiting for Lexi and Frank and the man they all worried about, their boss, Jonah. And he felt pretty sure this man wouldn't shoot him.

They all looked at Jonah with *fear and trembling*--Travis always loved that phrase--as if they thought he was evil or something. But they had no idea what it was like to be in the presence of a truly evil man. Travis knew true evil.

He was, after all, the nephew of the evilest man on this earth.

Travis considered this man, and then Jonah. He was sure they were more full of bluster than anything else.

So he pressed harder.

"Sarin gas is pretty scary stuff. I read about it in school.

"Did you know if you breathe in sarin, in its gas form, it will burn your insides and you'll puke out blood and parts of your lung? Do you think it would hurt to puke out your lung? I don't think your lung tissue has nerve endings, so maybe it wouldn't.

"I read that only a tablespoon of sarin could wipe out all of Miami." He knew this was not entirely true, because each person in Miami would have to have to have directly inhaled sarin, and it would take a lot more than a table-spoon's worth to get to every citizen of Miami. "I wonder how many tablespoons that drone spat out?" Travis shift-ed his gaze up to the ceiling of the cab for effect, as if the sky outside held the answer to his rhetorical question.

He kept his head fixed upward, but shifted his eyes toward the man to see if his words and actions were getting a reaction. They were.

The man was hunched over the truck's giant steering wheel, looking up owl-eyed. The endless silent tune in the man's head must have crescendoed, as his leg was practically jumping off the floor. Then, the man's rifle slid off his lap with a thud.

A curl of a smile creased Travis's lips.

The man rummaged for his rifle, and then grabbed his radio, parked on the space between him and Travis.

"Hey Jake, you think we're far enough away from the base to be safe?" the man begged into his hand-held. His voice fluttered as if he were speaking through the chop of a large fan.

"Stay off the radio, numbnuts," Jake's burly voice huffed on the other end. Travis could see the big guy in the pick-up pointed at them, glaring back through the windshield, his own hand-held pressed against his ear.

This was fun, but it was getting boring. He really didn't want to be here anymore.

As if in answer to his desires, four people shrouded in multi-colored blankets burst through the gate open-ing and shed their coverings, like flowers dropping their petals.

The man in front was barking something at the others and they began to pull their clothes off too, while hurrying in the direction of the trucks.

"Behind you, Jake. Soldiers are coming out of the gate," the man next to Travis shouted, his voice filled with inde-cision. "They're taking their clothes off?"

"They're removing anything that might have sarin on it, and getting it away from their bodies," Travis announced. "They probably need to hose off too. Do you have a hose or water?" Travis asked. Frank had already explained all about sarin gas and what they needed to do if they came in contact with anything that might have sarin on it.

"In back," the man mumbled.

"Did Jonah say what we should we do if someone came out besides them?" Jake asked, as the four disrobing figures approached Jake's truck, parked next to Jonah's 'Vette.

"I don't--hey, wait," the man barked at Travis's empty seat.

Travis had hopped out of the truck and was walking toward the approaching soldiers, now in their underwear. One of them was a woman, who looked very pretty, but also pale like she might throw up.

As Travis approached the four, he could see his sister, in her blue suit several sizes too big, and another man bounce through the gate, trying to catch up with the others.

"There are some jugs of water in the back," Travis told the soldier helping the pretty woman.

Lexi pulled her suit off, shedding it like a lizard would molt its old skin, only a lot quicker. She was able to pop out of her oversized boots and gloves easily, leaving them behind. She ran to her brother, pulling off her mask, and threw herself around him, huffing for air.

She felt wet with sweat, but Travis didn't pull away, not one bit.

"I'm so glad you didn't come with us," Lexi puffed.

That was all she said. She breathed rapidly and held onto her brother, seemingly relishing his embrace as much as he did hers.

"Come on," a voice demanded from behind, startling them. "Jonah said that we're supposed to take these four to the clinic and let Dr. Scott know who brought them in."

Jonah

"I can guess why you're here. So, why am I here?" Frank panted. He wobbled a little, grasping the side of a building, while he and Jonah waited for his other two men to finish searching the last building on the base.

"Okay, why do you think I'm here?" Jonah huffed, also out of breath.

"Weapons and other supplies." Frank stated this unequivocally as he would state any other fact, like Florida being a peninsula.

"Fair enough. You're here because I'm not as familiar with these suits and sarin contamination. I want to make sure that whatever we get out of this place can be used after we get it."

"But I've already told you that you can wash most of it off and then whatever is still on there will be inert after a few days. And you know as much about these suits as I do by now. So, what's the real reason?"

"All right, I guess it's more curiosity about you and the two kids and Stanley Smith, I mean Stanley Broadmoor's story." Jonah hopped up and down a couple of times, forcing the condensation to roll more abruptly off his faceplate, making it easier to see, at least for a moment.

"What's to tell? Stanley had many secrets. There are apparently many things you know about my friend that I don't." Frank eyed Jonah as best he could through their mutually foggy environs, obviously trying to read him, just as he was of Frank.

Although he didn't yet know the whole story, Jonah suspected Frank was being protective of Stanley's kids and their secrets. He couldn't blame him.

"Like how he became friends with a rogue like me?"

"Exactly."

"I couldn't help but like Stanley—still hard to believe he didn't make it, though ..."

Jonah took a few breaths while contemplating his late friend.

"... anyway, he saved my butt one day, and for no reason. He didn't want anything from me in return, so I felt like I owed him--"

"Hey boss!" an excited voice chirped in over their comms. "You better come in here."

"We're coming," Jonah said as he slogged in through the door. He glanced back and saw Frank was following him inside.

"Where are you?" Jonah asked as his eyes scanned for some sign of the man in the murk.

"Right here, boss."

Jonah turned to see him standing half in a doorway they had broken through earlier. He momentarily caught an ear-to-ear grin through his face plate, before the man's face disappeared again. His Maglight pointed inside.

Jonah stepped into the semi-dark room. The flashlight's glow gave him the sense that the area was not big, and was tightly packed with chest-high racks and crates. But he couldn't clearly see anything at all, even bumping into a large object in the middle of the floor.

His man's flashlight followed him the rest of the way inside, its beam finally revealing to Jonah that the "object" was actually stacked cases of ammo and grenades. And along the wall, in the racks, were dozens of military rifles. They had found the base's weapons.

"Now we're talking!" Jonah exclaimed.

Jonah turned back, curious if Frank could see the boun-
ty. But Frank wasn't there. "Frank, where are you? Being
a military guy, you'd appreciate this."

Jonah grabbed the Maglight from his man and stepped
back out of the room, tripping at the door.

He shined the light down and saw that he had tripped
over someone's blue boots. It was one of his bio-hazard
suits. At first he thought it was his other man, but then he
saw that fellow coming from deeper within the building.
When Jonah looked again, shining his light on the man's
faceplate, he could see it was Frank. He looked dead.

Chapter 13
Crystal Waters, Florida

Many of the community's men, and one young woman unaccompanied by a man, were crowded around the giant sign recently erected on the front lawn of Crystal Waters City Hall. Although they were riled up by the imam's words only moments ago, there was a hushed silence now as they attempted to understand what those words meant to them. After the first few phrases, it was clear to everyone.

To: The Crystal Waters Umhah (community)

From: Imam Ramadi

As-salaam Alaykum.

Praise Allah and his prophet Mohammad, peace be upon him.

I am happy to announce that we can now publicly testify to Allah's greatness in all that we do, by practicing what his prophet Mohammad—peace be upon him—has taught us. To this end, I declare as a servant of Allah, that as of today July 9th this umhah will practice Sharia within the confines of Islam's Five Pillars:

1.   All must openly declare their faith to Allah, Mohammad, their Mahdi, their imam, and to the holy precept of martyrdom;

2.   All must pray 5 times per day, and heed the public call to prayer;

3.   All must give 50% of their supplies and resources to their imam, who will distribute to those who need it more;

4.   All must fast during Ramadan; and

5.   All must make their pilgrimage. However, since travel to Mecca is impossible at this time, all men in this umhah are expected to make their pilgrimage with their Mahdi in the field

of battle. All men will start to train tomorrow at the soccer field, in preparation for the next phase of the war against the infidel.

Practicing Sharia will prove our submission to Allah and make us purer and more acceptable to Allah. In addition to the above, the following are required of all men and women:

> To protect and preserve the virtue of our women, no woman above the age of twelve will appear in public without her husband or father; will drive a car; each will remain chaste, not engaging in sexual behavior except with her husband; and will cover her body, hair, wrists and ankles so as not to entice others.

> Proselytizing against Islam is punishable by death

> The penalty for theft is loss of hand

Additional rules will be added.

All rules are subject to change by your imam.

All penalties will be decided by your imam and be carried out in front of City Hall, every day at Noon.

The crowds grew steadily throughout the morning, as more and more gathered around the sign. The din of discussion began first as a murmur, but then culminated into a clamor that could be heard for miles around. Long before the noon hour approached, the men were frantic in their chants for Allah, for their imam, and for sharia.

Some of the men and the few women who ended up in front of the sign, but immediately knew they didn't belong there, tried to slip away unnoticed. But these, who were perceived as either Christians or simply shirkers, were grabbed by those yelling and chanting in between their fist-pumps to Allah. The detained women were ushered to the front of City Hall, where they waited for the noon hour.

Some of the men who had tried to quietly leave, especially those known to be Christians, were summarily beaten. Two were beaten so badly that they eventually died on the City Hall's well-manicured lawn.

The few who were able to flee the multiplying mob, now numbering in the hundreds, ran for their homes, keeping to the shadows in hopes of escaping.

The hundreds of other Crystal Waters residents who had not yet witnessed the violence but could easily hear the uproar, understood what was happening from others who made their chanting pilgrimage down some of the town's streets and walkways. The parade of horror wound through the residential streets, and then returned toward the city center so that all could witness the festivities at noon.

Crystal Waters was effectively split in half: those adamantly supporting the imam on one side and everyone else on the other side. There was no standing in the middle or on the sidelines. The Imam and his supporters demanded public support, from everyone.

At Noon, the chanting crowd, now over one thousand strong, was once again silenced by Iman Ramadi, who exited City Hall like a pope coming from his apartment to address the crowd in St. Peter's Square for Christmas Mass. Imam Ramadi wore all the pageantry befitting a holiday announcement, including a fine new silk thobe. Upon reaching the dais, set up with microphones all connected to the city speakers, he held up his palms to calm his people.

"*Asalam Alekem*." His thick beard cradled a grin of pride.

"*Asalem Asalam*," the crowd replied, in perfect unison.

"Brothers and sisters. As I have told you and as you have just read, it is our time to come out of the shadows and openly pronounce our faith to the world. Further, this country of infidels will soon become part of the great new caliphate begun by our Mahdi only a few days ago.

"I will be brief today and attend to the proclamation of penalties. This is not so much a demonstration of punishment or cruelty, as it is a demonstration of our allegiance to Allah and his laws.

"First, bring up the women."

Several women, some detained from the crowds, and a few others already being held, were prodded as a group to an area of posts set up below the dais. Several men then bound their hands in front of them and around the posts so that their backs were to the crowd. All anxiously waited for what was coming next.

Several men from the *Matawi*, now dressed in black, their faces completely covered, approached the women, who ranged from 15 to 60. When each man reached a bound woman, he grabbed a collar and aggressively yanked—some using their knives to assist, tearing their clothes from their neck down, exposing their bare backs. A few only yelped, but most hollered or cried.

"These women," the imam boomed, "were in public, unaccompanied by either their husband or guardian. They've all been warned about this rule by *Matawi*. And because our rules were just proclaimed today, their punishment will be fair. It will be much harsher in the future. Five lashes!"

Some of the crowd looked away with fear, thinking that it could have been one of their wives or daughters up there. But most of the crowd cheered and called the women foul names in English and Arabic.

After the lashings, the women were unbound and allowed to flee to their homes, holding their tattered clothes and covering with their arms and hands what little dignity they still possessed.

The crowd then grew louder as they sensed the next phase of punishment would turn more gruesome.

Their wait was rewarded.

Three men, already showing evidence of torture, were escorted by three *Matawi* from the main entrance of City Hall.

"These three men are not only apostates to our beliefs, still holding onto their false Christian and Jewish teachings, but they also met regularly and conspired to assassinate your imam." Imam Ramadi looked over to one of his men, who tapped on a computer tablet, instantly filling the loudspeakers with sound.

There were sounds of hushed conversations and clinking china and the scuffle of shoes, then a clear high-pitched male voice. "So are we really going to do this?"

"Yes, we have no choice. Our families' lives depend on it," said a deeper voice.

"You are saying what I think you're saying then?" said the high-pitched voice again.

"Fine, I'll say what you're both unwilling to," a third voice said with purpose. "We're going to kill Ramadi tonight. But to—"

The broadcast was cut off.

Imam Ramadi pushed his face into the microphones. "I find no reason to waste our time any further. I find these men guilty of apostasy and sedition. Either is punishable by death. Execution to be carried out immediately." He stood back and looked down below the dais.

The three men had been bound just like the women to three of the same posts, except their heads were also bound to their posts. Behind each was a *Matawi* holding a long scimitar. The convicted were all speaking at the same time: one was sniveling pleas for his and his family's salvation, one quietly repeating words memorized from the Psalmist, and the third asked for forgiveness for the men about to execute them. They were all praying to God.

The *Matawi* peered up at their imam for the signal, and at a swoosh of his hand, they swung their blades.

Chapter 14
Endurance, Florida

Randall

He focused the pressure of each heel onto the lawn's wet blades, keeping his steps silent. The moonless night was his accomplice; its darkness consumed his shadows, making him nearly invisible. Then he heard the crunch of twigs behind him, and he flicked a glance in that direction to confirm its source. He exhaled in relief.

She seemed far less concerned about silence than he did. But she didn't see the final message: those bodies left, without their heads, in the public square; a warning to the town to comply with their rules or face the worst kind of punishment. They had already decided to leave, but this sign was what told him they had to run, leaving behind all their personal belongings. Not only was it a warning to all of Crystal Waters that their town was firmly under the yoke of sharia law, it was one step farther down their dark path to becoming an Islamic republic. It was not unlike so many places he'd read about in the Middle East. And without the supervision or authority of the United States, there was nothing to stop them.

What surprised him was that he hadn't seen it coming earlier. All the signs were there, long before the lights went out. By then Crystal Waters was their community. And because they were probably one of the few towns that was prepared for a calamity, they could survive the death and violence they had heard about outside their community. When that violence penetrated their boundaries, their rules and methods of enforcement were extreme. But to maintain a civil society, you must not only have rules, you must prosecute those who defy them.

He'd heard about a vagrant who had wandered into town. Unlike so many others who were immediately escorted out, this one stole food from several homes. His punishment, so Randall heard, was to have his hand chopped off. Before the EMPs, Randall would have thought this punishment was extreme in places like Saudi Arabia, and unthinkable here on American soil.

Yet what should have been the most troubling sign was the stepped-up rhetoric about Islamism and jihadism. His wife and he only spoke about it once, but he knew it weighed heavy on both their hearts. It just wasn't what they understood Islam to be. The imam's words were certainly from the Quran and the Hadith. But he and Leticia wanted to look at the good in their religion, and always felt that this darkness that infected a percentage of Muslims was just a disease that would one day run its course. He had hoped in his lifetime, he would see a reformation, not unlike the one that occurred over five hundred years ago with Christianity. But when the nukes went off and the power grid went down, Randall knew that day would not come while he drew breath. Islamists had done this, and he feared he was living among them in Crystal Waters. The imam's words made it a certainty.

Another crack—this one much more pronounced, and closer--preceded a form erupting from a tangle of trees.

They were making far too much noise.

He would quietly warn his wife again about making too much noise. They were only a couple of blocks from their target. Once they got there, he was sure they'd be safe.

He just needed to avoid detection by any other Endurance residents. Part of him even considered the imam's spies might be here, but that was just paranoia.

He repositioned his daughter, a fifty-pound dead-weight of skinny arms and legs. When his wife stopped in front of him, Randall offered a genuine smile that she returned.

She clutched their newborn, finally sound asleep. How could he be mad at her? The kids were finally quiet after several miles of whining about being tired, and his wife was obviously being as careful as she could.

He just held his finger to his lips, smiled again, and walked ahead.

The house was right on the corner, just as he remembered. It was a simple but spacious ranch-style home, owned by their friend, Emily Scott.

Emily

"**W**here's Dr. Scott?" Peter hollered to the ancient volunteer as he charged through the door, arms behind him, clutching one end of a stretcher. Jake shouldered his way through the opening, holding the other end.

The startled aide yanked his head up, eyes fluttering from just being wakened. He glanced at the unconscious man and then considered the question for just a moment. Rather than saying anything, he pointed into the bowels of the Endurance Health Center and put his head back down to pick up where he'd left off in his dream.

When they turned the corner, Emily was standing just outside of what had become the clinic's operating room, no longer a mere examining room. Her shoulders hung low and she wore several layers of blood and fatigue.

"Dr. Scott," Peter huffed. "Can you take a look at this one? Jonah thinks he wasn't getting enough oxygen through his hazmat suit, and then he passed out."

Emily's eyes didn't hide her dislike, bordering on disgust, before they flashed back to the patient. She probably should have been more careful, but she was too damn tired. She knew Peter was someone to be feared, and for good reason. Most in Endurance feared Jonah because of his power, but Peter earned these feelings from his reputation of cruelty, if the stories were true. But she'd known Jonah since high school, and because Peter worked for Jonah, she knew Jonah would do everything in his power to protect her against the likes of Peter or others. Still, she chided herself for the momentary lapse in her usual decorum. "Sure, Peter. Do you know his name?"

"Frank!" yelled Lexi from the back of the clinic. She dashed the span of the hallway—now lined with temporary cots and semi-conscious patients—in a flash, grabbing one of Frank's limp arms as she skidded to a stop.

Travis shuffled not far behind, bed-hair sticking up on one side. "Uncle Frank!" he croaked in a panicky voice.

One of Emily's fingers firmly pressed his carotid, while her other hand carefully held up his meaty left arm. "What's all the blood from?" She searched for the source, rolling up his sleeve, and then pulling at his collar.

"It's a gunshot wound to his shoulder, from a few days ago. I replaced the dressing earlier today," Lexi said, her voice several octaves higher than normal. As Emily peeled back the blood-soaked bandages Lexi added, "Is he going to be all right?"

Emily didn't answer right away, instead listening to his breathing.

"Yes, I think he should be fine." She said to Lexi with a smile. "Would you and Travis do me a favor and grab one of the oxygen bottles you helped put away and I'll get some fresh bandages. We can both clean up his wounds and change his dressings in a few minutes."

Lexi nodded back, and squeezed Frank's left arm, as if to tell him they'd be back, and ushered Travis back down the hallway to do as Dr. Scott had asked.

To Peter, now with a forced smile, Emily barked, "I have no rooms. So, find him an empty cot in the hallway here. I need to see to another patient."

She quickly stepped away, but stopped midstride and glanced back at Peter, who was already hoisting Frank's stretcher back up. "Oh, and would you tell Jonah I said thanks for the medical supplies?"

"Yeah, sure," Peter gruffed, as he and the other man trudged through the hallway, spotting one open cot. Peter mumbled something else under his breath, which Emily was probably glad not to have heard.

Emily briefly watched Peter walk the injured man to the back of the hallway, and wondered why Jonah wasn't here instead of his henchman.

Jonah

"Holy shit, Pop! That's a lot of guns?" Cain said while sucking on a beer bottle. He took a step toward one of the cases of guns already placed inside the ra- zor-wire fenced area, in between two warehouses.

Jonah leapt forward blocking his son's advance. "Don't you have something to do?" Jonah didn't want to be both- ered, but he also didn't want Cain or any of the other men to get infected. It was why he was isolating all of the Army supplies outside. He'd leave them here in the yard for a few days until he was sure they were safe. Jonah eyed the open enclosure and tried to consider what else he further needed to protect his new supplies, including the guns and ammo, from anyone who might want to take them, and in the process, unwittingly spread sarin residue before it had become inert. They were in the mid- dle of an open area, away from the warehouses and his workers. He'd planned to further post a guard to watch over the site for the next two days, before they'd move the supplies inside.

Cain ignored his father, eyes fixated on the growing stack of gun and ammo crates, no doubt wondering why he was storing them outside behind razor wire. "What if they get wet?"

Shit! Jonah looked up at cumulonimbus clouds—pulsating light in the darkness—threatening to do that very thing. He yanked at his walkie and spat into its microphone. "This is Jonah. I need someone to grab three of our canopies out from the supplies we got from REI yesterday and erect them out here."

Jonah then watched his men pulling the supplies they had taken from the base out of the back of the truck. Each wore a blue hazmat suit, which looked even darker outside the limits of the warehouse's flood-lamps. And with the suits' interior fog, he couldn't see their faces.

"Hey, you!" Jonah yelled at the closest man, just before he passed him.

The man looked up to regard him, struggling with two large green ammo cans. Each was so heavy it seemed to elongate the man's arms to an unnatural length, making him look like a big blue ape. It was probably an apt analogy, because many of Jonah's men were knuckle-draggers at best.

He spoke slowly and loudly, enunciating each word. "Make sure the supplies are in *three*"—he held up three fingers—"stacks. Put on pallets, so that they're off the ground. Each stack no bigger than nine feet by nine feet"--he held up nine fingers, palmed them and held them up again, then made a box shape in the air—"then place canopies"—he made a house over his head, outlining the roof and posts in the air—"that are coming soon, over each stack. You got it?"

The man nodded, but waited to see if his boss was done with him.

"Go on. I want to get this done before midnight." Jonah said, while thinking it would be a miracle if the man got this and communicated his demands correctly to the other men.

The man nodded again, and then pushed forward, almost scraping the cans on the ground with each step.

"Why not store this stuff in the big warehouse up north? You know the one that already has all the supplies in it?" Cain took his last gulp of beer.

Jonah let the question hang, not sure he'd bother to answer this because his son was not even listening to him. Then he barked, "Listen to me! We are leaving this stuff outside because I said. And the next part is important." Jonah paused to make sure Cain was paying attention.

Cain's head popped up, a little more alert.

"We're not using the big SBC warehouse—which is off limits—because that one is full already, with someone else's supplies."

Jonah once again scrutinized the blue ape, to see if he was complying with orders.

"What do you mean, someone else's supplies? I thought once the lights went out, you said all of this stuff was ours."

One ape was restacking a pile, just as Jonah had instructed. Another was making boot-measurements, pacing off nine feet in front of the others who had collected in the fenced paddock area. All seemed to be listening to the first blue ape's instructions through their comms. They might make this work.

"So is it our stuff or someone else's? Well?" Cain pushed again.

"That warehouse ..." Jonah glared at his son, annoyed at the constant interruption and inanely stupid questions. "That warehouse is set aside for a *very* special client. And you are to never go in there. You got that?"

"Special? We own this damned place, what yah mean special?"

"None of your damned business! Now, don't you have something better to do than stand around and drink my beer?"

"But Pop, I got sliced." He thrust out his two bandaged forearms as if offering proof. "Besides, the hot female doc you're too chicken to ask out told me to rest."

Jonah resisted the urge to cold-cock him, the vein on his reddening forehead throbbing as if it would pop. "You lazy-ass wimp! That's a flesh wound that I'm pretty sure you brought upon yourself. Nut up, son, and get your work done!"

Cain pulled his shoulders up and took a deep breath as if he was about to face down his father for the first time. His mouth clenched, his two front teeth held back the word he wanted to release, while his chest grew as far as his body would allow. But, he would do nothing more. He was all bark and no bite. Jonah almost wished the boy would grow a pair and take it further.

Then, like a balloon hissing out its heated gas, he deflated, turned and stormed off.

Jonah watched his idiot son stomp toward the open doors of the Number Four warehouse. It was just like he reacted when he was a little boy--he would never mature. To the side of the warehouse's giant opening lounged four young men—more of his lazy friends—who jumped off their chairs in response to some command

Cain directed their way. They shuffled behind him into the warehouse and out of site.

He wanted to laugh at the boy's behavior, but like the growing storms above, Jonah couldn't shake the feeling of dread at what was coming next.

Phase Three

*"The ruling to kill the Americans and their allies - civilians and military - is an individual duty for every Muslim...
We also call on Muslim ulema, leaders, youths, and soldiers to launch the raid on Satan's U.S. troops and the devil's supporters allying with them..."*
~~ Osama Bin Laden, Former Leader of al-Qaeda

"If we were united and strong, we'd elect our own emir (leader) and give allegiance to him... Take my word, if 6-8 million Muslims unite in America, the country will come to us."
~~ Siraj Wahaj, a convert to Islam and first Muslim to deliver the daily prayer in the U.S. House of Representatives

*"When Phase Three is complete, there will be a new caliphate in America
and its people will have only two choices, join us or die."*
~~ Imam Ramadi

Chapter 15
Endurance, Florida

July 10th

The day that would redefine the future of America appeared to begin like most mornings on the Gulf Coast.

Puffy clouds, darkened by heavy loads of moisture almost bursting, turned a bloody shade as the sun hinted at its steady arrival. When the delicate light breached the horizon, the heavenly billows appeared to cheer with a thunderous applause, which echoed throughout.

The storm's first drops fell upon Endurance, just as a barrage of footsteps tumbled upon its southern city limits, close to where Jonah had set up one of his roadblocks.

The immigrant swarm processing north on the highway was like a raging river flowing downhill, the roadblock no better than an insignificant boulder dropped in the middle of a torrent. The flow easily adjusted around it, seemingly unstoppable.

Not wanting to shoot people, including many women and children, the two guards were immediately overwhelmed. Ignoring their verbal threats, the horde streamed through and around their useless barrier.

Bagley reached into his '67 Beetle—one of the small pebbles that made up the roadblock—and grabbed his hand-held, frantically hollering into it. "We're being invaded by immigrants! What do we do? We need help!"

After long moments of silence on the other end, Jonah responded. "Stop them! You have guns, use them."

Bagley jumped into the driver's seat and slammed the door shut to get out of the torrential downpour now coming from the heavens. He needed to think, which he couldn't outside, so he could better make his case. He also needed to hear his boss's reply.

"But sir, they're mostly women and children... And, many of them have already gone past the barrier. There was no way to stop them, except to kill them."

Bagley bored his gaze into the radio, desperate for a speedy answer, but also apprehensive at what Jonah would tell him to do. He once again made sure the volume control was maxed when he didn't hear an immediate reply, afraid he had accidentally turned it down or off. The empty static, normally loud, was impossible to hear now with the clamor outside.

"Fine, I'll take care of it myself," the voice on the radio curtly replied.

Bagley felt an immediate sense of relief. He *really* didn't think he could shoot anyone, and certainly not women and children. He breathed out deeply waiting for the rest of his orders. Thinking of his wife and two kids, he considered that they might have been just like these people had Jonah not given them jobs to do in exchange for food. As someone who (until a few days ago) made his living from posting funny cat videos on social media, he possessed few marketable skills to exchange. Thank God he at least had one of the few working vehicles in town.

"How many and where are they?" huffed the radio.

"Hundreds, and they're still passing around the road-block. The first part of the group will be in town in less than five minutes."

"Get back here. I don't care if you have to drive over them. Set up a new roadblock, right before the health clinic. Don't argue. Don't say anything. Just go!"

Bagley tossed his walkie into the passenger seat, creaked the door open, and barked orders to the grunt assigned to him, who drove one of Jonah's big four-on-the-floor trucks. The grunt nodded and happily escaped into the truck's cab.

Bagley started up his Beetle. The sounds of its engine and ever present rattling were swamped by the thunderous storms coming from above and around them.

Lexi

While experiencing a nightmare about Abdul, the little ground tremors below them shook Lexi into semi-consciousness. The crashes above them jostled her awake. But it wasn't until the aroma from her brother's feet hit her that she finally moved.

Travis had the worst foot odor of anyone she'd ever encountered. And each time it assaulted her nose, aside from voicing her displeasure, she thanked her creator that she didn't get that same smelly-foot gene.

This stenchwas definitely Travis's feet.

She forced her eyes open, feeling at first disoriented and then scared. Images of an earlier nightmare about Abdul killing her attempted to work their way back into her conscious mind. She pushed them out by focusing on what she objectively sensed around her.

It was dark, and the drumming on the roof was deafening. A crack of thunder confirmed to her that the drumming was rain.

She tried to hone in on her last memory.

She had come into town yesterday with three men and a woman from the Army base, and one of Jonah's men. One of those from the base, an otherwise good-looking guy, had inflamed skin and was out of breath.

What was his name? She thought.

Robert O'Malley.

She remembered helping Dr. Scott at the town's clinic, then helping more of Jonah's men stack up medical supplies inside.

Then Frank was brought in, and for a moment she'd feared he was dead. But, he was just suffering from the same thing O'Malley was, and he'd torn his stitches, *again*.

Dr. Scott's office!

That's where they were. Frank was sleeping on Dr. Scott's couch. Travis and she were on the floor beside it.

"Travis," she said much too loud. She lifted her head up off the floor to check on Frank. *He's still sleeping.* Her brother snored beside her on the carpeted floor, under a shroud of blankets.

Propping herself up on her elbows to get a better view, she peeled back the covers, expecting to see Travis's head. Instead she was greeted by his feet.

"Wow!"

She reflexively pushed them away, whispering loudly, "Travis, your feet stink!"

He didn't move and neither did Frank.

When gunshots crashed outside, all three of them jumped out of their beds, and stood on wobbly feet.

"Where the hell are we?" Frank croaked, clearing his throat while he took in the dark room, sporadically lit by lightning.

"We're in Dr. Scott's office in the Endurance Health Center. You were brought in unconscious. The doctor said you're fine, and just needed some oxygen and rest. We replaced your dressings too, after she fixed your stitches: you'd torn them again."

During her summation, he had lumbered over to the window, his limp very pronounced, and angled his body behind the corner of the two adjoining walls. He slowly pulled back the blinds. His gaze shot from one direction to the other before he sprang back in their direction for the door. "Come on, we need to leave this place and get home, where we'll be safe."

They followed him out the door, down the hallway, to the entrance of the clinic, where a dozen or so people puddled around the windows and entrance. Their worried faces pasted against the clinic's glass. A few were just outside the entrance, speaking with cupped hands to each other. All were looking to their right.

Frank pushed past them through the doorway. Lexi and Travis trailed closely behind, glancing nervously around while trying to avoid the sting of the rain. They had broken free of the crowd, intending to go north, out of town and back to their home. But another shotgun blast halted them.

"Stop," yelled Jonah in the distance.

The three of them obliged. But the yelling wasn't directed their way.

Jonah, standing in the bed of a black pickup truck, arms raised and one hand clutching a shotgun, faced a threatening crowd of people. He looked like DeMille's Moses—except this version held a shotgun rather than a staff—trying to stop the coming flood, rather than parting it.

Even in the murk, it was obvious what was going on.

The undulating crowd of hundreds of people wanted into town. They were probably starving and looking for handouts from Endurance. A small show of kindness, that was usually common in these parts before the lights went out. But with each town in America suffering like all the rest—except maybe Endurance—that kindness was no longer possible. Their town had the resources, apparently thanks to one man.

Perhaps this crowd knew it.

A woman's scream pushed through the gloom.

"It's Dr. Scott," bellowed Lexi, pointing to some movement a few yards from them.

Frank

Frank squinted through the wet haze and saw that a man held a gun against the head of a woman, who he suspected was Dr. Scott. The man pushed her forward, while another woman clutching an infant and a little boy followed meekly behind.

As Dr. Scott moved toward the clinic, Frank could see the mugger was taking cover behind her, and he guessed the man's family was behind him. The doctor was wearing scrubs, which like her, were soaked. As they came into the light of the clinic, he could see she was covered in blood.

Frank ambled into their path forcing them to stop.

The thug's head popped up over Dr. Scott's shoulder, obviously perplexed why his human shield had become still.

"Hi," Frank said, extending his hand. "I'm Frank. You must be Dr. Scott. Thanks for taking such good care of me, and of course my godchildren."

Dr. Scott glared at him, her eyes whiplashing—as if pointing—to her side and her head motioning there as well, to silently say "Can't you see I'm being held hostage, you idiot?"

"What the hell's going on?" a voice, muddled by the downpour, and laced with a strong Ethiopian accent, called from behind her.

Frank stepped to Dr. Scott's side and faced the man, "Hi, I'm Frank, are you all right?"

"Get out of my damn way. Are you on some sort of death—"

What came next was as natural to Frank as sneezing.

Dr. Scott shrieked for just a moment, her eyes going wild, but the rest of her held still. She watched this man who looked dead last night leap forward, outside of her field of view, do something that caused her attacker to grunt—it sounded to her like a fist connecting with soft skin—and then the man who called himself Frank stepped back, jerking her away by the arm.

Now Frank was holding the gun on the attacker. When it occurred to her she was free, she scurried a few more steps toward the clinic and spun around to see the mugger, folded on the ground, grasping his throat, desperately trying to breathe.

"How did you ..." she started to ask, examining Frank, no longer worried about the attacker.

Feeling safer, she walked over to the man's wife who'd been following them, and now was bent over the hurt mugger. The wife was clutching an infant and both were crying. "Can I see your baby?" Dr. Scott asked.

Frank inspected the gun he'd taken from the mugger, pulling the slide back to make sure it was loaded. It was. All and all, a nice Glock. He handed it to Lexi. "Keep an eye on the man, would you? It's loaded and doesn't have a safety. Just squeeze."

"Emme," came a voice running in their direction, "you all right?" Jonah huffed, stopping beside Dr. Scott.

"Yes, I'm fine, thanks," she responded to Jonah. Then to Frank she said, "By the way Frank, I'm Dr. Emily Scott.

But in light of what you did, you can call me Emily." She flashed a big smile and walked into the clinic. The mugger's wife, cradling her baby, and her little boy followed them.

"Don't you have any police in this town?" Frank asked, motioning to the mugger on the ground.

"It's actually the sheriff." Jonah took a couple of breaths. "He and his deputies are ten miles away. I'm sure they have their hands full with their own problems," Jonah replied. Two of his goonish-looking men pulled up beside him, also after a run, but didn't say anything--just stood there, waiting for their boss's orders. "We set up a room inside one of my buildings to be a holding cell until the sheriff gets here. This guy will be held there." One of the goons jumped to attention and grabbed the man, aggressively hoisting him up from the ground.

"Looks like you've got a larger problem there, with the mass of immigrants. What do you plan to do with them?" Frank had more than a passing curiosity. What Jonah did next, since he was obviously in charge of this town, was going to determine their own wellbeing. There probably was no good answer to the question, though. If Jonah turned them away, these invading immigrants would probably show up on their own doorstep; normal family men would turn violent to feed and protect their families. If Jonah gave them some of his food, then word would get around and more would come, resulting in Endurance running out of its resources sooner. And that's not counting the evil men out there who someday would certainly set their sights on their town. Admittedly, no scenario would be favorable for Frank and his godkids.

"I'm telling them to leave, naturally. We can't very well give them food, if we hope to survive as a town."

There was another gunshot, this one from a large-caliber pistol, that drew their attention in its direction. One of Jonah's men had taken his place as the Moses-in-the-truck-bed and had fired it in the air as the horde pushed closer.

"You're not turning them all away, are you?" Emily pleaded. She had quietly come back through the clinic's entrance, and was listening to their discussion. "These people are hungry and I understand they've been kicked out of their homes from a town south of here. They have nowhere else to go."

Jonah hesitated, obviously considering what he was going to say in response. But Frank answered for him, "It's an untenable position, but the more food this town gives away now, the less its chance of survival in the coming days or months even. Imagine this town with no food anywhere, and Jonah's warehouses empty. That day will come much sooner if the town gives away its food, even just a little bit right now."

"Hey Jonah," a voice spurted from the radio, attached to his belt. Jonah side-stepped away from them, and gave a little bow, as if to apologize for the interruption. He then turned his back to them and answered his walkie.

They watched him become animated, yell a couple of expletives at his feet, and then return the radio to his belt.

Turning back to them, he said, "We're going to put everyone in one of my warehouses on Pine, a couple of blocks from here. They can stay there, out of the rain. We'll give them some food and water too." His voice was flat, emotionless, as if he were repeating someone else's words.

"Why?" was all Frank could think to ask, as surprised as the others appeared to be at Jonah's turnabout.

"I have my reasons. Emme," he said, flashing a faint sign at Emily, and then he turned and marched toward the horde.

"What was that about?" Lexi asked the question they were all thinking.

Chapter 16
Sunbay Cove Warehouse, Florida

Cain

"**Y**ou said yo father is holding all des supplies for someone else?"

"Quiet!" Cain barked. His head snapped around, goatee whipping, eyes searching for other movement. But the warehouse's blackness was thicker than the oil smell filling his nostrils. He turned in the other direction, slower this time, trying to focus on any other sounds from the darkness which might indicate they were about to be caught.

It was empty. They were the only ones occupying this vast space.

The screech of a nail being yanked from its woody mooring ripped through the gloom. Cain spun toward it, when the sound of another nail wailed; its origin was just outside of his flashlight's spray of light.

"You said yo father was gone," Artie's whiny voice continued.

"Yessss!" Cain breathed the "s" in a way to stress his frustration for all of his friends' lack of quiet. "But one of his idiot guards might hear us. And I don't want my father to know that we've been here."

"Wow." A high-pitched voice burst from the middle of the giant room, from the same place Cain had heard the nail-sounds. The vastness of the space seemed to consume the loud voice almost immediately. "Look at dis shit!" There was no expected echo; his friend's voice just tumbled into the void, never bouncing back to their ears.

Cain, Artie, and his only quiet friend hurried down a deep aisle bounded by trucks, lined up side by side. Nothing but their bumpers and headlamps were visible outside the beam of Cain's flashlight; its light bounced forward with each of their lumbering strides. When they reached a T-intersection made by pallets of stacked boxes spanning the limits of his sight in both directions, they stopped.

Cain flashed his Maglite's beam at Jordi standing gleefully in front of an open crate with what looked like Russian writing on its side. "Damnit, what yah do?" Cain bellowed, forgetting his own demands for quiet.

Jordi, who held a crowbar in one hand and something else out of sight in the other, hovered over the giant open container. Its lid lay dead on the concrete floor, the sharp nails sticking up and pointing directly at the culprit, as if to say, "He did it!"

"Man, look at this." He proudly displayed the object in his other hand: it looked like a brand new AK-47. Cain's father had a couple of these. A distant memory flooded his thoughts. His father had taken him shooting, each of them happily emptying mag after mag into useless targets. He remembered the smell of the cordite as thick as their laughter in the air. It was one of the few times he remembered having fun with his father. It was also one of the few times his father had treated him kindly, like a father should.

Cain pushed past Jordi, who had moved closer to show his find. Narrowly avoiding impaling his foot on one of the upended nails, he stepped to the crate and saw there were other rifles in it, packed side by side. All looked new, as if they had come directly from the factory that made them. He scrutinized the numbers of boxes to his left and then to the right and saw that the rows vanished from sight deep into the warehouse's void, out of his flashlight's inquiring cone of light. He quickly counted the number of boxes on each pallet and the number of pallets he could see and tried to do some fast figuring. *Shit, that's a lot of guns.*

Cain glanced back to Jordi, who was now pawing the rifle, salivating over it. "Put it back."

"But can't we each take just one? They'd never notice," Jordi protested. The other two gawked at the contents of the box and then at Cain, expectantly.

"No! In fact, close dat crate up now. I want it exactly like it was when you found it. Do it now! Then meet us up front. And you help," Cain told one of his other two yes-men.

"Come with me," he said to Artie.

Cain and Artie swam deeper into the soupy blackness.

Cain had confirmed his suspicions that his father had stored weapons in this warehouse he'd only been al-lowed in once before Jonah had leased it two years ago. Before he pushed his luck harder, Cain wanted to check on something else. He knew one of the guards probably heard their voices and would burst through the door they had come in any moment. They had to be quick.

Somewhere just outside of his flashlight's beam, when he was counting the gun pallets, he had seen another lone skid that looked interesting. Like a shadow that had sprung up unexpectedly, they found it.

On this skid were little crates, each crate no more than one foot square. Surrounding it were an uncountable number of pallets of shrink-wrapped dry foods. These seemed to span the other half of the warehouse. Each little crate on this skid had similar unintelligible symbols which he believed was Arabic, and a long word below the funny script written in English.

He pulled from the top, one box which was surprisingly light—he'd thought they were crates of ammo for the guns—and touched the English word, pronouncing each syllable: "Fen-eth-yl-line."

Cain snatched the crowbar from Artie, and carefully went to work on the top. "Hold this steady," he commanded.

It cracked open, and then he peeled at the lid. Nervous excitement flooded him, as if he were a child opening a present the day before Christmas, knowing he could be caught at any moment. When the top came free with a final squeak, he thought he'd heard a noise near the front of the warehouse, right where they had entered. *It was probably nothing.*

He shined his light into the crate and they silently stared.

"Do you know what that is, man?" Artie asked.

Cain pulled up a big clear plastic bag containing thousands of little white pills.

"Yes, I do."

The source of the sound he heard was now obvious. A large door slid open. The silhouette of a man stepped in and the floodlamps above bathed them all in light.

2 Years Earlier

Jonah stepped into the warehouse's void, feeling as if it would swallow him up in one bite.

Although if this deal didn't go through, the Second National Bank of Florida would consider him more like a nibble.

Waiting for his appointment, he couldn't shake feeling like he was dropping his last dollar into a one-armed bandit and giving it that final pull. Would this appointment be the jackpot that would turn the tide on his flagging real estate empire, and at the same time give him a solution to SNBF's foreclosure? Or would it be a bust? In his mind's eye the reels spun so quickly the images were beyond blurry, with no sign of ever slowing down.

He wished he believed in God, any god for that matter, so he could pray for success.

He had to make this deal.

His largest space, a 200,000-square-foot warehouse, had remained empty since he bought it. He was sure this space would make him a fortune. Although it was outside of town, Sunbay Cove was part of a failed development that he was able to buy out of bankruptcy using falsified financials and lots of financing at the local bank. What made it a potential jewel in his sagging real estate and business empire was its natural harbor. He figured all he had to do was find someone to lease it. The quicker it happened, the more money he'd make.

But after the so-called pandemic hit there were no takers, and his cash position dwindled down to nothing.

Then, out of the blue came the phone call; a businessman who had an export business and needed to store excess supplies. The potential lessor had already looked at it from the harbor side, and if the inside was as spacious and well secured as it appeared from the outside, he'd not only take it, he'd sign a three-year lease and prepay the full amount, in cash. It was, as he'd learn later, literally a deal too good to be true.

And still the reels spun.

As Jonah waited inside the dark warehouse, he grew ever more impatient for the warehouse lights. They were designed to be turned on remotely, but there were still a couple of parts he hadn't yet spent the money on. So, they had to be turned on at the breaker. He'd sent his son Cain to turn them on. Now he wondered if his son could be trusted with such a simple task.

His eyes impatiently floated upward, attempting to see through the darkness, to the ceiling. Although a large amount of light cascaded through the door's opening, it wasn't enough to penetrate the space. Once again, just like he did when he bought the place, Jonah marveled at this grand building he controlled.

It was the newest of his warehouses, and this one was in the best shape. It was sealed up tight: not a single shaft of daylight pierced its thick shell. So solid, it was designed to withstand the force of a category five hurricane. His other spaces, although closer to town, were much older and not nearly as solid.

He heard the soft engine sounds of a vehicle. And with it, his excitement grew.

The slot machine's kickers were clicking into place, slowing the reels, letting him see the images as one by one they stopped spinning.

Right then, the gigantic space was filled with light. Cain *finally* found the switch. He admired the space again, now with the benefit of light to reveal it vastness.

Click.

The crunch sounds of tires on asphalt told him it was close. Then the car's brakes softly squealed.

Click.

Jonah turned to it, sensing its presence. The silhouette of a man carrying a large case paused at the opening. The man looked around at the space and then walked toward him. He could see the case now. It *was* large enough to carry three years' worth of rent, in cash.

Click. Ding-ding-ding.

The bells and lights of the slot machine played in his head. He *would* hit the jackpot.

"Mr. Price?" the man asked. A thick but pleasant dialect accented his question.

Jonah thrust out his hand. "Mr. Ramadi. It's a pleasure to meet you."

Chapter 17

Randall

Present Day

Randall White woke to the same heavenly and earthly rumbles that shook the rest of Endurance to consciousness.

Although daylight was starting to trickle into the hallway, his mental cobwebs—mostly remnants of awful nightmares—conspired to keep him from finding the restroom.

He was familiar enough with the home's layout as his wife and son had stayed here a few times even after moving just south of here in Crystal Waters. He stopped after absently clumping up to the master bedroom, its door slightly ajar. He peeked in to confirm what he already knew. Emily wasn't home.

Then his mind started to clear—a cobweb being knocked down—and he remembered where the guest bathroom was. Now plodding in that direction through the small home's hallway he was careful to keep his movements silent, not wanting to make noise and wake his family. Stopping again, this time in front of one of the many pictures seemingly arranged without purpose, a disorganized jumble of family and friends. One was a picture of the team. Their team. Emily was there, along with everyone else and the other staff. Randall was not. Having just been added to the team after the season had started, he had missed the pre-season portrait. That was his only year with them. No photographic evidence to confirm he was ever a member.

Back then, Emily was a young doctor, focusing on or-thopedic medicine, when she received an offer to be the Tampa Bay Devil Rays team physician. After the team's first game, their right fielder fractured his knee in a car accident--the media speculated it was alcohol-related. Randall was acquired through a trade and boom, he was a Devil Ray, at least until they could develop one of their younger players. He didn't mind being a fill-in. He was happy to just play. As a new addition, but near retirement age, Randall visited Dr. Scott often to gain her help to get his old muscles through the long season. They became fast friends, and subsequently, Emily fell in love with Randall's wife, Leticia, and their new son. They often had her over for dinner, and considered her part of the family; Randall repeatedly referred to her as their adopted daughter.

A few games into the season, Emily was romantically involved with a teammate, and became pregnant. She confessed to Leticia, but Emily kept the pregnancy quiet to the rest of the world, until she could tell the father. During an eight-game home stand, she did and was sum-marily dumped by the ballplayer and the team before they went back on the road. She miscarried the baby a few weeks later.

Randall's release came shortly after this. He couldn't recover fast enough from his own injuries. Maybe Emily's exit had something to do with it. Before the end of their short season—they didn't make it to the playoffs that year—he was replaced by a teenager from their triple-A league. Boom, he was out of baseball.

In spite of the devastating losses, Emily rebounded wonderfully. She found a position at a small clinic in the town of Endurance, Florida. Emily's little home was only a few steps away from the beach, and less than a mile away from where she worked at the health center. Always welcoming, Randall's family traveled the short distance from Crystal Waters to Endurance numerous times to spend time with her at the beach. Sometimes, like now, they would arrive while Emily was on shift—she was always working.

He'd found the key in the same spot she had always left it.

He was so thankful for the place to stay and was anxious to tell her this. This was not just a weekend stay; they'd need to impose for a lot longer than just a weekend.

Randall decided then to quickly clean up, and get to the clinic to make sure Emily was okay with them staying here indefinitely.

Jonah

Jonah Price closed the door behind him on the immi-grants.

He housed them in a giant empty warehouse, really the last empty space he had left. He gave them plenty of food and water per his instructions. He was so done being told what to do.

This warehouse was the worst of all his buildings. It had a leaky roof, no cooling, poor ventilation.

The same door he had come from, popped open and a man as dark as night pleaded in broken English the question that maybe a hundred others had asked him this morning. "No!" Jonah barked. There was no bathroom.

That was another feature absent from this property. Not that it would matter. With the power out, restrooms didn't work. He told the man to find one of the big holes they'd set up outside, in the large walled yard behind them. There were shovels to toss in dirt and lye to stanch the smell.

As the dark man trotted around back, Jonah reflexively wrinkled his nose at the thought of how smelly it would get in and around this building in a few hours.

It may have been his worst property. But he'd picked this one up for only a couple thousand dollars, by fore-closing on a small carryback note he'd bought. Odd-ly enough, the previous owner sold reconditioned mattresses. So, when Jonah took over the building, he ended up with several thousand of them. He had no idea what he would do with them. They were mostly worthless, having sat in the warehouse for years. Fortuitously, like the hazmat suits, they found use once again.

He rubbed at his bloodshot eyes, and walked out into the humidity of the new day.

"Thanks, guys," he said to the two guards posted in front of the warehouse's only unlocked entrance.

"You're welcome, Mr. Price," they snapped in unison.

"Sir?" one of them asked.

"Yeah?"

"Are we here to keep them from leaving or to keep someone from getting in?"

"Both." He then repeated the words spoken to him. "Let no one leave the property."

The guards nodded obediently, albeit somewhat tentatively.

He walked away, needing to think and plan his next move. He was having difficulty doing this, feeling the weight of the world bearing down on him. He shook the fatigue out of his head—he hadn't slept since yesterday. He could sleep tomorrow, if he was given another tomorrow. There was just too much to do between now and then.

The burden grew heavier when he thought of what he'd have to do next. Like a growing migraine, it pressed upon his temples vise-like. He knew what he had to do. Walters already led a group of his men to complete the first step of his plan. Although Jonah was capable, he really wanted Peter to handle this. But Peter was MIA, and Jonah had started to have some doubts lately about the man's own motives.

Jonah wondered what time it was, getting a niggling need to confirm all was right with Walters. This would be crucial to what he had told Ramadi. Jonah felt his belt and looked around for his radio, but couldn't find it. "Where the hell did I put the damn thing?"

Chapter 18

Frank

July 10th

"**D**amnit!" He pounded the ground. "I was so focused on getting out of the clinic and away from the hordes of immigrants, I didn't think to grab us some water," Frank said, wiping his brow as they rested in the shade of a giant willow off the road.

"Here!" Travis held out a small bottle. Lexi snatched it with a snicker. Travis then reached into his overstuffed backpack and grabbed two more, giving one to Frank, and twisting off the cap of his before taking a giant gulp.

Frank and Lexi exchanged knowing grins as they each sucked down their bottles' contents in practically one swig.

"*Great* job, Travis. Have you been carrying those things around with you in *that* backpack since we left the house?" Frank asked.

"No," he choked a little, and then cleared his throat. "I picked up the waters at the clinic. I thought we might need them. I forgot they were in there until you mentioned it."

"I've been meaning to ask"—Lexi held back a belch—"where did you get the backpack?"

"My room; it has all sorts of cool things in it." He gleamed, feeling useful and knowing some factoid that they didn't.

Lexi grimaced, as if some thought had taken possession of her face. Then she pointed at him. "Okay, so how'd Jonah's men let you take that giant backpack with you?"

Frank knew where Lexi was going with this, having already heard her complaints about Jonah's men taking her revolver.

Travis yanked a clog of weeds by his feet, his shoulders sinking slightly. "Ahh, I put Dad's medals in that bag." His head shot up as he spoke quickly. "I didn't want to lose them, so I put them in the bag by the door—you told us to always be prepared—and when they pulled me out of the radio room, they said I couldn't take it with me ..." He spoke to the dirt, head down, while his eyes peeked up at Frank. "I sort of cried." He then turned to Lexi, his voice lowered. "It seems to work with grown-ups, so I thought ..."

Frank chortled at his godson's ability to manipulate. "I'm going to keep that in mind for the future." He winked at Travis. "Can I see the bag?"

Travis nodded, once again slurping on his water bottle.

Frank pulled the pack to him. "Damn, your dad sure was a model prepper," he said marveling at the well-stocked bag. It had been years since he'd seen Stanley, and yet every day he was learning more and more about his friend's preparations. Stanley sure did a better job than he did with his own preps.

A thought occurred to him. "Lexi, did you find a similar backpack in your room?" Since Lexi was sleeping in what had been Stanley's room, Frank wondered if perhaps she'd found that Stanley had stashed one in there, too.

Lexi's looked up toward the sky, an attempt to search her memory. She *did* remember seeing a similar bag in the closet, but she'd barely had time to get settled in, much less explore the house's nooks and crannies. "I think so, but I haven't had a chance to look yet."

"Well it looks like your dad had set up a bug-out bag in each of the rooms. I found one in my room. I'm guessing that one may have been set up for you. This one"—he motioned to Travis's bag—"had bug-out supplies, and a few things geared to Travis. He definitely was planning for this time."

They fell quiet for a moment as the sadness of their loss returned, like the pain of an injured muscle that you try to use, reminding you not to go there, not yet. Frank gave the bag back to Travis with a smile. "Thanks," he mouthed.

"Look!" Lexi proclaimed. "That house has a water catching system like ours."

While already scanning around them for any threats, Frank focused on the small house across the street. He had noticed the house before they stopped for a rest, as it was the only home they'd seen in their walk back from town that had a manicured lawn. The guy might as well have hung a sign out on the front lawn that said "Come here first, bad guys. I'm the one with supplies."

Still he was impressed with the excellent preparations: the southern span of the roof was covered in solar panels, a large propane tank jutted out of the back side of the house, rows of vegetables and other plantings were surrounded by fruit-bearing trees in the back yard, and an excellent system to catch and store water was in place. He thrust out his forefinger to the roof gutters. "You're right Lex; it's a water catchment system, exactly like ours. You can see the gutters funnel the water down to a large tank elevated just below the room, but high enough to produce a strong enough pressure so it would flow into the house without pumps. What you don't see is the filtering system that likely uses charcoal and sand to naturally filter the water that goes into the large storage tank."

"Uncle Frank?" Travis had begun calling him Uncle Frank lately, he said because it was easier than calling him Godfather Frank. "What's the other larger tank for, the one connected to the catching tank?" Travis asked, trying to suck in knowledge from his godfather, just like his sister.

Frank followed the pipe jetting out to another larger tank. "That's extra water storage. In the drier months, if the main tank runs out, they could pump water back int—"

Frank stopped midsentence, his whole body tense, on alert. He caught movement on the outermost edge of his periphery. He studied the home, now with more diligence. A curtain, in the second side window, abruptly flew back to reveal a wide-eyed man. He held up a large-caliber pistol for display and glared at them. It was a simple message, easily understood.

Frank nodded while holding his palm up, as if to say "Message received."

"Let's get moving. It's not safe out here."

The rest of their journey was mostly quiet and uneventful.

When they arrived at their driveway after another hour of walking, exhaustion took over, even though it was still early morning. He could see it on their faces as well.

It would have been easy to blame the Florida humidity and their five-mile walk for their fatigue. He knew it was the stress of always having to watch out for the next person, around any corner, who intends to kill you. It was one thing dealing with that stress when he was on tour, with the Army. But that was a lifetime ago, when he wasn't injured, he was younger, and didn't have two young people to watch over. His world, and theirs, had changed so much.

And even though he knew he should remain vigilant, he was sapped of energy. So, when he saw the house, their pace slowed. It was a mental acknowledgment that they'd had made it, this far. They would be able to rest again, before having to prepare for the next threat to come their way. He relished the feeling, even for just a short bit, as he limped the final few feet. That feeling didn't last.

As they approached the home's rear, Frank noticed the back door was slightly ajar, and he heard a voice coming from inside.

He froze and held up his fist--it was automatic for him. Lexi and Travis halted, each becoming rigid.

He then heard a creak, the telltale sign of weight moving along an older home's wood floors.

Someone was definitely in their house.

Chapter 19
Sunbay Cove, Florida

Stanley Broadmoor

Eight Years Earlier

"So, when was the last hurricane that hit this area?" Stanley Broadmoor asked.

"Because of its northern location, this area hasn't been hit by a hurricane in decades," the realtor proudly announced. It was a question out-of-towners often asked. She flashed him a manipulated grin, a salesperson's smile. "Let's walk around back."

Stanley followed the portly woman, who wore a bright blue flowered skirt way too short for her weight and age. He hated thinking critically of someone. But it was more than that. He just couldn't stand realtors, who had little training or knowledge about the biggest investment in a person's life. Yet they were a necessary evil as they were often the gatekeepers to the home he wanted.

Stanley stopped when he noticed the large tank on the side of the house, with tubing running to the gutter. He examined the plumbing and its quality. It looked good.

About a five-hundred-gallon tank, or more than enough based on the area's rainfall to service him and his kids.

"Oh, you have good eyes, Mr. Broadmoor." She swatted at a mosquito that was busily deciding where amongst its ample options it would land on her next. "That's a brand new water catching system that the owner installed. And you probably didn't notice, but new solar panels were installed last year. Isn't it wonderful? This home is totally green."

He of course knew all of this because it was on the listing. Besides its coastal access, being already off-grid or what she was calling "green" was the house's main attraction. Then there was the owner. This was an estate sale, and he knew why.

The owner was a prepper, who stupidly got himself entangled in a land-use dispute on the side of a rancher in Texas. The rancher was very connected with other survivalists on social media. And when the rancher made a stand against the federal government, this Florida prepper joined him, bringing with him a large selection of guns. When they started a firefight, he and several other survivalists were shot by the ATF. The newspapers released the names of the dead. But most reporters didn't do any further research, as they were onto the next story after the sizzle of this one died down.

However, Stanley, with his resources at the FBI, not only found this place, but also found out about the improvements to the home through filed permits. He learned that the owner's sole surviving relative had sold all of his belongings at auction, and then put the home up for sale. It was the perfect bug-out home for him and his kids.

The realtor, of course, ignored the whole prepper angle and the huge market that would have been interested had she marketed to it. Especially with the pandemic still on peoples' minds. Instead, based on her earlier comments, her choice of wording on the listing, and her white Prius, plastered with Democratic Party and Pro-Choice bumper stickers, she found the "green" living angle a much more palatable target market.

Although she had taken plenty of pictures of the inside, including several of the toilets--which was always gobstopping to him, and the ocean views, there were few images of the systems. Without looking at the inside, he was pretty sure he would buy this; he just wanted to make sure the systems were in good enough shape. He didn't have time for construction projects right now. So far, it seemed perfect.

He followed her around the northwest corner of the home to the back yard and was stunned by the view. Her pictures, no doubt snapped by her smart phone, didn't do justice to its true beauty. The home had a dock, with room for two boats, connected to a very small inlet, which led to the Gulf. With the property's incline from the water, and no other homes between this one and the ocean, the view was spectacular. "Wow!" he whispered.

"I know, it's amazing isn't it?" she said overly exaggerating her facial muscles.

Stanley scratched at his beard, discomforted by all this unfamiliar growth on his face, and his momentary reveal of emotions. "I saw on the satellite map an empty development south, and only one neighbor north, who shares this inlet. What do you know about them?"

"You are very smart to ask, Mr. Broadmoor." Her voice felt like nails on a chalkboard. "The Sunbay Cove Development, which you and your neighbor are part of, folded with the economy. It was supposed to be mostly residential development. There were other homes that were bought up and then razed. The owner of this house and your neighbor to the north held out and didn't accept any buyout offers."

She slunk over toward him, as if about to hand him something. Then she peeked in both directions. A secret was about to be revealed. "If you ask me," she whispered, plump hand partially obstructing her exaggerated red lips. "They should have taken the offer, which I hear was three times the price you can now get this house for. It's a steal, I tell you, believe you me."

"The neighbor?" Stanley said curtly.

"Oh yes." She righted herself, picking at her skirt, which seemed to be trying to ride up her thighs. "So, the developer only built a giant warehouse at the southern end of the property. Whereas all that vacant land, which was zoned residential and commercial, was ultimately purchased by a wildlife land trust, so you'll have no neighbors to your south."

He was getting annoyed as he already knew all of this from his research. "But to the north—"

"I'm getting to that, young man." Her face momentarily wrinkling with her own irritation, before the curl of her consistent salesperson's smile returned. "Your neighbor is a loner who keeps to himself. No one's heard from him in years. You'll never see him." She then motioned toward the house. "Shall we take a look at the inside now?" This was her plan. She'd have them fall in love with the outside views--the recent green improvements appeared to be an added bonus. Then, she'd walk him quickly through the inside of the house, where he'd be more likely to ignore the old pipes that often groaned when they were turned on, and the wood floors that creaked when you walked on them.

"No. That's not necessary. I'll take it. I want to offer full price, and I've got the cash. How quickly can the estate close?"

Frank

Present Day

Lexi drew her newfound Glock, but kept it pointed toward the ground—as he had taught her, with her finger resting above the trigger-guard. Travis clutched his backpack straps, wishing that he'd taken the .22 from under the radio room's desk and that his Uncle Frank had taught him to use it.

Frank motioned Lexi forward and held out his hand for the weapon, which she willingly relinquished.

Frank held the pistol in front of him with his right and slowly drew open the screen door with his other. When it started its creak, he rushed in, crouching low. He faced the storage/radio room's open door, where he'd heard the voice. It was the radio speaking. A figure on their couch moved, causing him to spin in its direction and greet the trespasser with the outstretched pistol.

The figure had a long gray beard and goofy eyes, and he thrust his hands up in submission. "Don't shoot. It's just me. Your doors were open when I came to check on you."

Frank lowered the Glock and his shoulders, stomping over to shake the man's outstretched hand. He turned his head to the door and yelled, "It's only Jasper; it's safe to come in."

Travis entered first. "Can I go to sleep now?" he asked. He pushed past Lexi at the door, bumping her—she shot a grimace his way—with his bulbous backpack, and strode right to his room, not waiting for an answer.

"I'm too wound up to sleep right now," Lexi huffed. "Think I'll grab the Prepper Brothers book and do like the song said and put my 'toes in the water and ass in the sand.'" She started toward her bedroom.

"Wait." Frank spun the Glock in his hand, holding out the butt-end to her. "You'd better get used to carrying this until we can get your revolver back from Jonah's men."

She sighed her displeasure, but snatched the black pistol and shoved it into her waistband. She had already emoted to Frank that she hoped they could reclaim her pistol and her holster from Jonah. She padded back to her room, no doubt to grab her book.

"Sorry I couldn't do much for you," Jasper said to Frank, who was busy examining the living room and kitchen before stepping into the storage/radio room.

"It's all right," Frank said to the empty radio room, then looked to Jasper. "I didn't want you to start a shootout with those men, and risk one of the kids getting hit. Thanks for looking out for us. You were obviously a good friend to Stanley." Frank plopped himself in the desk chair.

Everything appears to still be here, and in order, he thought.

The radio's static beckoned him and Jasper sauntered his way.

"Wow, this is a nice set-up. Didn't realize Stanley had all this. Much better than mine," Jasper said, his head nodding approvingly at all the radio equipment.

"Yeah, it's all above my pay grade, but it'll keep us in touch with our friends, and catch up on what's going on with the outside world."

"F this is G, are you out there?"

Frank and Jasper froze and glared at the radio speaker, as if it were a person and was reacting to their being there.

Frank slapped the microphone button. "I'm here. Is that you, Gri—"—he almost forgot Grimes's requested non-use of last names—"ahh, G?"

"So good to hear your voice again, buddy. You had us worried here. Please go to the next frequency."

Frank's left forefinger found the next written frequency on a list he'd scribbled from their last conversation. He had taped it to the desk below the transceiver so he could easily access it, and with the fingers of his right hand, he spun the transceiver's dial to that frequency. The speaker whistled at him with each broadcast he passed, or more likely just louder static since there were very few actual broadcasts anymore. When he found the noted frequency, he turned his gaze to Jasper.

Jasper hovered over his shoulder and seemed mesmerized by the radios and papers strewn upon the desk. His forehead was furrowed, unkempt brow-hairs pointing in all different directions. A little smirk hid behind his bushy beard, like he'd realized something. Then he met Frank's gaze and his face became even more animated. Frank continued. "We follow this frequency schedule so that we minimize the chances of the enemy listening in."

Frank gazed back at the speaker wondering why nothing but noise-haze was coming out of it. *Where the hell did Grimes go?* He returned his finger to the list, eyes darted from list to dial, and back. "Shit!"

"Do you need help, Uncle Frank?" Travis asked from the doorway.

"Shit-shit-shit! I must have chosen the wrong frequency. Yes, please. You seem to have a knack for this damn thing."

Frank arose from the chair, and Travis hopped in, knees first, planted to the back. He then flicked it once around before bracing himself back to where he was facing the radios.

"Which one were you on?" he asked.

Frank pointed to the second on the list.

"Are you sure?"

He nodded. "Mm-mmm."

"Oh, you see you have the day messed up. You're on yesterday's layout. Each day it cycles one, then two, then three frequencies on the list. We're on two." Travis spun the dial with the agility of a master safe-cracker, until he unlocked the radio's hidden frequencies, and out poured his friend's voice. Travis clicked the microphone. "Hey G, this is T. I have F here and J, our neighbor."

"T! Wow, I was getting a little frantic here," Grimes's voice sang out. He was crystal clear on this frequency, like he was next door.

Frank leaned in and pushed the button, "Sorry to worry you, buddy. Just so you know the gas didn't hit us after all. A bunch of birds must have passed through some intended for a secret Army base—that I guess wasn't so secret—just north of us. The spineless bastards killed most of our troops there, but we're safe. What's the word from your end?" He let go and stood erect, yearning for some information.

"Well, lots to tell. First, Porter hasn't shown up yet. We haven't heard anything from them, since they left Farook's base in Florida. I'm trying not to worry, but you know me." Grimes paused and although the microphone was open, all they heard was what sounded like a yawn before he continued.

"Sorry, but I haven't slept in a while and this waiting for your next killer thing sucks. Between the jihadis and the mystery group that's beheaded our man ..."

"What mystery group beheaded your man?" Frank asked.

"Oh yeah, sorry I'm not thinking straight. Paul, I don't think you know him, he was a lookout north of Winnie and he didn't report in. One of our guys, found him beside the tower he was glassing the road from and his head was missing. Our guy brought the body back, but he had to go around Winnie, which was burned to the ground. We suspect it's the same group and we thought they'd be here by now but ... What the hell? Hold on guys ..."

Grimes's voice trailed off, like he was speaking away from his microphone.

There were some cracks of gunfire coming from the speakers.

"What's going on at your end?" Frank asked.

"Wait," Grimes said. "Oh shi—"

An over-modulated *boom* shook from the speakers, causing a feedback squeak. Then there was only a hiss.

Their timer rattled noisily, telling them to change frequencies.

Chapter 20
Sunbay Cove, Florida

Lexi

exi's frayed nerves finally start to blanch away with the caress of each small wave lapping over her toes.

She was parked comfortably in a sand-chair, nested on a little stretch of the inlet's beach, along their dock. The water was warm, yet a slight breeze wisped over the water cooling her off just enough to be comfortable in the heat of the day. She longed for the freedom to swim and then to nod off at her leisure. But these luxuries were not possible in this world she lived.

There was no harm in resting her mind and body while she studied. And if she had to do it, she'd rather do it outside, by water.

She had already finished the Prepper Brothers Book. Now she knew everything about *Surviving the First Seven Days After an EMP*. She tore into the next how-to survival book, one of dozens from her father's bookshelves. This one was called *100 Deadly Skills*. She rose from her chair and looked around to make sure she was alone, self-conscious about what she was going to do next. She remembered how foolish she had felt knocking her head on the ground yesterday in front of Frank and Travis. So she moved farther into an area protected by long tufts of tall grass leading to the water. It was like a little room outside, walled in by green.

While standing, she scanned the chapter again and then put the book down. She would practice Deadly Skill No 61: Draw a Concealed Pistol.

Using her gifted Glock, purloined by Frank from the Endurance thug, she practiced her draw. It was frustrating at first because each time the weapon was getting hung up on her shirt tail. But as the book explained, all she had to do was hook the shirt with the thumb of her drawing hand, and assist with her free hand. This worked beautifully. After a few minutes of trial and error, practicing on an imaginary bad guy, she was able to smoothly yank the Glock and have it at the ready to shoot in less than a second.

She felt satisfied, but she wanted to do more. The simulations were growing tiresome. She needed to face her enemy and get rid of her ... fear.

That was it. She was afraid. The mental images of last night's nightmare returned. Abdul was chasing her, even though she had killed him.

She found herself hyperventilating, even though none of this was logical. She resolved to pick up her chair and go tell Frank about this. Maybe there was something more they could do together to keep her mind occupied and off her dead uncle.

She plodded back to her chair, leaned over to pick it up and then stopped.

There were several prints around her chair and they were all larger than her own. She scrutinized them: *Where they there before? What did Frank's boot prints look like?*

No, she thought, *these were new.*

Still unsure, she scanned around her area and found the next clue: a boat was tied off on their dock. Smoothly she drew her gun, and listened for movement.

Someone behind—

When she spun around, something large and hard met her square in the face, knocking her down. Her vision wobbled as did her strength, but her adrenalin was pumping full throttle.

She yanked her gun back up and toward a dark form just to her right when that same heavy object struck her arms.

Her gun fell away, out of reach.

One last option.

"Hel—" she yelled. A hand clasped around her mouth, stifling her.

Frank

"**G**, are you there?" Frank called into the microphone. He waited and commanded Travis. "Try the next one."

Travis spun the knob, finding the frequency,. "Okay."

"G are you there? Please reply." Frank waited. "The next."

Frank was frantic to find Grimes on the radio, holding onto the smallest of hope that what they heard was not what it sounded like. But with each turn of the dial, their hope diminished.

Chapter 21
Stowell, Texas

Grimes

The tooth-rattling explosion left his ears ringing.

Robert Grimes found himself on the floor of his radio room. The smell of dust and lemons filled his nostrils. Drops of coolness pelted his ankles—his freshly squeezed lemonade, probably overturned. The ringing sound was overwhelming, along with a million crickets bleating in his ears, all at once.

His eyes flickered open and this surprised him because he didn't realize he'd had them closed. They must've shut reflexively with the giant flash.

Mickey Mouse lay on the floor in front of him, staring back at him with his peculiarly happy face. Mickey's minute-hand pointed an accusatory finger at him, as if to say its situation was all Grimes's fault.

He did a self-assessment, glancing at and mentally focusing on all the parts of his body. It didn't feel he'd sustained any serious injuries.

What the hell happened, he mused.

Pushing himself up to one knee—his already splinted other was immobile—he faced his desk. It was a blanket of glass and dust and his overturned Zenith Trans-Oceanic radio. The portable short-wave from 1942 was his most prized radio. It was priceless, mainly because it was his father's. Now it lay upside-down with its belly opened, its guts—a tangle of tubes and wires—spilled out upon the desk's surface.

He glanced through his window, most of the glass now missing; only a couple of ragged pieces clung to its frame. A warm Texas breeze billowed through, but Grimes didn't notice. He was fixated on what was supposed to be outside the window: what he stared at every day and was now no longer there. Actually it was there, but not in the form he knew.

Grimes rose to his feet for a better look at his mangled antenna and tower. The tower's mast rose up only a few feet from its concrete footing. Then like a gargantuan metal erector set that had been pushed over by its temperamental creator, it was bent back at an awkward angle toward him. The majority of the tower ran to his left out of his field of view. He didn't even know what remained of the antenna arrays themselves. The storage shed it had been attached to, was now a bramble of rubble. He had constructed both not too long ago, with his own two hands. Now only fragments of his work-of-love remained, littering every square inch of his lawn.

More importantly, American Freedom Network was down, perhaps for good.

The constant high-pitched ringing in his head now included popping sounds.

He stuck his forefingers into his ears and rapidly wiggled them. He knew it was a futile attempt to clear up what would only take time to unblock. When he removed them, the pops were now more pronounced, and there were many of them. After what seemed like a minute, he realized what they were.

Automatic gunfire.

A hand grabbed his shoulder, startling him. It spun him around so that he was looking at Aimes. The man's face was a network of worry lines; his mouth twisted into shapes and muffled words came out. "Are you all right?" He was yelling, but it sounded like he was in the next room.

"Grimes, can you move?"

He nodded through his daze.

Aimes pulled him up and led him toward the front door. Grimes put his hand out to block their progression. "Wait, I'm not going out there unarmed."

Grimes stumbled to a hall closet, reached in, and grabbed his suppressed .300 Win Mag. "Okay, point me at the jihadis," he said as he slung his rifle over his shoulder.

"It's not jihadis. It's some other group of nut-jobs."

Corporal Ben Sparks

After the explosion he dropped the RPG launcher and ran, looking back to inspect his work only after he was a couple of blocks away. The radio building was destroyed and the antenna appeared to be down.

Several of the town's residents running to the explosion slowed, asking him if he was okay and did he see the explosion? He ignored them and continued his run. It was easier than killing them. He finally stopped when he reached his truck, a mile away in a dollar store's parking lot.

He never understood the American fascination with the dollar store. He opened his backpack and fished out a bottle of water, sucking it down in nearly one gulp.

He pulled out his RF detector once more and turned it on. Already having the known AFN frequencies pre-set, he checked all of them. There was nothing registering. He was successful.

Ali Atef smiled at the good fortune Allah had brought to his mission, and tried to consider what if anything else he needed to do as he slid into his truck. His handlers had provided him the truck and the radio equipment necessary to track down the infldels' radio station and stop them from further hurting their efforts.

He was able to track the signal to Texas, but to get any more specific was difficult because they changed their frequencies often. So, he'd pretended once again to be a Corporal Ben Sparks. It was his favorite American name. When he arrived in this country from Iran, to use his skills for the war to come, he'd taken it and the life from the American. As Corporal Sparks, he called out to G who ran the American Freedom Network, pretending to be need-ing help. When this G transmitted long enough over two frequencies, he was able to pinpoint the exact location of the broadcast.

After finding the antenna and the shack it was con-nected to by wires, he assumed it was the radio shack that transmitted the signal. The RPG worked perfectly and now he was ready to go.

He'd first check in with his handlers and then he'd hopefully be given the ability to fight the infidels at a place of his choice in two days. He had one in mind.

He pulled the microphone to his mouth and pressed the transmit button. "This is 1F8. Come in."

Ali started up the truck and pulled into the empty road. He'd go north on the main thoroughfare before heading west. He hoped to fight with Mahdi Abdul out East. He accelerated.

"1F8, were you successful?"

Ali stopped his truck abruptly.

A convoy of vehicles lined the road in front of him, blocking his way. There were men and women, most half-naked, sitting on top and outside the vehicles screeching. The lead vehicle was a semi-tractor trailer with spikes sticking out of its front grill. On the top of each spike was a decapitated head.

Ali stared, dumbstruck. He had never seen such a display in America, except in their films.

"Repeat 1F8. Were you successful?"

Ali jumped at the broadcast, more surprised that it had startled him. He reached down and grabbed the microphone again and raised it to his face, while glancing up. "This is 1F8. Mission was a succe—"

A 5.56 bullet, shot from the roof of the second vehicle in the caravan, crashed through Ali's truck windshield, burst through his nasal cavity and exploded out the back of his head, interrupting him midsentence. Ali's foot slipped off the brake as his head flopped forward, his chin onto his chest. His truck idled ahead and slid through the caravan unmolested.

The caravan growled its way down the road, the vehicles' occupants announcing their entrance to Stowell with shrieking brays and gunfire.

Chapter 22
Sunbay Cove, Florida

Lexi

The man who had whacked Lexi in the head and arms stood over her. His two bloodshot eyes glared at her through a full bearded face. His searing stare bristled over every inch of her, causing her to shudder.

She wanted to scream, but her mouth was taped so it would be no use. She tempered her anger, even though she certainly wanted to kill them, but the bastards had taken her gun and her knife from her. She was getting mighty tired of people taking her gun from her. She didn't even try to rustle away from one of the other two men who held her tightly.

She was just trying to understand what they were doing with her.

The red-eyed man held out a picture to other two men behind her for their examination. She couldn't see their faces only this one. He withdrew it, pulling it back to his own gaze. She caught only the briefest glimpse of the image, and with it came a rifle-shot of recognition. It was a picture of *her*, with Travis and their Aunt Sarah and Uncle David in Tucson, taken over a year ago. *How could they possibly have this?*

Lexi immediately had a flashback of her time of captivity at Uncle Abdul's compound.

Never mind what they intended for her. She was in a full panic over what this meant. *Can this really be happening again? And how? Uncle Abdul was dead.* She watched him die.

She told herself to breathe, to be calm and focus on first getting out of this, then she'd figure out what's going on. She listened to each of her senses now, concentrating on only those things she couldn't control. Her panic started to subside.

She'd learned this technique of boxing up your emotions firsthand, years ago and even much more recently over the last few days. It seemed to be the only way to cope in this crazy world: put your emotions aside and deal with them later, but survive now. With the added skills she was picking up every moment between her reading and Frank's training, she had many more tools than before all this happened.

Now she *needed* to use her abilities, both old and new, to get out of this one. Not only would her life depend on it, but maybe Travis's and Frank's too, as they still didn't know these men were here.

She had to get free and warn them.

So Lexi focused on all her senses, like a computer taking in data and processing it, churning out a solution.

One subtle thing she noticed, within the wet gentle breeze of the Gulf's salt air, was their smells, or rather lack of them. All people, but most especially men, stank now that showering wasn't practical. And although these men smelled sweaty and the red-eyed man was malodorous, even so she could pick up hints of soap as if they had just come out of a shower. She stored this piece of data for later use.

A small shudder hit her when she heard them unpack something and then roughly zip-tie her hands together. This brought another mental image. It was exactly what she needed. This was the thing that would provide her an opportunity for escape, or disruption, and certainly to warn Frank, Travis, and Jasper. She knew how to undo her zip-tie. She waited for the opportunity to start.

The two other men rose from behind her and withdrew their weapons—semi-automatic pistols by the look of them—and started toward the back door of their house. They walked carefully and quietly, obviously wanting to surprise whomever they found in the house. She had to work quickly.

She pulled a paperclip from the waistband of her shorts. She was glad she kept it against her back so as to not interfere with her survival knife, which she had carried--before they took it--up front. Frank had told her to always carry a paperclip on her, in addition to her gun and knife. He told her there were many uses for it as a tool, and a weapon. It would make a perfect tool in this instance.

Both now crept below the window line, hugging the rear of the house, only a few feet away from the door.

From one of her books she remembered a hack for un-doing zip-ties using a bobby pin. She didn't have enough hair for a bobby pin, but a paperclip should do just fine. Apparently, if one used the end of the pin or clip to wedge it under the interlocking ratchet, and force it from the teeth of the zip tie, one could pull themselves out of it.

She worked quickly, bending one end out and then sticking it into the zip tie, while watching all the men.

One of the two stealth men already had the screen door open.

Frank

"**K**eep trying, Travis." He glanced at Jasper. "Maybe it wasn't what we thought it was." Frank was sure that this guess was wrong, but he wanted to think the best. He didn't want to accept that Grimes was hurt or killed, and what that might mean for the rest of his home town, Stowell, Texas.

"I'm going to use the head, if it's all right?" Jasper asked, sounding almost uninterested.

He was right, Frank thought, what-ifs never solved anything. "Sure, it's off the hallway, and it's a normal flushing one, not one of those chemical things."

Jasper nodded and stomped across the creaky floor to the hallway. Frank stepped partially out the door to watch their neighbor. Before he entered the bathroom, at the end of the hall, he seemed to examine each inch of his path, like he was looking at it for the first time. Frank stepped back into the radio room and storage area of the house, and then took his place behind Travis. "Do you have frequencies on the other bands, or just these?"

Travis lifted his head up from the desk, with all the papers including their notes about the frequencies, and stared forward. "Sorry Uncle Frank, but this was as far as I got with Ga... Ga... Ga...." Like a broken record, Travis seemed to be stuck on G. His body became rigid and started to shake.

Frank peered down, over his head and put his hands on his shoulders. "Travis, are you all—" Frank lifted his head, now pointed, like Travis, toward the back door. "—hey buddy, don't shoot. You can take whatever you want. We won't stop you."

Frank lowered his hands behind Travis's back and clutched his rolling desk chair, getting ready to pull him out of the way.

Two Middle-Eastern-looking men stalked into their living room, guns drawn. Their eyes kept shifting from Frank to Travis.

"Step away from the boy," commanded the closest.

"Hey Mohammad," Frank said, intending to be disrespectful. He remained where he was. "That's not going to happen." Frank glanced past the men to the kitchen counter, where he'd left his Glock and shotgun. When he had realized Jasper was their intruder, he let his guard down and deposited his only weapons there. They were much too far away, and the men were closing their distance, slowly approaching.

"I will not warn you again," the man said smoothly. "Step away from the boy or both of you will die."

Lexi

*G**ot it**,* she thought to herself. She felt instant slack, and gently pulled until she was able to remove first her left hand and then her right. While the red-eyed man was staring at the house, away from her, she ripped the tape from her mouth and yelled, "Watch out, they have guns!"

Red-eyes spun around wildly, ready to strike her once again for causing so much trouble. But she was already lunging for him. Holding the paperclip firmly between the knuckles of her right fist, she punched him directly at one of his anger-filled red eyes.

He attempted to swing the gun at her, intending to make her pay for her disobedience, when multiple shots erupted from inside the house. He hesitated just enough for Lexi.

She grabbed his gun hand with both of hers, pulling and twisting up, bending his hand back painfully. At the same time, she pivoted, and swung herself around him, pulling him to the ground. This time, it was the man who dropped the gun when he hit the ground hard. But she landed on her face, already sore from where he punched her, and on her chest, taking her breath away.

Before she could react, she heard the man's footfalls, but they were scurrying away from her, toward the dock. Twisting her head up, but still lying prone, she could see the man was making a break for the boat. She turned away from the dock and caught her gun and knife still on the ground where they had thrown them.

Then she turned toward the house, fearful of what had just happened.

Frank

Frank was a bit taken aback by how things unfolded for them.

After the second command to move away from the boy, Travis swung his left hand around the chair, out of the view of the men. In his hand he was holding a .22 Ruger.

That brilliant boy must have pulled it from the scabbard underneath the desk. Frank accepted the gift, flicked the safety off, hoping there was a bullet in the chamber, and readied himself to push Travis farther into the room, out of the path of bullets. He would have to shoot quick and steady, using his weak hand.

He was about to make his move when two helpful diversions occurred. The first outside involved Lexi screaming; the next, the hallway toilet flushed and the door noisily opened with a clunk—Frank had just about forgotten about Jasper, who said from out of his field of view, "Howdy, fellas." That was all Frank needed.

He raised the gun and aimed for the first man's head, who like the other had swung his attention toward Jasper, away from them, when he fired the first shot; then another; and another. Joining the music of the little soprano-like *pop-pop-pops* from his pistol, was the beefy tenor of *ratta-tatta-tatta-tatta* of the Thompson—thank God Jasper hadn't laid his machine gun down too.

The two men danced, as if being electrocuted by multiple jolts, before dropping to the floor.

"Lexi!" Frank yelled, bounding to the back door.

Frank heard the sound of an outboard motor, as he raced out the door and down the stairs. He instantly saw Lexi standing between the house and the shore, arms down, gun in hand. She was watching the mouth of the inlet, out of his view. She turned back and acknowledged him by giving a thumbs-up. She was okay.

The motorboat quickly powered through the inlet, hugging the coastline. The invader's boat used the heavy growth along the shore to keep hidden. After a few seconds, the sounds of the boat faded into the Gulf.

Chapter 23
Stowell, Texas

Grimes

Once outside and away from his home, he took a moment to glance back. The shed had definitely been blown up, sending the tower over and antenna with it. However, other than some minor damage, his house was in good shape.

Either his ears were starting to clear out or it was their being outside, but the gunfire was quite loud—and it was everywhere.

They scampered across the street, toward Stowell Grocery, ducking behind a curved block wall on the street corner. Posted on each end of the wall was one of their town's militia, acting as spotters. Each was responsible for covering two directions of empty streets with an AK rifle—from the stash he, Aimes, and Cartwright had taken from the local terrorist cell responsible for torching Cartwright's home. One aimed his weapon to the north and then pointed it west. The other pointed to the south and then the east. Each looked for their newest enemy in one direction, scanning for a few seconds, before moving and searching in the other.

Grimes peeked over the edge of the wall. He could hear the gunfire, but couldn't see the shooters. In the distance, he also heard animal-like screeches, almost like primeval yells, as if they were being invaded by an Indian war party. He spun around and sat hard against the wall, examining his rifle and going through the mental checklist he always did before shooting. "Tell me what the hell is going on," he huffed.

"There's a crazed group of Mad Max wannabes that just drove into town, shooting up the place. They have Paul's head and others on pikes."

Grimes wondered if he'd sustained a concussion during the blast, because what he heard made no sense.

Then the sounds changed direction: they were now coming from the east. Their inhuman cries and pops of gunfire now mixed with echoing car and truck engine groans.

"They're coming," hollered the south-easterly spotter in a frazzled voice.

"We've got bogies coming from the east on Main," Aimes howled at his radio. "Pete, you and your men get your asses down Campbell. Maybe we can box them in once they come upon us. Grimes ..." Aimes spun to look behind him, sensing Grimes had already left. He caught a glimpse of his friend moments later hobbling up a ladder to the top of the grocery store's roof. At the northeast-ern corner, Grimes signaled thumbs up and erected his bipod.

"I need you," Aimes bellowed to his northwest spotter, "up against the horse facility across the street."

The young man dashed away and diagonally across the intersection, then over a fence and through a field of grass, as he made his way to the facility before he was seen. Aimes had just called in two groups from the south, and they were set up and waiting, their position protected by trees and bushes, making them invisible to the approaching horde from the east.

They were ready.

The Mad Max convoy—Grimes could see what his friend meant—rumbled toward them slowly, halting only a hundred feet from the intersection. The semi-truck in front was the one with spikes festooning its grill, a moving horror show of severed heads on every other spike. One of the heads looked familiar. That was obviously the intent. Their goal must have been to scare their victims into submission. It wouldn't work with Stowell.

Grimes sited in the semi driver.

The group of crazies was quiet, the growl of their idling engines making their only sounds now.

The semi driver revved his engine and then blew the horn, a blaring squeal that pounded Grimes's eardrums, already throbbing painfully. The driver let out an animalistic wail to match his horn, and all the others followed his lead, blaring their screams and horns in a cacophonous orchestra of madness.

The semi popped into gear and shuddered forward.

Grimes responded instantly, firing his first shot at the semi driver; then he cycled another and aimed at the next vehicle's driver; then another.

If Grimes had been watching the driver, he would seen a splatter of red cover the semi's windshield. The vehicle lurched off the road slowly and eased into the ditch. The other vehicles followed when everyone in Stowell joined in, firing on all the convoy horde's vehicles. The Stowell residents let loose with the power of nearly a hundred AKs.

Their enemy didn't stand a chance.

Mere seconds later, when it was all finished, Grimes stood up to take in the result. At first he felt a sense of pride for how their people performed. Then his pride turned to dread.

Aimes had been training their town's militia to prepare for a much more lethal enemy. The Islamic warriors they were expecting tomorrow or the next day, were far better schooled to fight than these drug-addled cannibals. Their true enemy wasn't scared and they relished dying on the battlefield as martyrs.

No, this band of drug-crazed thugs was no match for a little strategy and their AKs. The battle with the invading Islamist army would be different. Of that he was sure.

Grimes looked down to his friend. Aimes stared back at him, appearing just as worried.

Chapter 24
Sunbay Cove, Florida

Frank

July 11th

They rose early to prepare for the invasion.

There was no way to know if it would ever hit their area and if so, when. But they were going to be prepared for it just the same. No longer was this simply a matter of survival for Frank and what remained of his family. This was a preparation for war.

The rules of war were far different than those for survival. With survival, you prepared to react to the chaos that was foisted on you. Although you treated everyone with skepticism, even a suspicion that they wanted to do you harm, you still treated them with respect. It wasn't the rules of decorum that worried you, it was avoiding conflict. This was primary to survival. Conflict could mean injury, and injury led to a much higher probability of death. When faced with a conflict with someone who intended to do you harm, you would still be just as harsh in your killing, but you always did it with reservation.

Engaging in war meant being proactive, not reactive. You assumed that all those dressed in the enemy's uniform of choice were combatants. In the theatre of war there was only one thing you needed to do with combatants—and that was kill them before they killed you.

There would be no desire or thrill in causing pain or suffering to a combatant. Sometimes a combatant was a regular person like him, albeit a regular person who chose to be on the wrong side of the conflict. Regardless, in war, their job was to kill their enemy combatants proactively and as efficiently as possible. That was their primary focus from now on. As a warrior for the US Army who had been in involved in many battles himself, he would work with his family to accomplish this.

The first preparation was protecting their property. In a time of war anyone who entered their property without their invitation was considered a combatant. Their goal was to therefore kill that combatant quickly and effectively. To this end, with Lexi's and Travis's help, Frank set up their perimeter defenses and posted a clear warning. Across the front gate they strung a sign that spoke their intentions plainly: "Honk horn otherwise you will be shot."

Unfortunately, Frank didn't have any explosives for his defenses. So he opted for a few more jungle-warfare-style traps. They would be just as deadly as any explosive. In every simple egress and ingress area, he set up spearing devices, using saplings for their tension.

Frank cut and gathered the branches for spears and gave specific instructions to Lexi and Travis on how to make their points and their varied lengths. While they were busy doing this, he cut and gathered the sapling branches and trunks. Most of these were bundled to make them stronger and provide more tension, making the resultant traps much more lethal. Each constructed trap was taken to each area where he thought someone might try to gain access or sneak up on them by foot. Lexi and Travis followed him to each point, helping as he directed.

He did this not only to teach them both these skills, but so they'd know where each of these was located. That way, if they had to leave the property quickly, they wouldn't accidentally step on one of them. Frank even set up little red markers, twenty steps away from each trap, as a warning that a trap or snare was coming up.

Just before setting each trap, he added a poisonous cocktail to each tip. He'd made the concoction from a combo of some of the household chemicals they had on hand. Each time he did this, Travis went a little wide-eyed over how he'd feel if he was speared by one of these things.

"What about the boards with nails?" Travis asked. They'd made four of those and left them upside-down at certain places around the property.

"Those are for our secondary traps. Are you ready to dig holes?"

"Great," Lexi mused out loud. She had already ex-pressed her dislike for digging when Frank pulled out the shovels.

It was late morning when they were done and able to take a breather. They lounged in the yard for a few minutes and drank lots of water and snacked on some power bars from their food storage.

"All right," Frank announced. "Now we're going to take a few minutes for target practice."

He gathered Lexi and Travis together, and went over the fundamentals of handling a gun safely, how to load and shoot one. He knew Lexi understood this, as he'd already trained her, but wanted to make sure she had a refresher. This exercise was more for Travis though. Frank knew they'd have to leave him alone again, the next time they would go out. He wanted to be sure Travis could defend himself.

After letting the boy dry-fire several times, Frank set up a target for Travis. First he demonstrated, showing him what it looked like to shoot at a person. Then he had Lexi demonstrate.

It was utterly impressive and Frank squeezed her shoulder, letting her know. Then Frank warned Travis not to do what Lexi did, drawing her concealed pistol and shooting. It was too dangerous for him; Lexi had a special pistol for this and she'd been trained on the procedure.

Once Travis understood the rules, Frank let him have a try at firing several shots of the .22 Ruger.

Satisfied, Frank called it a day for their preparations.

It was about that time their neighbor joined them. Jasper said in his gravelly voice, "I heard the target practice. How did the kids do?"

"I hit the target twenty-five out of thirty times." Travis gleamed.

"They're naturals at it," Frank emoted, very sincerely. He was proud of what they had accomplished. "I'd hate to be on the receiving end of their weapons."

Frank posted a rooftop watch schedule for each, giving Lexi the first. Then he had Jasper set up the trap he had constructed for the walkway between their two properties. That way it wouldn't be a surprise to either of them.

Per instructions, Jasper set the red marker inside Frank's side.

Frank then took Travis with him inside. He was anxious to try the radio again, hoping they'd reach his friends in Stowell. He was beside himself with worry about his friends and his town.

Lexi

She knew the perfect spot for watch, where she could see everything coming their way.

Lexi went around to the garage, grabbed an aluminum ladder, and extended it to the western roof edge. She had found binoculars and after hoisting herself on the western crown, at the highest point she started to glass the area around her.

First she trained her binoculars on the eastern area of the property even though she wasn't as worried about invaders approaching from this side, as they should easily hear any vehicle or the cries of those speared by one of their traps. However, she'd never seen the property from this view and was interested to see what she could see.

The main highway road wasn't visible, but the cut in the trees made it obvious where this was. She scanned for their private drive and saw some of it snaking toward her, but the trees ate most of her view. Looking to the south, the dense growth only occasionally opened up, such as an opening cut for a development of warehouses just beyond her binoculars' reach.

She crawled over to the northern edge of the roof, seeing, without the binocular's help, Jasper's house and the small opening in between the two properties. But Jasper wasn't anywhere.

Finally, she flipped onto her back, using the roof's natural tilt to comfortably lie with her head propped up by her pack. The view of the Gulf was stunning from here. The water sparkled like billions of little diamonds reflecting the bright sunlight back at her. She had to squint to see. Looking through the binoculars got to be difficult because of the glare.

She heard what sounded like her stomach growling and thought, she wanted more than just a power bar. For just a moment, she let her mind wander over images of her Aunt Sarah making waffles for her and Travis. She snickered at the memory of Travis sticking an entire waffle into his mouth in one bite, smiling while he chewed. She could almost taste the syrupy goodness in her mouth. Her stomach growled again, and kept growling one long growl. But it wasn't her stomach.

Lexi sat up and slapped the binoculars to her head, letting her ears guide her to what was making the sound.

There.

It was several powerboats, maybe four or five. In each were men, lots of men. Each wore a para-military uniform much like those worn by Abdul's soldiers on his base that they had destroyed three days ago.

The lead boat disappeared among something that blocked her view.

She peeked above the binoculars and could barely make out the shrinking line of boats, between the glinting flashes of light around them. She looked again as the last boat disappeared behind the cover of trees.

They were headed to Endurance. The town was about to be invaded.

Chapter 25
Somewhere in Texas

Tariq

Tariq Aziz calmly transmitted one last time on the pre-designated frequency and waited for the response that never came. His team had been waiting for hours now, and their contact, who he suspected was the head of their cell, was not at the designated spot. They had arrived late, but their contact was supposed to wait for them. He checked his watch and then signaled his second in command.

"Mohammad," he said. The younger man was as devout and as serious as any he had trained with. Tariq clasped a hand on his shoulder. "It's time to go. We're going to go to our second meeting point. Get the men loaded into the trucks. You take the second truck and make sure you're ready to follow me out of here in ten minutes."

"When will we get our weapons?" Mohammad asked. It wasn't an emotional plea like some of the other men made, those desiring martyrdom. His request was more sterile, like a surgeon asking for his scalpel just before cutting flesh.

"That's where we're going next."

Mohammad didn't acknowledge. He just turned away from his superior and quietly gathered his men.

Meanwhile, Tariq took one final look over the boats to make sure they were completely cloaked, so that the only way to find them was to fall over one of them. And that wasn't likely, because this area was protected, marshy, and not frequented by many visitors. It was why this area had been selected for them.

He pulled himself into the first truck and started it up with the keys he'd found left inside the driver's-side front wheel well. He eyed the buzz of activity behind him, as the men loaded themselves efficiently into his and Mohammad's trucks. He heard the second truck turn over, and a quick flash of its headlights told him they were ready. They pulled out of the reserve, with the mission on all their minds.

They had followed the plans exactly as instructed. Last night, they had come in by way of the channel past Galveston, then through the Galveston Bay and then East Bay to the wildlife refuge where they'd be least likely to run into anyone. The trucks were found, camouflaged under cuttings that looked no more than a few days old. Tariq figured they must have been deposited there right after the EMPs. Their GPS told them exactly where they'd be. They were supposed to be met by their contact, who would assist them with picking up their supplies, and then they'd all convene at the safe house. Their contact not showing up at the pickup point was no more than an inconvenience. They would have to assume that he was captured or killed, and their safe house was compromised.

Other than their missing contact, all was going according to design. So, Tariq moved on to the next stage of their plan, sticking to the smaller roads until they found Monroe City, Texas. His GPS then led them to the warehouse that had been rented for them. In it waited all the supplies they would need and the list of their targets. Soon they would know which American cities they would be conquering.

For Tariq, his goals were twofold: to do his Mahdi's wishes and to inflict pain on this country. He would follow his Mahdi's plans for taking over the Great Satan, but in return his Mahdi would allow him to relish killing and perhaps torturing its residents. This is what motivated Tariq the most, ever since the Americans had killed his family in their indiscriminate bombing in Fallujah. He'd get revenge and be a part of bringing the Caliphate to America, just as the prophecies said.

When they found the warehouse (actually a group of warehouses and storage lockers off a mostly rural area), he was almost surprised how easy this was. *Why hadn't the Great Satan fallen before this?* He wondered. It was almost effortless to walk right up to it and pluck out its heart. These freedoms the Americans celebrated were a falsehood, because they chose not to protect themselves. When a shepherd leaves his sheep unprotected—each sheep certainly believes itself to be free to roam wherever it wants—he is inviting the wolf in to attack.

A perimeter fence provided no more than a cursory obstacle as Tariq hit the gas and barreled through the gate. The other truck followed easily behind. They pulled up to the rear of their warehouse and used a key on the truck's keyring to unlock the sliding door.

Once through, and the trucks parked inside, Tariq yelled, "All right, I want you men broken up into your teams and find your designated trucks. Mohammad, help me find the weapons and the medicine."

Tariq watched them all scatter, a deliberate chaos that he couldn't help but appreciate because of its exquisite execution. The men automatically split into pre-designated teams, or what the Americans might call a squad. Each team had a commander, with those men under him providing support for the mission of that team. Most teams were supporting the overall mission, but some had specialized functions, depending on their target cities. Their Mahdi had studied the American military's procedures and then made sure that they were taught to his men and to many other groups. All of it was part of this grand effort to destroy the Great Satan once and for all.

"Sir?" Mohammad asked stoically. It was a careful reminder to get back on track. He was anxious to get started on their mission; they all were.

"You try that box." Tariq motioned to a top-most crate on one of the many pallets in front of them.

Mohammad handed him one of the two crowbars in his hand and set to the first box, while Tariq took to what he was sure was an ammo crate. Squeaking nails and the thunk of wood on concrete announced their success.

Tariq nodded to Mohammad, who whistled to his next in command and told him to get the men armed up, one crate of rifles and one crate of ammo per team. Tariq now looked for the most important package in the warehouse. It should be easy to spot since it was smaller than all the others, and it should be by itself. He found it almost right away.

He knelt down to the small wood box, and reached out to it. It had Arabic written above a stenciled English word, "Fenethylline." Touching the writing, he smiled at what it said.

"May Allah be with you on your journey to paradise," said Mohammad, standing behind him. "The stupid Americans probably think it says something about the drugs in the box."

Tariq had the same thought, but didn't answer his man. Instead he applied his crowbar to the small crate. The top came off easily. Inside was a large bag of white pills. He handed it to Mohammad, who grabbed it but waited to see what their orders were. Now, the younger man's face was full of emotion, a longing for them to start their next step: kill the Infidel.

Nested below the bag under some of the packing material was a manila envelope. Tariq withdrew it and opened the clasp in back, and pulled out the paperwork inside.

Most of the pages were satellite maps of towns and small cities, spreading out for miles from one point, this warehouse. This would be their base and from here they would take over large swaths of American territory. They should have little resistance: their nuclear weapons and then gas made sure of that. The American people, now desperate for food and supplies, would be easily conquered. Finally, they would have overwhelming firepower since only the American military had automatic weapons.

Tariq forgot for a moment about Mohammad. He glanced at his man, who waited patiently, but still his eyes had a desperate disquiet, a longing for violence. He was just glad Mohammad was on his side.

Tariq handed him the first satellite map, which showed the first set of towns they would target. He studied the map and then handed it back to Tariq.

"So when do we leave?" Mohammad asked.

"In two hours."

"Then we go to Stowell, Texas."

Chapter 26
Sunbay Cove, Florida

Frank

H e heard the heavy scamper of her feet down their roof, her yelling something he couldn't hear that sounded like "invasion" and then the loud clang of an old dinner bell connected by the back door. Finally, Lexi burst through the door, her face twisted in a panic.

"We're being invaded." Her words came out like little coughs.

Travis's presence shrank from the desk where he had been on the radio. He glared at his sister with wide eyes.

"What did you see?" Frank asked smoothly.

Lexi took a deep breath and before she could let her words spill out, Jasper bounded up the stairs inside.

Frank held up his hand to Lexi. "Lexi has something to tell us. Go ahead, tell us slowly Lex." He smiled.

"Okay," she breathed, resting against the kitchen counter. "I just saw five boats. They were headed to Endurance. Each boat was filled with men in para-military uniforms"–she looked right at Frank—"just like at Abdul's place. They slipped out of view from my binoculars, but I saw they were headed south, and inland. It looks like they're headed for Endurance." Lexi took several quick breaths.

"Is that the invasion you thought was coming?" Jasper asked.

"What do we do, Uncle Frank?" Travis screeched, his voice much higher than normal.

"Yeah, what do we do?" Lexi asked.

"All right team, let's focus." Frank said calmly. "First, let's try to raise Jonah and anyone else in Endurance who might be listening and give them a warning. Travis, can you—"

"Here!" Travis said and thrust out the UHF base unit's microphone, his hand shaking just a little. They had been monitoring Jonah's frequency before Lexi's announcement. Travis turned up the volume with his free hand.

Frank grabbed the microphone and clicked it open. "Jonah, are you there? Jonah, this is Frank Cartwright, out at the Smith house. We've spotted the enemy headed your way. Repeat, we've spotted five boats headed just south of here, filled with enemy troops. They will probably go to wherever there's a natural harbor. Jonah, repeat, Endurance is about to come under attack."

They all listened to a solid hiss, not the undulating crackle they usually heard with the high frequency receiver. Then, there was a click.

"Hello, Frank," said a boyish voice. "Thanks fo dat heads-up. We've got it from here. Out."

They were all in the radio room now, glaring at the speaker.

"Was that—" Frank wondered out loud.

Jasper answered, "Jonah? No, that wasn't Jonah."

Frank processed all of this and then said to the group, "I'm going to load up our gear and head to Endurance to see what else we can do. I'm afraid if we don't intervene, regardless of what's coming, none of us will be safe here."

They all chewed on his unsavory proclamation.

To Lexi, he said, "If you're coming with me, you'll need to get ready to leave in two minutes."

"Wait," Jasper protested. "You can't take her with you! It's way too dangerous for a wo—" He stopped himself, probably not wanting to aggravate Lexi so that she'd do the opposite of what he wanted. Jasper's brows were furrowed and his deep set eyes were drilled into hers. His lip quivered like he wanted to say more. But he didn't.

"Um ... I can make up my own mind, thank you!" she huffed and snapped at Frank. "I'm coming." Not waiting for a reply from either, she trotted out of sight.

"Now that that's decided Jasper, you're welcome to come too." Frank ignored the mini-battle of the sexes in front of him as he grabbed water bottles from a shelf in the storage area, and then strode into the kitchen to drop them on the counter beside his two weapons.

"Very well. But I need to grab my gear too ..." Jasper hesitated. "Hey, why don't I approach by boat. We can keep in contact by radio and I can direct you or you to me?"

"Yes, of course!" Frank returned to the radio room. "That's a great idea." He grabbed one of their radios from a charging stand and thrust it at him. "Here. Let's use Channel 4."

Jasper snatched the radio and nodded. The sling to his heavy Thompson machine gun threatened to slip off his shoulder before he readjusted. "Yes, and if I get to town before you, I'll warn them."

"Great." Frank offered a hand. "And thanks for your support."

Jasper accepted. "My pleasure." He grinned through his bushy beard and returned the handshake before walking out the back. Frank watched him run past the living room window and out of view, no doubt around the corner of the house to his boat.

Frank grabbed more ammunition for their weapons. With only the two Glocks (including the one he borrowed) and a shotgun, they didn't have much to wage a defense against a well-armed jihadi army. Unfortunately, Stanley didn't have any secret cache of weapons—Frank had thoroughly checked the house. And Jonah, who was out of contact, still had his AK and Lexi's favorite pistol. Not that it mattered; they didn't want to directly engage the enemy. They just wanted to warn the town before it was too late, and maybe monitor the enemy. Then, they'd try to get their weapons back and hopefully find some way to fight before the enemy reached their home.

Lexi shuffled down the hall and stopped in front of his bag, already cinched down.

"Ready?" he asked her. She fidgeted with her super-stuffed bag, adding the extra waters and loaded magazines he gave her. Then she stood up, with confidence. He was taken back for a moment at the transformation that had taken place over the last few days, and it was more evident now than ever.

She wore cargo shorts a couple of sizes too large, held to her meager waist with one of her father's newly repurposed belts. Her faded T-shirt, also new, looked to be a perfect fit though, maybe even a little tight for her frame. Perhaps it was one of Travis's. She'd even found time to remove the blue highlights in her hair, now jet black and serious. With a gun in her belt, a knife clipped beside it, and a steely determination in her eyes, she was starting to look the desired role of a badass in this real life play.

"I'm ready," Travis announced, dropping his bag on the floor at his feet and positioning himself at attention.

Frank fought the urge to grin, composing himself before answering. "Thank you for your offer, soldier, but I have a much greater mission for you."

Travis wrinkled his face. "What? What is it?"

"I need you to monitor the radio for Robert—"

"—you mean G?" he interrupted.

"Yes, G in Texas, and also you need to monitor the UHF here. Much more importantly, I'll need you to coordinate for us. Also, see if you can raise Jonah again and warn him about what's coming. If you hear from him on any of the UHF frequencies, you'll need to let us know. Finally, report to us if you've heard any intelligence from anywhere else. You are our base station: our mission control. So, in fact, your job is probably much more important than ours."

At first, Travis looked a little put out by not being allowed to go, but he perked up when he realized how important he had become to them. Only he knew how to work the radios, at least better than his Uncle Frank did. And they did need someone here. Who better than him.

"Yes, sir," he said with a salute.

Lexi snickered. "You're so goofy."

Travis crossed his arms, about ready to deliver an angry retort, but then seriously looked back at Frank. "What if someone tries to come in again?"

Frank knelt down so that he was looking at him eye to eye. "Remember what I told you, son. You hide in your secret place. But if your cover is blown, you shoot to kill. Anyone who comes in uninvited is your enemy. You got it?"

"Yes, sir," he said reluctantly. "And Uncle Frank?"

"Yes, Travis?"

"Please be safe," Travis said through the lump in his throat. He wrapped his arms around Frank and Frank hugged him back.

Frank hated having to leave Travis alone and put so much responsibility on this kid. But Travis no longer had the luxury of childhood.

Lexi waited for their release and offered him a hug as well. "Don't open that door for anyone."

He gladly accepted. "I won't. I love you, Lex."

"Love you, too, Travis."

Frank and Lexi quietly left, but before they secured the back door, they heard Travis already on the radio. "Hello, this is Travis calling Jonah, or anyone else who can hear me. The town of Endurance is under attack. There are armed Islamic fighters headed your way, by boat..."

What they didn't hear was what came next.

"Kid, get off the radio," the base UHF unit blared back at Travis. The voice was high-pitched, not the deep timbre he remembered hearing behind the blue space suit. He understood why their neighbor, Jasper, said this wasn't Jonah. "I told you, I've got this covered. Now get off the radio."

Travis heard a voice in the background, "You should make the announcement on channel 5."

Travis flipped the channel selector to 5 and heard only one word: "Nuts!"

Cain

C ain was pissed at that kid on the radio, afraid the kid would spoil his plans. But he was more pissed at the boy's sister. He glanced at his bandaged forearms, lines of reddish brown just visible below the dressing's first layer where he had bled. Both pulsated with an aching pain as he clutched the steering wheel with one hand and the radio with the other. He adjusted the frequency once more, and pulled the radio to his lips and called out, "Nuts!"

It was his call to those people who were loyal to him that it was time. It was time for the takeover of his father's empire.

Now was the perfect opportunity. Most of his men were unhappy with Jonah's recent moves, which showed way too much kindness to the people of Endurance, especially to that bitch doctor. And how he handled the immigrants was perfect proof to all the men that Jonah had gone soft. He was messing with everyone's survival when he started giving out food and medical supplies. And it needed to stop.

But he had to hurry, while his father was occupied and before anyone did anything crazy.

He swerved once, nearly losing control of the truck, and narrowly avoiding a collision with one of the many stalled vehicles in the road.

In the days since the nuclear attack, Cain had been quietly trying to get a sense of the political winds within Jonah's organization, only approaching those men he'd heard were openly disgruntled. That included almost 50 percent of Jonah's men. After hearing Cain's plans, especially the promised perks, each proclaimed their allegiance to him. All wanted something in return and early on, he gave them what they asked: a higher level in the organization, their own home, women, alcohol, drugs, and so on. Once the takeover occurred, Cain figured the remainder would join when offered either allegiance or death. Meanwhile he continued his act of being the drunkard loser of a son that his father knew him to be.

He had no problem stabbing his father in the back, literally if he had to. He'd been looked down upon by Jonah ever since he had told Cain he was an accident by some whore he'd gotten pregnant. Jonah seemed always resentful that Cain even existed, never treating him with the respect he deserved.

Cain pulled on the wheel once more and lightly touching the brakes to get around some debris in the middle of the road. He knew he was driving at an unsafe speed, but every moment that passed, reduced his safety, and his chances for success.

He stomped on the gas pedal and gained a little air over the last rise, before jamming on his brakes and screeching to a halt.

Jonah's truck was parked off the road, pointed in his direction.

Cain had stopped only a dozen or so feet from it. And he glared at it like it was some predatory animal that would at any moment leap up and eat him.

His chest pounded, and he was sure he'd been caught by his father. His plans unraveled before his eyes.

When the sun peeked out of a dark cluster of clouds, it bathed Jonah's truck in a shower of light. But he still couldn't see the driver.

A thick arm stuck out the window and ushered him forward. It didn't look like Jonah, but at this moment he couldn't be sure.

Cain inched his own truck forward, and pulled alongside the larger one, so that he was staring directly inside its cab.

It was Peter.

"Shit, man." Cain blew out a puff of air. "You nearly gave me a damned heart attack. I thought my father had caught me."

"No worries, kid. I grabbed your dad's truck and his radio while he was giving away our food and offering sanctuary to all the illegals ..." He paused and asked, "So why the secret word, 'Nuts!'?"

"You ever see Jericho? It was on TV."

"No," Peter said gruffly. He had no time for these dalliances.

"Never mind. Just follow me," Cain said as he threw the truck into reverse, before Peter could even respond. Cain backed up and then guided his truck through the entrance, Peter following closely. The sign beside the entrance said "Sunbay Cove... with natural harbor access."

Chapter 27
Sunbay Cove, Florida

Frank

The truck's cab was thick with their quiet anxiety.

Their truck bounced down the private road and then to Endurance, but they couldn't shake the feeling that they'd be too late when they got there. They had not taken that long to get ready. And the three-mile trip to Endurance certainly wouldn't take long. But the boats had long since made it to their destination by now and if their men were fully armed, Frank wasn't sure that they could do much to stop them.

Frank's mind was also racing trying to consider the possibilities. And he couldn't quite a lingering thought that he was missing some vital clue.

"Get Jasper on the radio." Frank yanked the wheel, nudging them around a thicket of green deposited in the middle of the road by last night's storm. "Ask him where the harbor is."

Ready for this, Lexi pulled the walkie up to her face so quickly, she clunked herself on the chin. She clicked the on button, rubbing the sore spot with her free hand. "Jasper, this is Lexi ..." Momentarily, she wasn't sure if she should wait for his acknowledgment or just ask the question. "Can you tell us where the harbor is located—"

Frank cut in. "—in Endurance. Is it by the health clinic?"

She continued her broadcast. "Where is the harbor in Endurance? Is it near the health clinic?"

The radio crackled back at them and then Jasper's raspy voice stated stoically, "Endurance doesn't have a harbor ... There are maybe a dozen inlets in and around Endurance. They could have landed anywhere by now."

Frank jammed both feet on the brakes, screeching the truck to a long stop.

Lexi held her palms out, bracing for impact, but there wasn't any. "Why are we stopping?" She leaned forward, thinking there must have been some sort of threat in front of them.

Frank didn't answer. He shifted into reverse, turned to look over his shoulder, and gassed the engine. When he had backed up twenty feet, he threw it into park and pointed to a sign. It was right beside them, just before the entrance to a commercial development. The sign read "Sunbay Cove Commercial Warehouses." Below that: "With natural harbor access."

Frank jolted them into drive and slid his foot off the brake. "Better tell Jasper where we'll be."

Imam Ramadi

"**D**id you take my guns?" Ramadi hollered at Cain, who had his hands up, and stood just outside the open door of the truck he'd been driving.

Ramadi was bursting with anger. Someone had stolen from him. He suspected he knew who it was, until this boy arrived conveniently at the same time he discovered the theft.

Ramadi stomped toward the truck, snatching one of his men's rifles and pulling back the charging handle to make his intent clear. He pointed it at Cain's head. Ramadi almost pleaded with his eyes to give him a reason to squeeze the trigger.

"Whoa there, Mr. Ramadi! I know who took your guns. That's why I came here when I heard your men were coming by boat." Cain said this so fast, it almost came out as one complete sentence.

Ramadi hesitated, his movements stating with absolute certainty that he was ready to pull the trigger. Then he lowered the weapon. "Talk, but I better hear the correct answer or you and your man in the other truck are dead."

"It was my father, Jonah Price. He took your weapons. I saw him do it. He screwed you and me. I can give you everything you need for all your plans." Cain's voice was so high-pitched, he almost sounded like a girl.

"You don't know our plans, boy." Ramadi glared at him.

"Actually, I do. Your men inside are part of many groups here to take over America. My men and I do not plan to stand in your way."

"You couldn't stop us if you wanted to."

"And I don't want to."

Ramadi considered what this Infidel was telling him, all the while trying to guess at the boy's motivations. Ramadi had made a deal with this boy's father, and it seemed that Price had followed his demands for a while, without question. But now it seemed the whole time, Price was planning to take his things. The evidence was his missing rifles in a warehouse only Price and he were supposed to have access to.

Now Price's spawn wishes to make a deal for his own weapons?

Ramadi started to lift the rifle again, to finish off this boy and go find the missing rifles himself. But he didn't have the time. So he calmed himself down. He would make some sort of deal with this boy, so that he could get his guns back, and then move into their next phase of the war. After that, he would shoot the boy and his father. For now, he would bite his tongue and get what he wanted.

"What do you want?" Ramadi asked.

"The same thing my father did: a little slice of my own territory."

"But why do I need you? Now that I know your father took my weapons, I'll just find him."

"Besides trying to find the weapons, which if I know my father, will be difficult if not impossible, I have the loyalty of many men. They'll follow me, and we'll stay out of your way. We can even help you stay in control of this area. Florida is a big state. You can't run it all."

"We have plenty of men devoted to the cause of Allah."

"I'm sure you do, but you can't be everywhere. By dealing with me, Endurance and the surrounding area will be one section you won't have to worry about, and you won't have to put any of your men at risk."

Ramadi thought the boy made good points. *And as Mohammad, peace be upon him, taught, it was better to make deals with your enemies until you were strong enough to take them over.* That's what he'd do.

"All right, you have a deal. Now show me my guns."

Cain motioned to his cab, "My men are looking for them right now. But first, I have your crate in the back of my truck. It has your drugs and your targets. I've shown it to no one else."

This surprised Ramadi; he thought Price had taken those as well. Now, he wondered if this boy was talking from both sides of his mouth. "But you didn't take my guns?"

"No, and I'm not sure exactly where they are. But until we find them, my men are bringing you a bunch of military weapons and ammo in a few minutes. Then I'll help you find your own weapons."

"Very well," said Ramadi. He wanted his guns, and to be done with this whining dog.

Frank & Lexi

They watched everything from a short distance away, using binoculars they had in their bags.

When Frank and Lexi parked the truck off the road and behind a small structure, they could see the boats had already arrived at the inlet, they called a harbor. The boats were parked on the launch, but empty. But their timing couldn't have been any better. They found a stand of trees they were able to hide behind and watch Cain talking to the enemy, a man wearing traditional imam's clothing. At first, Cain looked tense, and the imam looked like he was going to shoot him. But after a few minutes, they looked like they were old friends. Based on what they've seen and heard, it appeared that Cain was going behind Jonah's back to make some sort of deal with the enemy.

"But why?" Lexi asked. "What would he gain by helping people who want to kill everyone who isn't their type of Muslim?"

Frank wondered the same thing, but it didn't matter. What mattered was their security and the security of their town. "Let's get out of here. Then we'll try raising Jasper again."

"Remember," she whispered, "he's not answering."

"Come on." He offered his hand. "We'll tell Travis. Maybe he's reached Jonah. He can relay the info to both of them."

"So where are we going?" Lexi asked as Frank pulled her up from where she had been lying prone.

"With the enemy here, we still have a chance of warning Endurance. Maybe we can track—" Frank stopped. Lexi, following close behind him, didn't see why until she came out into a clearing. She raised her hands.

Two men had their rifles pointed at them. One spoke into his radio. "We have them."

Chapter 28
Stowell, Texas

Grimes

"Just a little further... Another foot ... All right, that's good," he proudly announced over the radio.

The antenna teetered and all who were watching held their collective breath. Two men at the base worked rapidly, affixing their brackets on each side. They then tightened the bolts, holding the newly sawed-off base to the newly straightened tower. The driver kept the truck idling in gear, keeping the tow ropes taut while she waited the command to bring up the slack. It only took a couple of minutes, but after a final grunt by both men, they rose and examined their work. A last-second shake of the structure to verify its sturdiness, and both were satisfied. The taller fellow gave Grimes an "OK" sign.

"We're good, back up and unhook. Great work," he told the truck's driver over the CB.

Although not as tall as it was earlier, and a little bent in places, Grimes knew it would do. The antenna was more of a wreck than the tower, having absorbed most of the toppling impact. So it had to be rebuilt using parts they picked up from donations from the town's people. The rotor was shot and there was no time to find a replacement, so he had the antenna fixed in a north-south position. They'd not be able to receive some of the UHF transmissions from the East Coast, and even Florida might be sketchy. But it would have to do for now. He already had some helpers measuring out the copper wire for the forty and eighty-meter dipole antennas. They'd go up in an hour or two.

"We're ready with the coaxial," a voice said from the other side of the permanently opened window. Its owner handed Grimes the coaxial cable's end, and then fed in another dozen feet before Grimes connected it via a bracket to the window frame. The remainder of the cable looped across the yard to the fifth ring of the tower and then up the middle to the antenna. The previous cable was buried, but damaged. So Grimes thought it better to string up a new cable through the window. He'd weatherize or find a more permanent solution later—if there was a later.

He stripped off an inch of the outer plastic jacket from the end, pulled the metallic shield back, and slid the connector through. A quick crimp using a wrench and a trim of most of the core wire, and it was ready. "Not perfect, but it will do." He screwed it to the back of the transceiver, and turned the radio on.

The response was almost instantaneous: jubilant voices jumped out of the speakers.

Grimes turned up the volume and then added his voice to the chorus of happy expressions, cheering "We're up! We're up!" out the window. Several others outside joined him.

Then Grimes wondered why the radio's transmissions sounded so jubilant. What had been going on in the world in the few hours since they'd been down?

"It's the gosh-darned US Army. They drove right into our city center and said that the US Military was now in charge," a man with a Californian accent stated triumphantly.

"They arrived in our town bout an hour ago," said a thick Louisiana drawl. "They said we were saved. But there'd be a fight coming. So they ask everyone with a gun, who wants to fight des assholes who done this to us, to meet in the city hall. In fact, I gotta go. They should be meeting soon."

"I think we might actually survive this, now," said the Californian. His voice crackled with emotion.

"I think you're right," said the Louisianan.

"Thanks for the report, Cajun Shrimper. God bless you."

"You got it, Dodgers Fan. Out."

"Hey Dodger's Fan. This is Don't Tread on Me in Texas. You still on?" Grimes transmitted, adjusting the dial up a couple of kilohertz to make sure he was on the exact frequency.

"Sure am, DTM. Texas you say? That's a long way. Are you close to the folks at American Freedom Network? They went off the air yesterday."

Grimes grinned. "That's us. Somebody blew up our antenna. We just got her back up and connected."

"That's more good news. Have you heard what's happening?"

"I just tuned in. So tell me about the US Army. What's going on?"

"Well, several Army trucks just drove right down Broad Street, honking their horns. My son chased them down, listened to their announcement and ran back to report. Their captain said they came from San Louis and they're going from town to town to prepare everyone for the coming invasion."

"So they're asking for civilian recruits?" Grimes asked, slurping on a water just handed to him by Aimes, who was now listening attentively.

"That's what they made it sound like. They asked for everyone with a weapon to meet right away, just like the Cajun Shrimper said. They plan on giving them some suggestions and then they're going to move on to the next town. They're trying to cover ten towns per day, he said."

"Did they say what happened with the rest of the Army and why they need help?"

"No, they said they were just warning us and wanted us prepared if the enemy comes our way."

Grimes scratched his beard and glared at the radio. There was something off about this. For one, he thought it was weird that the US Army would be trying to solicit the help of armed townspeople. Maybe they were depleted more horribly from the gas attacks than he thought.

"Hey, I probably should get going too. My son and I are excited. It's kind of like we're getting drafted. Wish us luck."

"Good luck and thanks," Grimes told him and then sat back. He wondered if this was real and if the US Army would visit Stowell soon.

Meritville, Alabama

The rumble of their tires on asphalt shook the glass panes of the houses on either side of the road. It was an olive green parade of US Army trucks. Their horns blared, bringing the anxious faces the town's residents to the windows.

Most of Meritville's residents had been hiding, since the shooting began. It was their town's protracted version of the Hatfields and McCoys. Only their two warring families were the Merits, who founded the town, and the Boykins, who'd resided there almost as long. The members of these two families had hated each other since the town's start, long before the world ended. The war just brought the worst of them out. When the Boykins ran out of food yesterday, they attacked the Merits. The fighting started with fists, but then devolved into gunfire. All day long they'd been taking pot shots at each other, like some surreal, never-ending western gunfight.

When the half dozen US Army trucks drove down Commerce Street the shooting stopped. As the last truck in the convoy passed a home, its occupants poured out onto the street cheering, "We're saved!" or "Go Army!" It was a time of celebration when there had been nothing to celebrate since the war started.

Each resident who joined in the cheering had similar thoughts: *Was this the end? Would the country go back to normal now? Would they finally be safe?*

The older residents ambled after the trucks. The younger ones ran after them, matching the convoy's pace easily. All wanted to meet the trucks downtown where they were headed and celebrate together.

Those who were near city hall had taken cover from the gunfire. But when the trucks rolled up and stopped in front of city hall, men slowly rose from their places of protection. Most were tentative in their motions, afraid that someone would shoot at them while they were out in the open. But as the men in US Army uniforms emptied out of their trucks, and the cheering crowds swarmed the city center, those worries were cast aside. And everyone forgot their differences for just a moment to join in the celebration.

An Army captain trotted up the steps of City Hall, and into the building. Moments later he emerged, stopping at the edge of the top step, above the crowd. He raised his bullhorn and spoke clearly. "Everyone please gather around. I have an announcement."

The captain waited, letting the bullhorn drop, as more and more people gathered to hear. Their cheering had subsided; all were anxious to hear the news the US Army had for them. Any promise that they were no longer on their own.

After repeating the announcement twice more, the Captain told them his reason for being there.

"I am Captain John T. Smith with the US Army." Smith paused to wait for the murmuring to die down.

"Although we are here now, we need your help. We expect an invasion by the enemy at any time. We are going to go engage them directly, but if they come through this town, we want to make sure you will be ready."

The crowd spoke in apprehensive whispers. Their mumbling crescendoed until Smith put his hands up to silence them.

"Please, may I have your attention?" he hollered.

They were mostly silent when he continued. "You should be safe, but we want to advise everyone who has a weapon and is able in this town to fight."

The crowd reverberated, some saying, "I'll fight." A few raised their weapons to show their support.

"Please," Smith pleaded again. "We ask that everyone who has a weapon and is able to defend your town, if that's needed, to please come to this building and meet us inside in thirty minutes. Bring your weapons and your ammo when you do. We will speak to everyone else after this meeting. Thank you."

Some of the troops had already made their way up the stairs and now were creating a barrier of soldiers around city hall. Several of them went inside and moved people outside of the building. Those people joined the others crowded around, sharing with each other what they had heard and what they suspected it all meant. Nearly half the crowd began dispersing, anxious to spread the captain's message to the rest of the town who hadn't heard.

Within twenty minutes, every resident of Meritville knew about the US Army presence. And everyone celebrated. Supplies of alcohol and food, intended to be made to last as long as possible, were pulled out from storage, passed around and consumed. Many no longer worried about tomorrow's supplies as they assumed the US Army was a portent to the country returning to the days of grocery aisles flowing with over-abundance. Those who worried only did so because they planned to participate in the Army's call for men with guns.

No one in Merit concerned themselves with what would happen after this.

Certainly nobody doubted whether this Army was the genuine article.

Chapter 29

Peter

He drove the truck up to the two guards who had been given instructions to shoot anyone coming to this gate.

Peter stuck his head and arm out the window, offering a slight wave. The guard who had the cross-hairs of his weapon trained on Peter let it drop. The other guard pushed open the gate, allowing him to pass. From the side mirror, Peter could see the guards paid no further attention to him. They closed the gate and returned to watching for the next threat.

Peter squeaked to a stop in front of a US Army truck backed up to a fenced-off area near the Number Four Warehouse. He fought the urge to rub his eyes in disbelief. What was a US Army truck doing here? Did that mean that Cain had been caught? Or was it more likely that the Army found out about the weapons that Jonah had stolen from the base and they were here to reclaim them?

As if to confirm this theory, he watched men wearing US Army uniforms carry crates from a fenced area shaded by three haphazard canopies and load them into the Army truck parked in front of him. Directing this odd show was a skinny man with a long goatee.

Peter got out, slammed his door in anger at this development, and marched over to Cain. Keeping his voice low and directed he asked, "What's going on?" Peter figured that Cain had been compelled by the Army to hand over the stolen weapons in exchange for not getting arrested. He expected a muffled retort like "Yeah, I had no choice man."

Cain smiled at Peter and said, "They didn't want to wait. Guess they needed them now."

Peter shot this funny little man a questioning WTF glance, before asking another question under his breath. "So you knew they were going to come here directly?"

"Yeah, once I told them about the stash of weapons that Jonah had taken from the Army up north, they insisted on coming down themselves."

Peter was getting angrier now. "Why in the hell did you have me risk getting caught with one of Jonah's trucks and drive it all the way here if you didn't need me to?" he huffed, still trying to keep his voice down so that the grunts from the Army didn't hear their conversation.

"Oh, no worries man, Jonah's been cut off from most of his men. As you told me, he's probably in hiding right now. Even if he saw you, he couldn't have done anything."

He was right about that. "But we haven't found him or the missing guns yet."

"Yeah, but I know you and the men will."

"I'm sure you're right. Still, you could have called me. You know, let your partner in crime know about this development."

"Yeah, well I was a little busy, you know?" He threw a condescending glance at Peter, reminding him why he didn't like this boy.

He calmly reminded himself that Cain was an end to a means. He didn't have to like the kid. He only had to pacify the little shit to get what he wanted. And in spite of the kid's annoying persona, he was performing up to task. And Cain had been straight with him ever since he first disclosed his plans to stab his father in the back.

It was far better treatment than he had received from his now former employer. When Peter had learned about the weapons and supplies Jonah had recovered from the Army base, he was shocked that Jonah hadn't told him about it. Instead he was made to play baby sitter to the Smith kids and a few of the injured. Cain may have been far from perfect, but he was doing what he said and always gave Peter the respect he deserved.

Peter watched the men work to load the last few boxes of weapons. "You still haven't told me how the US Army found out about the guns."

Cain thought about the question for a moment and then chortled, his head nodding like he just got the big joke. He slapped Peter on the back and said, "That ain't the US Army."

Jonah

J onah Price had his head down when he marched into the Endurance Health Center.

"Dr. Scott?" he asked the volunteer—he thought they seemed to get older each time he entered—but he didn't wait for an answer, and walked around the corner to Emily's office. He expected to find her to reading about some ailment or treating a patient, as she seemed to do day and night. Instead she was sound asleep on her couch, at peace.

He hesitated over her, not wanting to wake her. She obviously needed her sleep. But he wanted to know where his son was. He wanted to strangle that illegitimate little shit for pitting half of his men against him and for making a play on what wasn't his, and all while their town of Endurance was in jeopardy. But more importantly, he needed to find the two men from the Army base, and Lexi and Frank. He couldn't do what he planned without their help. He reached out to touch her shoulder, to jiggle her just a little. But he couldn't.

He withdrew his hand and just stared at her.

For a moment he let his thoughts of her linger; his heart longed for her. He had yearned to be with her for a long time. One day, he had hoped to wake up next to her. To see her like she was now, but know that she was his. As if responding to him, she softly murmured something, her lips lightly trying to speak from a dream.

He shook himself awake from his woolgathering.

He wished it were a different time and place. But it wasn't. He knew they would never be together. He wasn't the type of man she would ever have been attracted to, even before all this. And when who he really is and what he's done comes out—how could it not—she would certainly hate him even more. They all would. Maybe this was his penance for a life wasted pursuing his own wealth and not paying attention to what he already had.

He took one last look and wondered if this would be his final memory of her. It's not a bad way to remember her: beautifully at peace.

Jonah spun on his heels and walked out, leaving her and the Center behind.

"Mr. Price?" a commanding voice called out behind him.

Jonah was generally unflappable, fearing few things. But the sound of his name caused a nervous shudder throughout his body. He turned to face the monster of his making.

But it wasn't who he thought it was. It was Sergeant Reynolds and PFC O'Malley, who must have been looking for him too.

"I'm glad to see you men. I need your help."

Chapter 30
Endurance, Florida

Jonah

After seven days without power, and people having gotten accustomed to most things mechanical not functioning, the sound of one car was nearly as novel as it was when the automobile was first invented. But when a convoy of US Army trucks thundered into Endurance, the residents could only watch in stunned silence: their skeptical brains couldn't accept what their eyes saw. Even after understanding took hold, the town's jubilance at witnessing help arrive was certainly more tempered than it was received in most towns that day.

Endurance was perhaps unique in that it was doing better than a lot of places in America. Many of its residents were already prepared for hurricanes, having enough supplies to last at least a few weeks. And those who didn't had Jonah Price to help them out. The belief that circulated around Endurance was that they were on their own and that life would become more difficult in coming weeks. Many had heard the call and were buckling down for the worst. So, the last group Endurance's residents expected to see, after a week, was the US military.

Still, just like other towns that were experiencing this—many around the same time—they were drawn out of their homes like moths to a flame.

Jonah was one of the few who didn't hear their arrival, as he was busy ducking from building to building, attempting to not be seen. He arrived at 280 Liberty Street late, hopeful that at least some of those he asked would be there. It was one of his in-town office/warehouses. This one he kept off the books, owning it through a Delaware LLC that didn't report its ownership publicly. The secrecy was necessary for some of the more questionable merchandise he trafficked. Only a few people knew about it, the men he really trusted. No one else was told about this place. So, he hoped that while Cain was occupied with his attempts to steal everything, this place hadn't yet come across his radar.

Walters was in the shadows, guarding the side door entrance to the room where they were all meeting. Jonah warmly gripped his hand. "Thanks for having my back."

"Jonah, you know you're the most wanted man in this town?"

"Yep, my illegitimate shit-for-brains son thinks he has me backed into a corner."

"Well, he sort of does since you're the one hiding in the shadows. Cain has got all of his sycophants scouring everywhere for you and the guns."

"I know, but we still have a few tricks up our sleeves, don't we." Jonah grinned.

"That we do. And, he still thinks that I'm with him. So, after you break up this little shindig, I'll have to get away, and pretend I'm searching for you."

"No problem. This shouldn't take too long. If you have to leave early, just make sure you make it to the appointed time and place."

"Will do, boss." Walters smiled back and released his grip. His shoulders straightened and he fixed his gaze into the night, confirming to Jonah he would keep watch. Jonah couldn't help but grin.

Jonah continued through the door, grinning until he entered the room.

It was a small meeting room, like the office, partitioned off from the warehouse, but sharing one vast ceiling, twenty feet above them. A random collection of 30 chairs were filled and facing a podium.

Their anxious heads snapped back to see who had come in.

As Jonah walked through them, he could see everyone he had asked was here, and a few more he didn't invite, Including Emily.

When he approached her chair, he asked, "What are you doing here?" He scrutinized her mannerism to, attempting to gage her tenor.

She rose to greet him, wearing only the weakest hint of a smile. "You said to others that it concerned the safety of Endurance. This is my town too." Her tone was not entirely friendly.

He knew it would get only worse when he was done.

"I didn't tell you because I also said that this would be very dangerous."

"What can I say, danger is my middle name," she said and sat down, facing the front of the room. Her face was a humorless wall.

Jonah shook off his feelings and stepped to the podium, facing his town's people. He considered his words and spoke in an even, almost unemotional tone.

"About two years ago, a foreign businessman approached me to rent my largest warehouse north of here, at Sunbay Cove. I was desperate at the time and didn't ask questions. I needed the money, or I would have probably gone bankrupt. I have come to find out that man is an Imam and one of the leaders of the terrorist movement that brought down our country on July 4th with nuclear explosions, and only two days ago, killed probably hundreds of thousands of our military with sarin gas."

The room was filled with gasps and angry whispers.

"Further, I found out that my warehouse was being used for the next stage of their plan, the full-out invasion of our country. Since my warehouse appears to be a staging area, I suspect Endurance would be an early target—"

"What'd you get for screwing your country?" said an understandably very angry sheriff, who lost his son to the gas attack.

"Rory, at this point what they promised me is unimportant. Here's why I asked most of you here. When I realized what was coming next, I stole from Imam Ramadi the guns and ammunition that he had obviously planned to use to kill more Americans. Without these guns, he's effectively neutered."

"That doesn't excuse what you've done." Rory pointed a finger at him, tears streaming down his face.

"Look, I'm not asking for your forgiveness. Yes, I was a willing accomplice in all of this because all I cared about was the money. And so I willingly aided these monsters and looked away while receiving my Judas ransom. I'm probably damned to hell for what I've done. But that's on me. This thing is much larger than me, or any of you. And regardless of whether you believe it, I still care about this town; I guess I always have, even though I've been a selfish bastard all of my life. I want to do what's right for this town and I want all of you to survive this. But we need to work together to accomplish this.

"You want us to trust you now?" asked Sheila, the pretty base commander's wife—she'd found out yesterday that her husband had died on base from the gas attack.

"No, trust yourselves and each other. I'm just trying in a small way to make things right. I would ask you to pay attention to two heroes in our midst: men who risked their lives to pull out four others from the Army base, Sergeant Reynolds and Private First Class O'Malley." Jonah shrunk away to the side of the room where the sergeant and private stood, unmoving.

A few hands clapped, including two of the Army servicemen they had saved from the base. Most were still in shock over what they'd just heard.

"Thank you," Reynolds said. "Mr. Price told us everything that happened and asked us to lead the effort to defend Endurance. PFC O'Malley and I are going to go over our plan for all of us to fight against the Islamic Invaders. Then, we'll teach you how to use one of these Russian-made fully-automatic rifles." He held up the one slung around his neck. "Because when we meet again in a few minutes, you'll each be handed one of said Russian-made rifles, courtesy of the same assholes who attacked our country.

"Hopefully, together we'll be able to save this town and send some of these damned terrorists to hell where they came from."

O'Malley and the two other Army soldiers from the base yelled "Hooah!" The civilians in the room remained mostly quiet, although a few, like Sheila cheered. None of them wanted to face what was coming next.

Walters

Walters was just about to slip away, out of fear that Cain or the men would question his being gone so long, when out of the darkness a figure appeared. It was Cain.

He had to think of something quick or hopefully, the monitor checked out the door's peephole before they were surrounded.

That's it! He thought. He'd let Cain warn them.

Walters waved and then ran over to Cain, like he was glad to see him.

"Good, you got my message" Walters said enthusiastically. He eyeballed all the men Cain brought with him, who were now watching him. He was glad to see Peter was not among them.

"What? What message? We're here searching every place Jonah might be hiding. This was next on the list."

Walters knew how Cain operated, but he still took a chance with what he said next, hoping it helped Jonah, not hurt him, or the others. At the same time, Walters wanted to strengthen his own position with Cain. He might need the bargaining power.

"My message was that I think Jonah might be here," he said several decibels louder than normal.

"Jonah, here?" Cain almost begged. He turned to his men and yelled with his shrill voice, "Surround the building."

He really isn't too bright, Walters thought to himself, trying to not let his expression change.

One man stayed with Cain, handing him a bullhorn. The others raced around the building like cockroaches exposed to light.

Cain waited impatiently for them to be in position.

Jonah

"**S**o if anything goes wrong, you know where to meet," Reynolds finished.

The group nodded, but not equally. Some did so strongly and certain, while others did so more meekly, and unsure.

"Okay, they're ready," O'Malley told Jonah.

Jonah gave a furtive glance at everyone in the room. They weren't soldiers, but all agreed to fight. He couldn't have been more proud of them. Regardless of their position in the community, all were willing to risk their lives to protect their town, his town.

"All right..." Jonah started, but abruptly looked up when he hear the high-pitched voice outside. "That sounded like Cain. Check the door."

The man who was supposed to be on watch at the door slapped his head, acknowledging his mistake and ran back to his position. He looked out the peep sight and then to the group wide-eyed. "There's a bunch of men surrounding the building."

Reynolds whispered, "I assume there's another way out?"

O'Malley, who was already looking announced, "I think I found a way up and out." He shimmied up a small ladder, which led to the roof above.

"The private found the entry to the roof. There's also an exit through the warehouse and out the back," Jonah said as he pointed at the back of the room.

"All right O'Malley, I'm right behind you. Once in position we'll lay down cover fire, drawing their attention to the two sides and front of the building."

O'Malley nodded.

"You all get out the back," Reynolds told Jonah and the group, while heading up the ladder. O'Malley was already on the roof, holding the hatch open. "Wait until you hear the shooting before you run for it. Good luck," he whispered as he slunk up through the hatch and let it close behind him.

A loud squeal and a crackle of feedback blared outside the meeting room, followed by his son's shrill voice, "Jonah? Are you in there?"

Jonah's head shot up again in surprise. He couldn't believe his stupid son found out about this place, then found him. But, he remembered that Peter knew about this place too. It confirmed to him that Peter had joined forces with his son.

Reynolds and O'Malley's boots thumped overhead, across the roof to opposite corners.

"Come on," Jonah beaconed. "Follow me." He switched on a mini Maglite he now carried everywhere and led them into the mostly dark warehouse and then quickly through its clutter to a far door. The group followed him, occasionally bumping into one of the obstacles, while others in the group *shushed* the offending klutz.

He heard the muffled sounds of another bullhorn announcement, Cain's high-pitched voice more numbing and unintelligible than he could remember.

Just before they reached the door, the shooting started.

Jonah twisted the door handle, unlatched the deadbolt and threw it open. His Maglite flicked off so as to not draw attention. After confirming none of Cain's men were around, he huffed, "Go!" The new recruits of the Endurance militia streamed out the door, and ran for the woods.

Jonah remained at the door and ushered them through, offering "See you at the meet up point, " to each.

The last of their group at the door was Emily. She paused to glare at him before exiting. He couldn't really see her eyes in the darkness, but he felt her gaze. Then, for just the briefest of moments, she pressed her lips to his. "You did the right thing. I'm proud of you." Before he could react, she burst out the door, dashing for freedom.

Time seemed to stop for him, but it also seemed to for Emily and several others as they weren't moving.

"Freeze!" commanded Cain through his bullhorn.

A flood of realizations hit Jonah all at once: their cover fire had stopped, Cain was uninjured, and several of them were caught.

He poked his head out the door, and saw that besides Emily, Sheila and at least five others were among those who wouldn't make it out. Maybe the others got away. He threw his rifle on the ground and thrust his hands into the air.

"Father. So glad to see you're safe," Cain said arrogantly. "Mr. Ramadi asked that we not harm you, so he could talk to you himself, before he shoots you."

Chapter 31
Meritville, Alabama

W ilber Merit sauntered up to the two Army officers, standing by the entrance to City Hall's meeting room and several tables full of guns and ammo. Wilber was ready for war, at least he hoped so.

He laid his Browning Automatic Rifle or BAR on one table and a can each of 30-06 and .45 ammo on a separate table with the others.

The gun table was filled with countless rifles, shotguns, and pistols of every variety. The ammo table must have had ten thousand various caliber rounds. A lieutenant held out a clipboard and said in a gruff voice, "Your name and address here, list what you brought here, and sign here."

Wilber grabbed it, scratched the requested information and handed it back to him. "I miss much?"

"Hasn't started yet," the sergeant said.

When Wilber entered, all heads turned to look at him. A few men mumbled sarcastic comments—they'd dare not say what they wanted to his face. The others turned back to face the podium. Two of his own—both Merits—sitting up front rose and offered their seats to him. Wilber chose the seat in the front corner of the room.

"Wilber," said a heavy-set man in the back, everyone knew to be Meryl Boykin.

"Meryl," Wilber responded, without looking at his adversary.

"You bring that antique museum piece with you?" Meryl asked.

"That museum piece is fully automatic and it won the Big One. It's kicked Nazi ass and Jap ass; figured it was time to kick some Muslim ass." A few men mumbled affirmations. "You bring that pea-shooter of yours."

"That pea-shooter or at least something similar to it has kicked Muslim ass throughout the Middle East. It will do the same in America."

"At least were here for the same thing," Wilber said.

"Just don't expect me to kiss and make up after we kick Haji's butt back to Syria."

"Speaking of which, where are our US Army friends?"

As if on cue, a high-ranking officer stepped onto the elevated podium. He looked like he was doing some mental calculations, before speaking. "Is this all the men and all the weapons of this town?"

Several of the men in the audience, turned in their seats to examine the room. Each wondered why the thirty or so men and all their guns and ammo weren't enough for the US Army.

"So what did you expect, Captain?" Meryl asked, not trying to be a smart-ass, but genuinely wondering why this wasn't a good amount for such a small town.

"My name is Captain Smith. We just wanted to make sure that we didn't forget someone."

"When are we going to kill some gosh-darned terrorists, Captain?" asked Meryl, spitting a brown wad of tobacco into a paper cup.

"Hold on please," the Captain said, and then stepped back behind the curtains.

A young man rose from his chair. "C'mon already, how long do we wait?" He was one of the younger Merits.

"As long as I say," bellowed Wilber.

Wilber's young cousin sat down.

Four men dressed in US Army uniforms stepped from the curtains and stood before and above them.

For a moment, it felt to Wilber like they were going to perform some sort of musical arrangement with their AK-103s.

It was then that Wilber realized what had bugged him all along about this offer. He wondered why the US Army would ask the men to bring their weaponry to a meeting. And why the US Army would even need their help. It felt funny giving up his rifle to begin with. But then he knew the answer when he saw the AKs, still brand new looking.

"They're not the US Army," Wilber hollered.

The men on stage pulled their charging handles back together and aimed their rifles.

"Son-of-a-bitch. The bastards got us again," Meryl stated.

They fired.

Chapter 32
Stowell, Texas

Grimes

The new long dipole antenna would let Robert Grimes hear and speak to much of the world, even if he would miss signals too close to home. He would fix that another day.

He worked the needle-nose pliers, pulling the end strand of copper wire around itself, making sure it remained bound to the insulator. To relieve some of the strain it would absorb during windstorms, the insulator was connected to a tension spring strapped around his chimney.

The sixty-five-foot length of one half of the dipole now spanned his chimney to just below the top of the tower. The other end of the dipole extended to a tree on the other side of his property.

Just then he felt a small tremor, and he froze.

The top of his ladder shifted an inch across the fascia, its rubber scratching to a stop.

It slid another inch and felt like it would let go, so he released the ladder's rung and grabbed onto the antenna line with both hands. The slipping stopped. But he waited just in case. He didn't want to repeat the casualty that occurred seven days ago on this very same roof. He wanted to laugh at his near stupidity, but held firm.

The last time this happened, he had seen a flash and so he ascended this same ladder to get a look west. When he saw it was a mushroom cloud, he was so startled he lost his footing and fell off the damned roof. He later told Aimes that it was the Jacksonville nuke. Aimes had to point out how ridiculous that was since Jacksonville was over 800 miles away and line of sight is only 50 miles on a good day. Yes, of course he was right, it would have been impossible. But he certainly saw something.

He felt the ladder move again and remained still, swearing to himself that he was done climbing up ladders until his leg fully healed. But the ladder wasn't slipping; it was shaking, like from an earthquake.

Now he heard the accompanying noise too: a deep rumble like from a highway full of cars on their daily commute, only more substantial. The rumble grew, getting louder and deeper. Grimes held on and listened intently.

Then the sounds exploded from the tree line, and directly in front of him passed six separate US Army trucks. A convoy of trucks such as these would be used to transport more soldiers to a battlefield. Only these were older. *Maybe that was all the Army could get back into service?* he wondered.

After the convoy passed and the rumble subsided, Grimes carefully navigated down the ladder. He was dying to find out if his new antenna worked, and what the hell the US Army was doing in Stowell, Texas.

He still had less range than he did before on the UHF frequencies without the benefit of a rotor and the extra twenty feet of tower. But he definitely had more options on the SSB frequencies, and that meant he was just as likely to hear a signal from Houston as he might from Honolulu or Helsinki.

When he made it back to the safety of his desk chair, he urgently twirled the dial, hoping it would land on the right combination of frequency, time of day, signal strength, and distance away.

Nothing.

He also listened with his other ear, to the chatter on his base unit, for news on the Army trucks.

He twirled slowly to the next frequency, having had some luck before in this area.

A whine and warble around 3.5 MHz, until he homed in on it: "...Army. They aren't real. First it was all men with a weapon need to report to them..."

A repeating signal, like a radio beacon noise, bled over the transmission, making it impossible to understand. He tried to dial around it, but it was no use.

Then the clutter of noise disappeared and the broadcast was clear again.

"Repeat, we have been invaded by what appeared to be US Army trucks"—Grimes immediately flashed an image of the trucks that just drove by: US Army trucks. He turned up the volume. "They are not US Army. There are Islamic terrorists, the same ones who attacked us on July 4th and they are now masquerading as US Army. When a group of us reported to them, giving up our guns, they slaughtered us. Repeat, if they show up in your town, ask to see their orders. If they cannot produce them, shoot them on sight, or they will do it to you. I repeat ..."

The noise clutter bled in again, but he had heard enough.

Grimes twirled to AFN's main broadcast frequency, clicked on his amplifier to make sure the signal covered as great a distance as possible, and flicked on the microphone. He also clicked open the base unit microphone. He wanted everybody to hear this.

"This is the American Freedom Network, broadcasting from Texas. You crazy asshole bastards from Iran or wherever you're from. You didn't get us. Yes, you blew our antenna tower to shit, but in less than a day, we're back. And your man died anyway. My fellow Americans, I have much to report to you."

Chapter 33
Endurance, Florida

Commander Bahia

Less than a dozen men showed up in a room designed for forty, unknowing that they were waiting impatiently for their own deaths.

Most of those were old men, who possessed ancient weapons that didn't look functional, like their owners. Only one man in the group brought with him an arsenal. Like his weapons, he looked serious. It was more than ten minutes after the stated meeting time, so Commander Bahia assumed no one else would be attending. Perhaps these were the only town residents they'd have to worry about.

The commander turned his attention from the little window in the room's side door entrance to his five well-trained warriors. They would normally be more than enough to extinguish the apostates in the room. But something was wrong with them.

Each of his men scratched at their arms and hands; their skin in the irritated areas was red and angry. One warrior was coughing loudly. After each bout of hacking, he desperately gulped for air. Unsuccessful, he started to wobble, like he might fall over at any moment.

"Soldier, you stay here," he commanded the sickly warrior. "The rest of you, stop scratching and be ready on my command."

The coughing one shrank back; a bout of hacking took over, as he tried to muffle it with his hands. The other four shrank away from their sicklier brother, stepping closer to the meeting room's entrance. They held up their M4 American rifles to show their commander that they were ready.

The commander examined the four warriors once again. The warrior closest to him clawed at a cheek, now radiating its own plume of red. The commander slapped at the warrior's scratching hand, and then he plucked the warrior's weapon right out of his free hand in an attempt to demonstrate how unready he was. The warrior became rigid, throwing a frightened gaze at his superior, who had caught him in a moment of weakness.

"Both hands on your weapon, and your safeties should be off," Commander Bahia said, flicking the selector to "Auto." The embarrassed warrior nodded furiously and accepted his rifle back. Sweat poured down his temples and onto his cheeks, giving him an even more flushed look.

The commander lamented to himself about the weapons his warriors were forced to use, watching another warrior fumble with the selector. His men were trained with AK-47s. And upon arrival to the States, he was expecting to receive the much newer AK-103s. Instead they were given these American-made rifles which used foreign ammunition and operated differently. But since the cell's leader trusted an American, this is what they would have to use. And because he was their commander, it was still his responsibility to bring honor to his men and to his Mahdi, in spite of Imam Ramadi's mistakes.

There was a tingle in the commander's fingers and on his neck, which he reflexively satisfied with an unconscious scratch. His nose then started to run. He quickly rubbed his palm across his nose and mouth before it could. Then he licked his lips, which felt dry—they were always dry when he had to speak to a group—and walked through the meeting room's side door to address the Infidels.

He was greeted with agitated glances, which grew more serious upon seeing him. Even the older men looked like they had come to attention. He decided then that he should not take them for granted. His pulse raced, and his throat felt raw. Involuntarily, he barked a quick cough, which grew to a long spastic bout. When he was done, he looked up and saw several of the Infidels looked at him with sympathy and concern. He didn't want their sympathy. The tickle in his throat grew, and now he was afraid that whatever cold he and his men had would silence him, allowing no more words but only coughing. He decided not to wait. So he signaled his warriors to enter. But none of them came through the door.

"Sir," said the serious looking man in front, "can we get you some water or something?" The man stood up from his chair and glared at him.

The commander ignored the question, stumbling to the door he'd entered, and pushed it open. Behind it all his warriors were coughing in spasms, oblivious to their commander's demands. The closest had his back to his commander and the door. The commander barked out scratchy words in Arabic, comparing them to dogs. Then he found his voice, and forgetting himself, yelled in English, "Kill these American whores."

Two of the warriors stumbled through the door, the first aiming his American rifle at the closest infidel, now walking in their direction. The warrior squeezed the trigger.

Buford

The serious American sitting up front was Endurance's most colorful resident, Buford Justice. He was an author and survivalist who mostly kept to himself. When he heard the Army trucks roll down his street, he followed them to the city center, curious if his country was finally taking it to the terrorists. When he heard their call for volunteers, he decided to take action, rather than wait in his house for the invaders to come to him. He went back home and grabbed what weapons and ammo he could carry. He knew he'd probably be giving up some of his weapons to another townsperson. But if it helped to defend his home, it was worth it.

While waiting in the meeting room, he started to have doubts about the whole affair. When he saw how few volunteers showed up, and especially being older himself, he thought that his decision to come into town might be a bad one. He was about to go, when the Army captain came out and started his hacking spell.

Buford rose to offer assistance for the man. At first, he was so shocked at the captain's command to kill the "American whores," he froze, not believing his ears. That moment's hesitation should have ended his life. But providence may have been on his side.

When he saw the two US troops rush through the door with the intent to shoot them, he went for his concealed weapon. They had asked for all his weapons before he entered. But he wasn't about to give up his Taurus Slim, cradled to his back in an Uncle Mike holster. He moved quickly, but the soldier had already drawn down on him.

The soldier aimed his rifle right at him, and he was almost at point blank range. The soldier's finger curled around the trigger and squeezed, just as Buford lifted his pistol up. Thankfully the soldier forgot to take it out of safe. This gave him enough time to thumb off his own safety and fire two rounds into the soldier.

The explosive sounds of an automatic rifle's report burst beside Buford's ears, as the second soldier fired several rounds at another direction. The soldier stopped his killing to cough up blood. He looked up and saw Buford's barrel. Buford squeezed his trigger twice.

"Get out the back door," Buford roared at the uninjured men, though it sounded like he was yelling into a pillow. Buford turned to the back exit and galloped toward freedom.

Suddenly, he felt a need to turn around and face the front of the room.

The captain, after seeing that his first two men went down and the others not responding, picked up a soldier's dropped weapon. He pulled back the charging handle, and rushed out the door, into the room. Appearing to look for his first target, he found Buford promptly. But Buford was already aiming his pistol at the captain. Bufford squeezed his pistol's trigger once more and dropped him.

Chapter 34
Stowell, Texas

Tariq

To Tariq Aziz, it wasn't just wearing a US Army captain's uniform that felt foreign. It was that nothing seemed to be going according plan.

Now, no armed men—not even one—had showed up at the appointed hour to give up their weapons and volunteer to fight for their town. Mohammad proclaimed that it was simply that the men of this town were afraid and that meant they would be compliant during their demonstration. His intuition, forged over years of fighting his enemy on and off the battlefield, told him this meant something much more.

One of Aziz's warriors reported seeing some men, with rifles slung around their shoulders during the announcement. So, this town certainly had men of fighting age with rifles, but no volunteers. He had never tried wearing their enemy soldier's uniforms and then offering to allow their citizens with weapons to come in willingly. But from what he understood of the American people, he thought this part of Mahdi Abdul's battle plan would work well. He certainly didn't expect no takers.

Aziz walked through the designated meeting area, which was a break room of the Saw Buck Store they had taken over. He stepped through the side entrance to ask his men a few more questions, stopping first to gaze up at the roof. It was why he chose this building to take over Stowell. Since they had no obvious "city hall" or "central meeting place," this place stood out with its vast parking lot, indicating a majority of the citizens came to this store to buy useless devices for their homes and idols for their walls and lawns. But it was the roof that was the most useful, as it had the best view of the whole town. Until after the execution and sharia announcements, which they may have to do sooner rather than later, he had Mohammad and several of their men waiting on the roof to provide protection, if their armed citizens decided to fight back.

Aziz stopped at the two empty tables by the door. They were set up to collect guns and ammunition, their emptiness now plainly telling Aziz what he already knew; for whatever reason, no one was coming. His two warriors snapped to attention upon seeing him, their eyes following three men approaching from the back of the property. He asked, while he examined the approaching men, if there had been any other townspeople coming forward, even to ask questions. Their "Nos!" were as detached as his question.

"Maybe these are recruits," said one of his warriors.

The three men who marched in their direction were led by a thick bald one. Aziz knew even from at this distance that these men were soldiers, like his own men. These three walked with the presence and purpose of hardened warriors.

At first Aziz thought that these men were going to comply with their orders. But his years of experience fighting and dealing with other men told him otherwise. There was no hesitation in their step; each man had a rifle slung behind his back, so as to not look like a threat, but the weapons could be brought to a ready position quickly; and each man's eyes were studying them, examining their occupied store and Aziz's other men up front in the parking lot. No, Aziz knew these men were not here to volunteer.

But Aziz couldn't do anything to reveal who he and his men were, until he presented the executions and made the final announcement. Until then, they were to pretend to be friends, wearing this country's military uniforms.

The short but solid leader said something to the other two, now close enough that Aziz could see he bore a tattoo on his bicep that said USMC. But it wasn't until he and each of his men unslung rifles that Tariq understood that this town knew their real identity.

Aimes

Aimes couldn't believe their luck.

When the US Army trucks had come into town, for a moment he was filled with the same hope he imagined others were: that they were the real thing. When he heard the Army captain announce their request for male volunteers to show up in an hour with their guns and ammo, he was instantly suspicious. But none of them knew for sure until Grimes shouted over the radio that they were actually terrorists. This was the invasion they had been waiting for.

Their plan was brilliant, really. Rather than coming into town shooting, like the Mad Max discards who had tried unsuccessfully earlier, these invaders came in masquerading as US Army. By doing so, their town would have their guard down, trusting in the belief they were here to help. But the true brilliance was their plan to defang the Americans by convincing their armed population to surrender themselves and their weapons by volunteering. They would kill that town's militia and take their weapons, making sure the town became compliant.

Once he and his group had uncovered the terrorist cell in their own town and their plans for an invasion, Aimes doubted how these terrorists could succeed. Even if they were able to kill all their active military, which he didn't believe they could, there were just too many armed citizens who would fight back. It was true that most of the population no longer could stomach war, but he knew there were enough patriots, in addition to retired military and survivalists out there to put up a real fight.

They were just lucky to find out about their enemy's plan before they could succumb to it. But they had very little time. They spread the word to all the townspeople to stay away from the Saw Buck Store and that their militia was to meet to plan how to take on these invaders.

After the militia had met and understood their plan, they decided that Aimes would lead an attack directly at the enemy.

When they approached, he could see that they were perplexed by them. He had planned for them to get closer, but he could see the fake-Army captain was agitated. So Aimes barked off his command, and that's when the fake officer jumped for his rifle, while yelling to his men in Arabic what Aimes guessed were orders to shoot. He wouldn't let them.

Aimes swung his AK around and squeezed the trigger less than a second later. He led a trail of bullets from the captain to the other two men, who weren't able to reach their own weapons. When he let go of his trigger maybe three seconds later, his men were firing upon the other enemy soldiers visible in front and back of the building. Aimes could hear other gunfire start around the building. They had the building surrounded; he watched the remaining fake Army men pile into the building for protection. That's when the militia's luck ran out.

Several heads popped up above the roof's lip and Aimes forced them down with cover fire. Then the side door they were going to try and enter popped open and two soldiers stuck their rifles out and fired blindly. But the message was clear, they'd be sitting ducks in that location. "Retreat!" Aimes yelled at his men as he replaced his magazine, fired at the doorway, and then ran after them.

A barrage of bullets zinged around them. They were only a few more strides before they could turn down the street and behind the cover of trees when Pete, a young man who fought so well against the crazies yesterday fell. Aimes stopped, turned and fired back at the roof and the door way, but was pounded in his leg, which exploded in pain. He ignored it, slung his weapon and grabbed Pete by the arms.

The young man's eyes found his as he dragged him the last twenty yards to safety. Aimes had watched men die in battle, and usually just before their time, their eyes were wide with fear. Pete's gaze was different, which he would almost expect from this young man who followed orders without question, and learned so quickly. His eyes seemed at peace. "They got me, didn't they, Sergeant?" he yelled above the gunfire sounds surrounding them. Aimes glanced at the bright red circle now covering his entire chest, and then back behind him to find the road.

"You'll be all right, son. You're too damn good of a soldier to ..." Aimes didn't finish because the young man's eyes were already closed. He had a slight smile on his face.

His feet touched the road, with the intent to run back toward the building and further engage these bastards, when he felt a blow to his arm and then one more to his head.

The road came fast and greeted his face with brutality. Before the world went black, Aimes thought of Pete's peaceful smile.

Chapter 35
Endurance, Florida

Lexi

Lexi worked at the screw. When it came undone, she knew she had found her ticket to freedom.

The other women, who shared this room—their mock-up jail cell—watched Lexi attentively, wondering what she was doing. She didn't say, only telling them to be ready when she "executed her escape plan."

After removing the armrest to the office chair, now repurposed into a club, Lexi drew their attention to her. She whispered, "I need help lifting a desk, not dragging it, to just before the door. It will take maybe six of us, I think. But we have to be quiet for this to work." Several of the women nodded their approval and so Lexi rose and found the closest desk and waited for their help.

She motioned for them to hurry, and five of the women stepped quickly over, as Lexi pointed one to each of the four corners and the middle opposite her.

Lexi mouthed, *one-two-three*, and they lifted. It was a Steelcase and it *was* heavy. "My way," she grunted, leading them to within a foot of the door.

They tried to let it down gently, a couple of the women fighting furiously with the weight, expelling grunts. Sheila, who held the far corner, let her end slip and it crashed hard.

"Shit. Sorry," she whispered.

They waited and listened for movement beyond the door. There was nothing.

"Okay, I need to get set up," Lexi told them.

She pointed them to the other end of the room and she went to work on her para-cord bracelet. She unraveled the smaller inter-white ropes and then using a sharp edge from a piece of metal in the desk, she cut it. She tied one end of the thin white line to the desk leg, moving it up a foot high and then she walked over to the other side, with her club held taught in hand. She looked at the group to see if they knew what she was doing. There were a few nods, but she had forgotten the most important part.

Lexi scurried over to the group and whispered her plea. "I need bait now. Someone who doesn't mind being attractive to the guard."

"Honey, I got this. I'll use the same technique I used on my husband twenty years ago."

Lexi heard enough and trotted back to the door, pulling the line tight with both hands. She nodded to Sheila.

Because of what the woman did next, Lexi thought Sheila who could definitely have made a career out of acting, at least in B movies. She grabbed one of the office chairs and rolled it to the middle of the room and then kicked it hard. It banged against the other desks and a stack of chairs against the same wall they had pulled the desk from. The chair bounced off and fell over with a large clatter. The impact caused the stack of chairs to wobble one way, then the other, until the mass came crashing down, just missing Emily who had to jump out of the way. The noise was near deafening.

Sheila looked at her position on the floor, and then ripped the front of her blouse, exposing an ample amount of her healthy chest. "Owe! Shit, my leg's broken. Please won't you help me?" she wailed.

There was movement behind the door and then a guard yanked it open, his gun pointed inside. He glared upon the women grouped together, who didn't meet his gaze. There was no question that he was angry for having to deal with them. Then his gaze found a pile of chairs toppled over and movement from a couple of women attending to Sheila, who was lying on the floor. Then his eyes found Sheila's target. Drawn to this vision, the guard stepped forward.

Lexi could only see the guards head and rifle, as she tried to make herself small against the wall, and out of his vision. She glanced at the women attending to around Sheila, seeing their mutual feelings of shock, then horror and then panic. Sheila never broke form until the guard moved, and then Lexi saw his foot cross the threshold, immediately snagging her line. She dug a boot into the doorframe and yanked back with all her strength, propelling him to the floor.

Like a jackrabbit, Lexi let go, grabbed her armrest-club and leapt at the guard. She swung at the man's head, but instead caught him in the larynx. He clutched his throat, convulsed in a long gasp, and painfully attempted to draw in a weak, raspy breath not once but twice.

Sheila sprang up too. She had her own target in mind, walking around the flailing guard; she kicked with all her might, connecting directly with the man's groin. He groaned and balled up. But he also whined.

He is making way too much noise, Lexi thought.

She grabbed his rifle and commanded the women, "Get out of the way." Mid-scurry, Lexi flipped the rifle around so that she was holding the barrel. Then she swung in a long arch, using the heft of the gun to do her work. It connected with a *thunk* to the back of the man's head. He grunted no more.

There was a commotion outside as one of the other guards stepped to their door. His shadow entered the doorway and then stopped, silent. Lexi swung the gun back around, pulled the charging handle back, aimed at the empty doorway, and waited.

Another shadow crept up from behind and joined the first—she didn't hear any footsteps on the hard floor. Then the second shadow moved and merged with the first. There was a muffled grunt and the first shadow folded onto the floor. The second shadow remained outside the doorway opening. "Ladies are you alright?" it asked.

Lexi recognized the voice, but demanded anyway, "State your name."

"Sergeant Reynolds, ma'am, and I have PFC O'Malley with me as well. I would ask that you don't shoot." Reynolds appeared in the doorway, a splatter of blood on his face.

"Howdy," said O'Malley, filling up the rest of the doorway.

They casually glanced at the crumpled body on the floor, Lexi was crouched beside him with the guard's gun pointed their way.

"Guess they didn't really need us, Sarge," O'Malley stated with a snicker.

"Miss Broadmoor," Reynolds said, "So glad to see you and the other women are safe, but we really need to get going."

"Don't need to say it twice. Come on everyone. I think we're free." Lexi breathed with a heavy sigh.

"Well not quite. We have a few more guards to get through. I don't think with all of you, we'll be able to be as stealthy as the sergeant and me," O'Malley thought out loud.

"Who else has used and is comfortable shooting a gun?" Reynolds asked. "We have these two rifles from the guards we've taken out."

"I'll take one, if you don't mind." Sheila rose from the floor and repositioned her shirt. "My husband took me out a few times to the firing range." She walked over to O'Malley, and snatched one of the two AKs he held out. She smiled at him and winked, "You're just as cute with your clothes on Private."

Lexi could have sworn the private blushed, if only just a little.

"I'll take the other," Emily announced. "I can shoot."

"What about that Hippocratic oath Doc," Reynold's asked.

"It doesn't apply to these animals." She pulled back the charging handle. "Ready?"

Reynolds turned to O'Malley. "Okay, you heard the ladies."

Lexi, Sheila, and Emily followed the two soldiers out of their prison cell to the exit door, which led out the side of the building. The others shuffled up behind them.

Reynolds whispered, "All right, the private will lead you outside and to the back of the property. There's an alley about one hundred yards away. That alley leads to a storefront. If we get split up, we'll meet at the back of that store. I'll bring up the rear with one of you ladies who have a rifle," he said this motioning to the three armed women.

"Please don't look at me," Sheila said. "I'd prefer sticking close to the private, at the front of the line."

"I've got your back, Sergeant," Lexi said.

O'Malley cracked the door open, scanning in all directions and then lightly shut it. To the group he said, "All right, since Ms. Thompson volunteered, she and I will go through the door first and protect the doorway. Then one at a time, I want you to run when I tell you and wait at the alley entrance. Dr. Scott, would you go first and then when you're set up at the alley entrance, shoot anyone who comes our way?"

Everyone nodded.

"Okay, go!"

Emily

Dr. Emily Scott, the head physician at the Endurance Health Center, held her gun at the ready and sprang out the door, dashing the hundred yards to the alley behind the city hall. She didn't look back the entire time, until she was at the alley's entrance. Then she spun around, dropped painfully onto her knees, and aimed her rifle toward an opening between City Hall and Endurance Water & Sewer, past PFC O'Malley and Sheila Thompson.

The Private waved the next woman, who ran toward Emily, who signaled her with her hand.

When the third woman leapt out the door, and started her run toward Emily, a man wearing Islamic robes peeked around the front corner of City Hall. The private got him with one loud booming shot.

That's when the proverbial shit hit the fan.

PFC O'Malley signaled wildly and all the women poured out the door, sprinting the long one hundred yards to Emily and their freedom.

At the same time two streams of Islamic soldiers—Emily couldn't think of what else to call them—rolled around the two corners of City Hall in their direction.

Emily took aim at the lead soldier coming around the back corner, hoping the sergeant and Sheila would be able to engage those coming around the front to the side.

A collage of thoughts momentarily raced through her mind: she'd never shot anyone, much less pointed a gun at a person; when she volunteered to take a rifle, at that time she wasn't sure she could do it; she had just figured she was the best person for the job.

But then just as quickly she looked at this like a surgery, stripping all emotions from the decision to act. She needed to do her job right now, to save these women.

The lead man in Emily's sights took a shot in the women's direction. Emily squeezed the trigger.

The rifle seemed to explode with a long rapid succession of bangs, while at the same time rearing her rifle barrel up to the sky. She let go of the trigger, and it stopped its bucking. She knew instantly it was set on Automatic Fire. Examining the selector switch, which was in Russian, she saw that it was down midway. Thinking that up was probably "safe," she pushed the switch down all the way, hoping that was semi-auto. She also wondered how many bullets she had left after firing off so many. She'd been told it held thirty. She hoped she had at least half of her ammo left.

She glanced back and caught O'Malley leading four of the women to the north, along the back of the Water and Power building. The women dashed ahead, and he followed, but turned around frequently to take an occasional shot.

A *ping* passed right above Emily's head; a sign beside her wobbled and shook. They were shooting at her now.

She aimed again at the soldier firing at her, this time squeezing the trigger and letting go, then squeezing again, firing off one shot at a time.

She watched the enemy drop.

A man was running in her direction, firing off bursts at her.

Only three women reached her; the others held back as this crazed man screamed a fusillade of Arabic her way. He seemed set on getting her. Each time she attempted to pull up and take a shot, the man fired multiple rounds in her direction. She'd get a shot off, but she missed him each time, as he did her.

When the man was almost upon her, she had had enough. She quickly rose and steadied her rifle, aiming carefully. The man fired another burst of bullets, but she ignored this—-ike the others, his shots never came close. She squeezed the trigger, but nothing happened.

She was empty.

She was about to turn and flee down the alley when the man's head rocketed to his side and he fell to the ground hard, maybe twenty feet from her. Emily looked for the shooter and saw that it was Lexi.

When she gave Emily the thumbs up, Emily saw a flood of men come out of the same exit they had used. Their exit appeared to be a surprise to Lexi, Sheila, and the Sergeant. Emily could hear the hollering for them to drop their weapons. They were caught.

"Come on," Emily said to the three women, "Let's go. We can't help them if we get caught too." They raced down the alley and out of sight.

Lexi

When she lowered her weapon to the ground, she felt like she was committing suicide. She wondered if it wouldn't have been better to just turn and fire: she'd get one or two of them before they got her.

At least we got some of these pricks, she thought quietly.

Before being tugged inside, Lexi glanced at Emily and three others in the distance, running down the alley. When she blinked, they were out of sight, but she also saw the carnage. At least three of the women had been killed, but so had several of their soldiers. When someone yanked her through the doorway, Lexi was shocked to see Reynolds was shot. He was holding his gut. When she glanced up to his face he smiled to her, acting as if it didn't hurt. But she knew it must have. She'd read gut wounds were the most painful.

O'Malley escaped. Last she saw, he had taken several of the women in another direction. She hoped they all made it.

They were roughly ushered back to their prison room, the same furniture storage area they were in before. This time they were commanded to sit on the floor and each had their hands bound behind them with zip ties. Then each had a hood placed over their heads.

As the hood covered Lexi's head, she could no longer hold off her emotions. The adrenaline had worn off; she knew there was no getting out of this one. She started to sob.

Chapter 36
Stowell, Texas

Grimes

G rimes couldn't stand not being in the fight.

He had made the announcement several times now, his attempt to warn the world about the terrorists' invasion plan. But when he heard the gunfire outside, he couldn't wait any longer. He was a soldier and not a radio man.

He grabbed his sniper rifle, slung it to his back, then grabbed a tactical vest and an AK and hobbled out his door while he attempted to dress for battle. He probably looked ridiculous, hopping and moving weapons around as he attempted not to fall on his face while racing down his street to the fighting a couple of blocks away. He didn't care. His pulse quickened and he mentally prepared as he approached the Saw Buck Store.

Aimes had told him his basic plan of directing their fire to all the openings in front and back, but they would gain entry from the two opposite side entrances and fight them head-on, inside the building.

When Grimes came to the first parking lot entrance from the street, he could see the enemy firing from the building's side entrances and the roof. It looked like they wouldn't be able to do what Aimes had said.

One of their militia ran over to him. He was frantic and had a splatter of blood on his shirt and hands. "Sir, what should we do now?" he begged.

"Where's Gunny Sergeant?"

The man looked down and then back up. "Ah, he's been shot."

"Shit, is he all right?"

"Don't know, but he was shot in the head." The man looked at the blood on his hands.

"Son, help me to the command center." Grimes hoped Aimes had told the rest of their militia about their command center.

The young man nodded and took a shoulder, helping him hop a little more quickly to the Texas Mini Mart on the other side of the street.

Just before they entered, a loud horn honked and all heads turned to see a yellow firetruck roaring down the road, approaching the Saw Buck Store. Driving it was Hunter Barrow, who hooted and hollered out his window. Hunter's yellow firetruck was known everywhere in these parts, leading their Independence Day parade every year since he'd bought it twenty years ago. This year he announced that it wouldn't work and he was tired of fixing it. He must have gotten it fixed.

Aimes could see the firetruck was already attracting a lot of gunfire, as it rolled through the intersection and into the store's parking lot.

"What the hell is Hunter doing?"

"It was his idea. When the gunny sergeant was shot and we couldn't get any closer, Hunter said he would drive the truck into the front of the store and our militia could follow in its cover from behind and then pile in."

Grimes was going to argue, but the plan was already in play, and it wasn't too bad, as long as the enemy didn't have—

A whoosh sounded from the roof, and a projectile raced toward the firetruck trailing fire and smoke.

—an RPG.

It was a direct hit into the cab of the truck. The smoke trail raced in and fire and debris exploded out the sides and the front windshield. The truck continued its march, no longer driven by anyone, now halfway through the parking lot.

Another RPG whooshed down from the roof and connected with the truck's front axle, momentarily lifting the firetruck off the street. When it crashed down, it ground to a stop. The ten or so of their militia were now trapped behind the truck.

Grimes barked off a command to two of their men lingering, to give some more cover fire. He let go of his escort and started to hobble in that direction, stopping momentarily to fire off a few rounds toward the roof. He didn't expect to hit anyone, simply wanted to help his people get away.

Two of their militia darted away from the firetruck following the trail it furrowed. But they were quickly cut down by the enemy's shooters on the roof.

"Dammit! Get those bastards there," he howled to no one.

Another RPG sang its deadly song from the roof, but this time it was headed toward them.

"Hit the deck!" Grimes yelled.

The mini-mart, their temporary command center that he had almost walked into, spewed out shattered glass and other debris.

He waited a solid minute before he pushed himself up off the ground, dislodging himself from a shelving unit of flaming Doritos and Cheese Puffs. The mini-mart was destroyed and so were their plans. They were losing this battle and needed something to turn it around fast.

Tariq

Aziz knew his wounds would be fatal. But before he found Paradise, he wanted to crush these Infidels.

Mohammad had found him outside and pulled him in, bandaging his wounds as best as he could. He felt quite weak, but wanted to see the battle to its end, so Mohammad propped him up on a seat near the front entrance where he could watch.

Mohammad was doing an expert job fighting the Infidel's advances. After the RPGs, Aziz knew that they had the Infidels near defeat.

A cluster of their warriors, already having discarded their Army uniforms, prepared to advance from the store and attack the Infidels directly. They would crush them once and for all in the next few minutes.

Mohammad walked through the store, striding up to his men in pride, ready to lead the next assault. He stopped in front of Aziz and said, "Are you ready?"

"Yes, stand me up."

Mohammad pulled his superior up and handed him his rifle, commanding one of his warriors to provide assistance.

Outside the gunfire had slowed to an occasional pop, but the sound of a low engine was fast approaching.

"What is that, Mohammad?" Aziz asked, urging the warrior to help him closer to the jagged opening in the front of the store.

It was a truck, coming from the same direction as the firetruck, but heading toward a side corner. It raced along the side of the parking lot and then turned toward them, its engine howling like it was stuck in a lower gear.

They aimed all their gunfire at this truck, but it wouldn't abate.

Most saw a man roll out of it and take cover behind a line of dead vehicles in the parking lot.

All their attention was focused onto the oncoming truck, until it finally exploded and veered farther off to the side. The men stopped their shooting, and that's when they heard the other noise.

A white Toyota quietly, but quickly, came at them from another direction. A woman rolled out of this vehicle and it seemed to accelerate. Before they could focus their fire, the Toyota crashed through the window and narrowly missing Aziz.

Then it detonated.

Grimes

At the moment Grimes was thinking that maybe they should retreat and find a spot to defend, a truck raced from the side street and barreled past the firetruck toward the side of the store, with its engines roaring like it was in second gear. It seemed to be heading for a side wall, which might do nothing, when it hit—if it hit.

"Now who the hell is this?" he cried out at the insanity of the ploy, until he saw the other vehicle.

"It's a diversion," he huffed.

The enemy stopped the truck; its gas tank ruptured and exploded in fiery blackness, but they didn't hear or see the white car careening their way. The trees obscured his vision, but it looked like someone bailed out of it and a moment later, the explosion that followed almost shook him to the ground again. He recognized the severity of the blast immediately. It was plastique. And the results were total.

They had just won the battle.

Grimes and the rest of the town walked or hobbled toward the black mushrooming cloud, billowing from where the Saw Buck Store once sat—he always had hated that place.

Neither he nor the rest of his militia knew who the two were who worked in tandem to deliver this epic blow to their enemy, but their heroism was epic and he couldn't wait to thank them.

A woman he didn't recognize hobbled in their direction. Perhaps it was she who had driven the Toyota.

Someone yelled a single word, and all eyes, including the woman's, turned toward the voice. A young man, who looked strangely familiar, ran to the woman and embraced her. They hugged and then both started toward Grimes and the crowd gathering near the front of the burning building. First Grimes and then crowd stopped short as the heat from the fiery rubble was a little intense. They waited for their heroes to catch up.

The smiling couple was covered in soot and other debris, mostly hiding their identities, but their smiles were visible.

One of them was Porter.

"Hi Dad," Porter said. A grin wrapped around his face. "Let me introduce you to Major Wallace," he said to the woman whose arm was slung around his waist.

Grimes couldn't say anything. He folded his arms around both of them and let his tears of joy flow.

Chapter 37
Endurance, Florida

Ramadi

This demonstration was not part of the overall plan given to him, but sometimes plans had to be changed.

Each cell leader would follow their invasion plans in the same way throughout America. They would go from town to town, being welcomed as liberators, wearing the colors of the Infidel's military. Then they would execute all those who had the willingness to fight and who possessed weapons, taking those weapons to use for themselves. They would then post and institute the rules of sharia and demonstrate their power by executing at least two of the town's people, including one woman. Preferably they would be apostates, but it wasn't even necessary that they actually commit a crime. It was necessary however that there be at least a public display of their intent. Then, they'd move on to the next town, leaving two warriors behind to administer the town's eventual conversion to Islam.

Assuming everything went as planned, they would have executed the only men who possessed the will or means to effect a resistance against them. And the execution of two members of that community would be more than enough to force the rest of its members to be pliable to their will. But that was if everything went as planned.

Ramadi's own plan was even more elaborate than the one handed down by the Mahdi. Besides storing up twice the weapons and supplies recommended, he had planned for additional contingencies over the last two years by having the leader of Endurance join in an alliance. Ramadi even built up an Islamic community just south of the town. All of this, he believed would make the transition to the Islamic Caliphate, especially in Florida, that much easier. It did not.

The Endurance leader or his son (which one didn't matter) broke his alliance, stole all his weapons, and then infected his warriors—killing several—and allowing their town's armed men to slip away. Because of this, he needed to provide a demonstration to this town that was much more gruesome and fitting for this treason. He would take care of his enemies and show what happened when anyone in a population crossed him. So, in spite of all the problems he'd had with Endurance, he could use this to his ultimate advantage.

His Mahdi Abdul taught him to always use one's own failure against one's enemy. He would do this today.

He stood at the top step of the small city hall building, wearing his finest thobe, and faced his new subjects, the residents of Endurance, Florida. His presence, with the US Army troops, brought obvious confusion to them and they chattered wildly, asking questions like "Who is this man?" and "Why is he here speaking and not someone from the Army?"

Normally, he would have had the weapons and ammo they'd confiscated beside him to show the town that they controlled their weapons as well. However, since they had confiscated only a few guns and very little ammo, he would go directly into the punishment phase of this demonstration.

Ramadi signaled and over a dozen men and women were marched out by his warriors, still dressed like US Army troops. With their hands bound and pillow cases over their heads, it was obvious to all who watched that they were being held as prisoners. The troops forced the prisoners to stand against a wall, where each had their ankles bound so that they couldn't run away.

Then their hoods were removed, revealing their faces. All who were gathered around and could see them expelled a collective gasp. These were their own people: their friends and family members.

Jasper

Jasper watched the whole display from a rooftop across the street only a simple one-hundred-meter shot away.

The black roofing material leached out its fiery breath, adding at least twenty degrees to the outside temperature, which was over eighty already.

He had to ignore the searing heat, even though it added to his ratcheted panic.

Through his gunsight, he watched them bring out the prisoners and reveal each. Frank Cartwright was among them. So was the Army sergeant, who looked to be suffering from a belly wound; his face was pale and sickly. Others he recognized but didn't really know. More importantly, Lexi Broadmoor wasn't among them.

Jasper hated this situation, because it offered very few options. He had few choices. If he had to take a shot, he would do so, even though it increased the risks, and lowered his chance for success.

For now, he'd have to watch and wait.

Their mouths were taped shut, but their eyes spoke of fear. Some were crying and others tried to scream through their gags. Cartwright and Reynolds were both stoic, as he would have expected. They were looking for a way out, even when there was none for them.

Then for show, the troops took off their US Army shirts, each revealing a cream-colored tunic, which was then pulled from their waistband and let to fall over their trousers. This elicited further gasps and a few shrieks.

Ramadi held up his hands, to quiet them.

Ramadi

He spoke into a microphone, its cord snaking down to an all-in-one public address system, amplifier, and speaker. "As-salaam Alaykum," he offered to the crowd.

All his warriors, including those who shed their American uniforms and others still wearing them around the crowds, responded saying, "Alaykum As-salaam."

A woman in the audience screamed.

"People of Endurance. I am Imam Ramadi. May the mercy of Allah be upon you. This is a momentous day in your new lives. Soon you will be given a choice: to pledge your allegiance to me, our Mahdi, to the Prophet Mohammad, peace be upon him, and to Allah ... Or you can die." He breathed the last syllable, drawing it out so long the speaker reverberated with feedback.

"This town is now under sharia law. Although we don't expect you to understand this completely, we have posted a sign to my left"—he pointed to a new sign attached to the banister of City Hall—"which lists the rules of sharia.

"The rules are simply this: You will submit to our will or you will die." Each time he said "die" he paused to see the faces on the crowd.

"In a few minutes, we will show you how we administer our laws. You see these prisoners standing before you. Each participated in a plan to kill our men or me. As the chief lawgiver, I have found them guilty of treason and they will pay with their lives. Each will be beheaded.

"But before this, I have a special treat for you."

Ramadi signaled his men and they brought out Lexi, Cain, and Jonah. Ramadi had them stand in front of him with Jonah closest to Ramadi, one step down. Then Cain and Lexi in front of Jonah, one more step down. All faced the crowd.

"You know this man," he pointed to Jonah, "as Jonah Price. Jonah and I have been working together for over two years. Jonah says that he's still loyal to me, but I have reason to doubt him. So he will prove his loyalty to me by executing one of these two prisoners. I don't care which one."

Muhammad who wore similar clothing as Ramadi, although not as regal-looking, handed Ramadi two pistols. One was Lexi's revolver and the other a Glock.

"In this pistol," he showed Jonah, with the cylinder open, "is one bullet." He closed the cylinder. Ramadi handed it to Jonah, while at the same time pushed the Glock up against Jonah's head. "You, Jonah Price, will shoot either your son, Cain, or this young woman, Lexi Broadmoor, whom I'm told you've already saved once before. If you don't shoot one, my men will shoot them both and I'll shoot you. If you try to shoot anyone else, my men will shoot them both and I'll shoot you. You have ten seconds to decide."

Jasper

Jasper heard all of this, as the speakers transmitted very well across the one-hundred-meter span.

He examined each of them. Cain's eyes were animal-like with fear, while Lexi looked reserved, almost calm. She's a strong one, that's for sure. He understood Mahdi Abdul's interest in her.

But like Jonah, Jasper knew that he also had a decision of his own to make.

If Jasper took his shot, Lexi would most likely be killed. If he didn't shoot, Lexi still had a high chance of being shot by Jonah, who surely wouldn't choose to kill his son over someone who was a stranger only a couple of days ago.

Jasper whipped at the sweat pouring down his face as he considered his own next move.

No matter what, he couldn't let anything happen to her. He had been charged to protect her, and keep her safe. He had been succeeding at it, until Imam Ramadi deviated from the Mahdi's orders.

This Imam was going against the orders handed down directly from their Mahdi himself; the same Mahdi to whom both he and Imam Ramadi had sworn allegiance. Their Mahdi had directed him to protect Lexi "Smith" Broadmoor, at all costs, even if it meant giving up his own life.

Chapter 38
Northern Panhandle of Florida

Jasper

July 5th

The truck pulled up to him. A small plume of dust arrived a few seconds later. The door groaned open and a dark-skinned man wearing a full beard hopped out. Smiles of familiarity lit both their faces.

"Good morning," Abdul said, welcoming the driver.

"Yes, it is."

They embraced like brothers, separated by many years. And this was true in many ways, since it had been many years since they had seen each other, only communicating by radio. And this man, Abdul thought, was more like a brother than his brother by blood, Stanley Broadmoor.

"Come, Imran, let's sit by the river so that we can talk about what you've accomplished and what I have for you next.

"Of course, my Mahdi." He pulled himself away, getting ready to bow. He had forgotten his place.

"No, my brother. We are equals in Allah's mind. I shall always treat you no less. Please call me by the same name you have always known me." He put his arm around Imran's neck and led him from the drive to the dock, where Leo had set up two chairs and tea.

"Tell me, how was your drive?" Abdul asked, letting go of his friend as they walked slowly to the dock.

"Well, Ma—sorry, I mean Abdul—it was not without some peril, since there are many dead cars on the road, blocking access. But otherwise no troubles. The first phase went as planned, I trust? Jacksonville's destruction was very satisfying."

"I'm sure it was, since you were right there. Yes, Phase One went off mostly as planned, and the other two phases should as well." He beckoned Imran to one of the seats.

Imran sat and glanced at the smooth river, a delicate carpet of green glass, gliding by them on its way to the ocean. "This is a beautiful property."

"Yes, it is, but no more lovely than the one you've been living in," Abdul picked up the teapot and motioned to him.

Imran nodded, drawing up both cups to the welcoming pour. He then offered Abdul his choice from the two full cups after the teapot was rested back on the platter between them.

Imran held his cup, but didn't yet drink. He stared at the brown liquid, looking for the courage to ask the next words. "Sir, I have been waiting for years, doing all that you have asked. I can only hope that I can take my place and lead your warriors in this glorious fight against the infidel in the next few days?" He took a sip of his hot tea and then watched his Mahdi for his reaction, hoping he hadn't pushed him too far.

Abdul slurped a large amount of his cup, and examined Imran, considering his words carefully.

He had expected this from his loyal brother, who was designed for fighting. Imran's eyes bounced around, plaintively waiting for his reply. So many looked at this man and thought him crazy, with his strange eyes that seemed to be unconnected, and so they thought him to be the same. But Abdul knew this man too well, and what he had done to help the cause.

His brother Stanley had disappeared after his wife's death and the world had thought him dead. But Abdul knew better. He was in hiding somewhere. His people found a purchase made under the name "Abby Smith," his sister's married name, for over a million dollars. Abdul knew that she didn't have that kind of money, so it had to have been made by Stanley. The contract confirmed it, with the buyer as "Stanley Broadmoor, and or assigns."

Abdul then guessed that Stanley was going to someday disappear with his kids to this home in Florida, and he didn't want that to happen. So, Abdul asked Imran to help him.

"You've done so much for me and the cause, Imran. You took the home next door to my brother's, killing the occupant and taking over his identity. You found the warehouse where we could store the supplies we needed for Phase Three, coordinating with Ramadi. Then you've patiently waited for your next orders."

"I am ready to serve you, my Mahdi. Just say the word and I'll join the fight. I've been waiting so long for this."

Imran was about to fall to his belly in supplication, but Abdul thrust out his palms to keep him seated.

"My brother, I have one more favor to ask, before you join in the fight. This is a personal favor to me."

"Anything," Imran said this, but he felt burdened, afraid that he would lose his Mahdi's respect, by disappointing him.

"I want you to return immediately. I'm expecting my brother and his two children to arrive any time now either here or at their own home in Florida. I want you to wait for them, and when I tell you, I want you to take his children, a young woman and her younger brother, and bring them to me."

"But Mahdi, what if your brother disagrees with this?"

"Kill him. He is lost to me and to Allah. But I want you to protect the young woman and her brother with your life. She will become my wife when you bring her to me and he, my son. Once you have confirmed Stanley and the woman and boy are there, call me on your radio at our normal frequency and I will give you further directions. Until then, protect the woman and the boy."

Mahdi," Imran exclaimed. He was going to ask him why and ask him to reconsider, but if this is what he wanted, he would do as he was asked. His shoulders sunk with acceptance, already feeling the weight of this burden. "Yes, Mahdi, I would be honored to do this personal favor for you." He rose, feeling his Mahdi's sense of urgency.

Abdul rose with him, restraining his sense to grin. "Thank you Imran for your loyalty. You have earned a place in Paradise for sure. But, please call me Abdul." He raised his hand to shake his friend's.

"Okay, Abdul. Then you better continue to call me by my current name, until I am finished with this mission for you."

"Very well. Thank you, Jasper."

Endurance, Florida

July 9th

J asper watched from the bushes as the man, who he was sure wasn't Stanley Broadmoor, was teaching the very attractive young woman how to fight like a man.

He knew he shouldn't look at her with longing, but it had been a long time since he had been with a woman, and this one was beautiful. He understood his Mahdi's interest in her.

With a great effort, Jasper shook away his own lust. He was charged to protect her and her brother, and he would do as he was asked. He would need to get to know this man, who seemed to be their protector. He would earn their trust and when he received word from his Mahdi, he would kill the man and take the woman and the boy from this place. He just wished he could reach his Mahdi on the radio, but he had been silent.

He was startled when she ran by. Her pretty face seemed determined and her gait set to go somewhere.

He would wait for her and his moment.

Chapter 39
Endurance, Florida

Jasper

He squeegeed away another sheet of sweat with his palm, whipping the moisture on his back, and focused his peep-site on Jonah.

Jasper watched his eyes. When they flitted to Lexi, Jasper's finger curled around the trigger and he squeezed it slightly. But then Jonah's eyes moved decisively to Cain's head, and Jasper knew both their decisions.

Ramadi had been counting down from ten.

"Three ... two ... one," he bellowed over the loudspeaker.

Jonah squeezed his trigger and so did Jasper.

The sound from Jonah's gun seemed to reverberate from far away, as both Cain and Ramadi fell.

Then multiple shots rang out from some distance and several of the guards fell, while Jonah stood transfixed at his dead son.

Lexi pulled her bound wrists around each foot so they were now forward and then jumped toward Ramadi. She kneeled beside him and then pulled her arms hard toward her trunk and the zip tie broke from her wrists. She picked up Ramadi's gun and fired at the guards coming up the stairs. "Come on Jonah, we need to get out of the open."

Jonah sprang to life and followed her up the stairs and into City Hall.

Two of the Army trucks exploded, and townspeople who were transfixed only moments ago scrambled for cover.

The prisoners moved as a group from the open to the safety behind the building, led by Frank and Reynolds. Frank used the brick corner to saw his bindings free and raced back to the front of City Hall to help Lexi.

Two groups of men, one led by O'Malley and the other by Randall White raced to the city center, firing their weapons at the remnants of Ramadi's army. Some ran, but most were cut down.

Several of the Islamic soldiers ran from one of the burning trucks to the city hall's front entrance. Two fell, taken out by Jasper's rifle. But the rest slunk inside, took cover, and hid.

Four or five shots came from inside the building and after a few long moments, Lexi strode out carrying two rifles.

Jasper could see she fought better than many of the men he fought with. She was a natural warrior, even if that was not her proper place in this life. He couldn't help but admire the woman.

He was tired of watching all of this from a distance, and thought that he might perish if he spent any more time on this hot roof. So, he left the building and walked out into the city center. It had quieted down and there was only an occasional gunshot. The battle seemed to be over.

Frank

Frank was in awe of his goddaughter. He knew she had it in her, but he was amazed at how she handled herself. She was completely calm, even though her fate was being decided by Jonah and Ramadi's guards. And then she had complete poise in taking cover behind Ramadi and breaking free, then shooting the guards. He so wanted to help her, but she didn't need his help any longer.

Frank marched up the steps of Endurance's city hall. And although he felt the battle was done, he had one of the dead guard's rifles in hand.

He stepped beside Jonah, who had his arms draped around his dead boy, sobbing. Dr. Scott, also toting a rifle, brushed past Frank and stopped near Jonah. She hesitated and then wrapped her arms around them.

Frank took the final steps up to the level area on which Lexi was standing. She looked wired, almost high, with her eyes darting around. She hadn't settled down yet, afraid the fight was still on. But he knew it was done.

She quickly raised her rifle pointing at something or someone.

Frank spun around and saw it was Jasper. He was finally joining them, *although he missed all the action*, Frank thought.

He turned back to Lexi, pushing her rifle down. "It's all over, Lex."

Frank swung his own rifle around to his back and offered his arms. "You did an amazing job. I'm so proud of you."

She gazed at him, and then her shoulders sank and her lower lip started to quiver.

She collapsed into his arms and wept.

Chapter 40
Sunbay Cove, Florida

Lexi & Frank

They were euphoric over crushing the Islamic Invaders and they looked forward to telling Travis.

They hadn't heard from him since just before the battle. They had heard from several of Jonah's men that Travis was on the radio, parroting Grimes's message about the Islamic invaders dressing up like the US Army. Travis was part of the reason why they won.

It also told them that Grimes was safe and that he made it through the explosion they heard and was back up. That meant the American Freedom Network was back in operation. He couldn't wait to tell Grimes and then make sure that the word was spread. They now knew the invaders' plans and how to defeat them, and the quicker they got that information out there, the quicker America's towns and cities would be able to extinguish the threat.

Frank had always believed that they would prevail. He knew now after seeing it first hand and hearing stories circulating about other communities that the answer rested with America's militia. Based on reports that the American government and the Joint Chiefs were nuked, along with all of DC, on July 4th, and knowing many military bases were damaged by the enemy's attacks, he suspected the US Armed Forces were still days away from mounting any coordinated response.

Their new community still had many battles in front of them as Peter and some of Cain's people went into hiding, and he understood the town of Crystal Waters was an Islamic jihadi enclave. But he had hope that with Jonah and the rest of Endurance, they would be able to hold off any future threats.

"Do you think Travis is all right?" Lexi asked as Frank swerved around new debris in the road. They had borrowed one of Jonah's trucks to get home. She turned on the hand-held radio and it squealed an ear-splitting tone that she immediately switched off.

"Yes. As you can hear, no one is getting through those frequencies."

"What is that anyway?"

He wished he knew. But technology was his Achilles heel. All he knew was that some strange interference popped up on several of the frequencies. Hopefully Travis would know, or Grimes.

When they arrived at home they walked to the back, as this had become their front door entrance. Frank and Lexi smiled at each other but Frank's smile slipped away instantly.

The back door was propped open. That was strange; a tension spring automatically closes it, unless there's something blocking the door's closure. But why would Travis do that?

Frank automatically drew his gun and approached the door quietly. Lexi had hers drawn as well.

This felt way too familiar.

Frank immediately saw the problem: a dead man lay on the floor. His feet were inside the doorway, propping the door open, a sort of human door stopper. As Frank bounded the stairs, he trained his eyes around the house before lowering them again to the dead man. The man had been shot in the head and face by a small-caliber weapon.

Travis's .22.

Frank stepped over the body and into the house, staring into the combo radio room and storage area, where he expected or rather hoped to see Travis. But he wasn't there, and the chair he sat in was over-turned.

"Travis, are you here?" Lexi screeched right behind him. She ran past Frank, hollering Travis's name. He knew it would do no good, but he let her be.

As she called out stopping in each room, Frank's eyes found an object on the kitchen counter.

He approached it carefully, seeing it was something with a hand-written note wrapped around it. He twirled it so the writing was facing him. He caught the word Travis in the letter.

Lexi ran up from behind, "He's not anywhere. Did you check in the storage room? What's that?" Her words falling over one another.

He reached out and picked up the note-wrapped package, and undid the rubber-band tether that held the note to a wooden box that looked familiar.

Frank unfolded the note, and laid the box down. Lexi snatched it up. "It's... Dad's box, it had medals in it. Travis kept it in his pack." They both quietly searched the house with their eyes, both realizing the pack was gone as well.

"Oh shit. Oh shit ... what does it say?" she begged.

He held the note down so that they both could read it. The first sentence took their breath away.

I have taken Travis for two reasons.

First I wanted you to know that there is no place that you can hide from me. And I wanted to make sure that you came to me. I want you and not Travis, although I'd rather have both of you. I will kill Travis if you do not come to me. But my preference is not to kill him.

I promise you that if you come to me, I will protect you and Travis. I will also offer protection to anyone who accompanies you.

I have drawn a map with coordinates so that you can find me.

Finally I've provided you with proof of my intentions. In the box, you'll see what I'm willing to do to get what I want.

I will see you soon, Suhaimah.

Abdul Raheem Farook

Lexi shrieked.

"What's in the box?" Frank asked Lexi.

She hesitated, her hands shaking violently.

She slid open the drawer and dropped it onto the counter.

They watched the box bounce up once and off the counter, but the object it held landed on the counter in front of them: a shocking proof of Abdul's cruelty.

Travis's pinky finger.

Lexi fainted.

Chapter 41
Sunbay Cove, Florida

July 12th

Frank and Lexi stared at their well-wishers, showing no emotion.

Jonah saluted Frank and promised to make sure their home would be looked after, as well as taking care of Endurance and its people. He smiled at Emily and squeezed her hand as she walked around to the other side of the Plymouth Fury, to talk to Lexi.

Frank knew that the pain of shooting his son, in spite of all that Jonah said, will one day slam into him like a freight train. He understood how emotional pain worked; he had bottled up enough of his own over the years. He didn't say this. Instead he thanked Jonah again for the windshield he'd installed for them.

"You take care of this one," Emily said through the passenger window to Frank. "But also take care of yourself..." She trailed off, obviously wanting to say more, but piping up before she did. She had promised him she wouldn't say anything to anyone "I will, Doc." he said.

Emily nodded to Frank and then to Lexi she asked, "Do you have any idea how long you'll be?" Emily immediately shrugged back, her face twisting in pain. "Sorry," she whispered, obviously regretting her question.

"As soon as we get Travis back," Lexi said, feigning a smile.

Emily reached out to her hand resting on the car's open window and squeezed it.

"I almost forgot, Em?" Jonah looked through the driver's side windows at her. "In your purse..."

Emily nodded and pulled out Lexi's Rossi Revolver.

"As you probably can guess, I don't want anything to do with that gun. Besides it's yours."

She accepted with a slight grin. "Thanks," she said softly, laying it on the seat, beside her.

"How far is it anyway?" asked Jonah.

"Mt. Weather? Oh, about 800 miles."

"Well, take care of each other and we'll expect to see you both soon ... oops, sorry Jasper, you too of course," Emily said, bending down on seeing see Jasper in the back seat.

He nodded once as his acknowledgement.

"We'll be fine and we'll take care of each other." Frank laid his arm over Lexi's shoulder and softly squeezed to show he meant it.

Unseen by anyone, Jasper glared at Frank and strangled the neck of his rifle, only letting loose when Frank removed his arm from around Lexi.

"Bye guys," Emily said.

Frank and Lexi waved back, watching them fade in their mirrors and both wondering if they'd ever return again.

Epilogue

Stowell, Texas

"This is the American Freedom Network.

"I'm happy to announce that America's militias are taking up the mantle of defending our country against all enemies foreign and domestic.

"There was a reason why the framers put this into the constitution and in spite of political motivations to change this, we can be thankful that our country has private militias.

"Our US military has been severely damaged by the Islamic invaders, and with the loss of many of our Federal Government on July 4th, it may be a while before we see any battle plans from our Armed Forces.

"We've already told you of the invaders' latest ploy, pretending to be the US Army. They are arriving in old US Army trucks and their forces masquerading in Army uniforms. Do not fall for it! If you see US Army trucks in your town, beware! They are doing this as a means to take your town's weapons and potential militia members, by executing each potential militia member and taking their weapons.

"I repeat if you—"

A pulsating loud tone shot through the speakers, cutting off his broadcast.

Grimes twisted the dial up a few kilohertz and then back down and that tone was there.

"What is that?" Aimes said.

"What the hell are you doing up? You should be resting after being shot three times." Grimes glared at his friend, but then turned back to the transceiver. Grimes knew Aimes would do whatever he did, regardless of whatever ribbing he dished out. He was far more concerned with what this might mean.

"Actually I was shot twice, the third just grazed my head. I'm fine. Now tell me what the hell that tone was."

He punched in the next pre-set frequency. It was also where Grimes broadcast the AFN signal.

The same pulsating tone blared through the speakers.

"Shit!" Grimes huffed to himself, and punched in the next one.

It didn't matter whether he went to a frequency which was either a common broadcast frequency for AFN or one of the often communication frequencies from some of their sources on the ground. In every case, that pulsating tone burst through the speakers, bleeding out every broadcast on or around that frequency.

"What does this mean?" Aimes asked again.

"We're being jammed."

"Jammed? But how? By who?"

"There's only one place with the capabilities to do this. And our enemy must have taken it over.'

"Where?"

"Mt Weather, Virginia."

**To be continued in
RESISTANCE (HIGHWAY Book 3)**

Did you like *ENDURANCE*?

Help spread the word about this book by posting a quick review on Amazon and Goodreads.

Reviews are vital to indie authors like me. If you liked this book, I would really appreciate your review.

Thank you!

Want to read more about Frank Cartwright?

Learn what happened before *HIGHWAY & ENDURANCE*, in the USA Today Bestseller, *True Enemy*. Just tell me what email address to send it to and you'll have it for free. This exclusive book is no longer available anywhere else but here.

https://www.mlbanner.com/teshort

Who is ML Banner?

Michael writes what he loves to read: apocalyptic thrillers, which thrust regular people into extraordinary circumstances, where their actions may determine not only their own fate, but that of the world. His work is traditionally published and self-published. Often his thrillers are set in far-flung places, as Michael uses his experiences from visiting other countries—some multiple times—over the years. The picture was from a transatlantic cruise that became the foreground of his award-winning *MADNESS Series*.

When not writing his next book, you might find Michael (and his wife) traveling abroad or reading a Kindle, with his toes in the water (name of his publishing company), of a beach on the Sea of Cortez (Mexico).

Want more from M.L. Banner?

Receive FREE books & *Apocalyptic Updates* - A monthly publication highlighting discounted books, cool science/discoveries, new releases, reviews, and more. Just go to:

MLBanner.com/free

Connect with M.L. Banner

Keep in contact – I would love to hear from you!
- Email: michael@mlbanner.com

- Facebook: facebook.com/authormlbanner

- Twitter: @ml_banner

Books by M.L. Banner

For a complete list of Michael's current and upcoming books: MLBanner.com/books/

ASHFALL APOCALYPSE

Ashfall Apocalypse (01)
A world-wide apocalypse has just begun.
Leticia's Soliloquy (An Ashfall Apocalypse Short)

Leticia tells her story.
(This short is exclusively available from link at end book #1)

Collapse (02)
As temps plummet, a new foe seeks revenge.
Compton's Epoch (An Ashfall Apocalypse Short)

Compton reveals what makes him tick.
(This short is exclusively available from link at end book #2)

Perdition (03)

Sometimes the best plan is to run. But where?

MADNESS CHRONICLES

MADNESS (01)

A parasitic infection causes mammals to attack.

PARASITIC (02)

The parasitic infection doesn't just affect animals.

SYMPTOMATIC (03)

When your loved one becomes symptomatic, what do you do?

The Final Outbreak (Books 1 - 3)

The end is coming. It's closer than you think. And it's real.

HIGHWAY SERIES

True Enemy (Short)

An unlikely hero finds his true enemy.
(Get this USA Today Bestselling short only on mlbanner. com)

Highway (01)

A terrorist attack forces siblings onto a highway, and an impossible journey home.

Endurance (02)

Enduring what comes next will take everything they've got, and more.

Resistance (03)

It will come down to citizen militias to resist the jihadi's march.

Revolution (04)

A 2nd American revolution might be required to save the country.

STONE AGE SERIES

Stone Age (01)

The next big solar event separates family and friends, and begins a new Stone Age.

Desolation (02)

To survive the coming desolation will require new friendships.

Max's Epoch (Stone Age Short)

Max wasn't born a prepper, he was forged into one. (This short is exclusively available on MLBanner.com)

Hell's Requiem (03)

One man struggles to survive and find his way to a scientific sanctuary.

Time Slip (Stand Alone)

The time slip was his accident; can he use it to save the
one he loves?

Cicada (04)
The scientific community of Cicada may be the world's
only hope,
or it may lead to the end of everything.